MURDER TAKES THE STAGE

MURDER TAKES
THE STAGE

Amy Myers

severn
House

This first world edition published 2009
in Great Britain and in the USA by
SEVERN HOUSE PUBLISHERS LTD of
9–15 High Street, Sutton, Surrey, England, SM1 1DF.
Trade paperback edition published
in Great Britain and the USA 2009 by
SEVERN HOUSE PUBLISHERS LTD

British Library Cataloguing in Publication Data

Myers, Amy, 1938-
  Murder Takes the Stage.
  1. Marsh, Peter (Fictitious character)–Fiction. 2. Marsh,
  Georgia (Fictitious character)–Fiction. 3. Private
  Investigators–England–Kent–Fiction. 4. Fathers and
  Daughters–Fiction. 5. Missing persons–Investigation–
  Fiction. 6. Detective and mystery stories.
  I. Title
    823.9'14-dc22

ISBN-13: 978-0-7278-6789-6   (cased)
ISBN-13: 978-1-84751-158-4   (trade paper)

All Severn House titles are printed on acid-free paper.

Typeset by Palimpsest Book Production Ltd.,
Grangemouth, Stirlingshire, Scotland.
Printed and bound in Great Britain by
MPG Books Ltd., Bodmin, Cornwall.

AUTHOR'S NOTE

Broadstairs is a delightful and attractive coastal town in Kent, in the Isle of Thanet. Thanet is no longer an island, but it retains its special atmosphere, and Broadstairs is one of its gems. I must apologize to the town for giving it a fictional theatre at the end of its pier and to both Broadstairs and London for several fictional roads and buildings. For information on the town in the 1950s I am very grateful to Alan Robinson for all his help, and to local history books by Bob Simmonds (*Broadstairs Harbour*, 2006) and John Whyman (*Broadstairs and St Peter's in Old Photographs*, 1990). Any mistakes must be laid at my door, not theirs. That this novel came into being at all is thanks to my agent Dorothy Lumley of Dorian Literary Agency and to Amanda Stewart and the splendid team at Severn House, and I am most grateful to them.

ONE

'I *like* fish and chips.'

'So do I – normally.' Georgia shivered, surprised that Peter wasn't having a similar reaction. There was something about this cafe that disagreed violently with the simple pleasures of battered cod and surprisingly crisp chips. All too often these were soggy, but not in Gary's Fish Bar. In a seaside resort such as Broadstairs she had expected to find good fish, but today the chips were the better part of the experience. Not that it was fair to blame the food. That was probably first class if only she could appreciate it. The cause was more insidious than that.

At first the restaurant had seemed inaccessible for her father's wheelchair, but Gary himself, a portly black-haired man in his thirties who flaunted a moustache that spoke of true Italian rather than Kentish descent, had spotted them outside and immediately rushed out to escort them to the rear door reached through a small yard at the back.

And that's where she had begun to have severe doubts about Gary's Fish Bar. On their way in, something had made her glance at the flight of steps leading from the yard to the living accommodation upstairs – not that there appeared to be much life up there at present. There were no potted plants on the small balcony to suggest that tender loving care was being devoted to those rooms. Nothing seemed out of the ordinary about the steps, and yet it was while passing by them before entering the cafe that her stomach had turned decidedly queasy. *By the pricking of my thumbs, something wicked this way comes* had been her instant reaction. Then she regretted it. Quoting from *Macbeth* even in her mind was not a good idea – and anyway, she had comforted herself, it was entirely her imagination at work.

Now she was not so sure. She made an effort to explain

to Peter, as much for her own sake as for his. Putting something into words often helped. Her father ate on with
apparent pleasure, even adding another dollop of tomato
ketchup as a defiant gesture. 'It's not the food – it's this
place,' she said.

Peter sighed. 'I'd been trying to ignore it.'

He laid down his knife and fork and met her eyes for
the first time since they had entered. The unexpected reaction wasn't being caused by this room, Georgia decided, as
it was bright, clean and cheerful, but was definitely being
triggered by something outside. Something near those steps,
and not a something that had material existence. And that
meant—

'Fingerprints?' she asked in trepidation, and Peter nodded.

The advantage of working with someone over a long period
of time, as she had with her father, was the development of
a shorthand method of conversation, and for Marsh &
Daughter, fingerprints on time, as they called them, were at
the top of the list. The cold cases they chose to investigate
arose from such fingerprints, caused by the unfinished business of violence or injustice in the past imprinting itself on
the atmosphere of a place or building.

She and Peter had long since agreed that they shared a
'nose' for fingerprints, but there had been many a false trail
when one of them had been convinced of their presence,
only for them to fade. Today Georgia had hoped against
hope that Peter was not going to share her reaction to that
very mundane flight of steps. After all, she reasoned, they
were in Broadstairs on a more important mission than
looking for a new case for Marsh & Daughter. Even so,
she had to admit, it was relatively unusual for them both
to react in the same way at the same time, although that,
Georgia told herself defiantly, making another effort to
finish her fish, did not mean it was a valid path to follow.
They were both on edge about the coming meeting with
Christine Reynolds. Nevertheless, Georgia reluctantly
acknowledged that this matter of the outdoor steps had to
be settled.

Peter cleared his throat. 'You or me?' he enquired.

'Me. I'll test it again and then drop a casual remark when I'm paying.'

Georgia was glad of the excuse to leave the shame of her uncleared plate, and she went outside, ostensibly to the whitewashed annex housing the toilets. She didn't reach it but stopped short at the instant sense of revulsion, so strong it felt like an invisible wall. There was no doubt about it. It was those steps that seemed to be crying out to her, and she had to force herself into the toilet (a physical necessity now) before hurrying back inside to rejoin Peter and pay for their meal.

She could sense Gary's unspoken disapproval of the insult to his fish and made haste to explain that she and her father had a difficult task ahead of them (true enough) and it had robbed them of their appetite for his *wonderful* fish and chips. He looked mollified, and so she decided to ask casually, 'I know this sounds ridiculous, but is there any history to this house? Broadstairs is such a fascinating town, and this seems to be a very old building, and full of atmosphere.'

The words sounded gushing even to her, but the town was indeed attractive and atmospheric, peppered with associations with Charles Dickens, whose favourite resort it had been. Basically, she thought, the town could vary little from what it had been like in its Victorian heyday, and in today's May sunshine it was easy to conjure up the past.

She could hardly have asked Gary straight out about the repellent atmosphere outside. Ten to one, most people walked past the steps without a sniff of anything awry. Nevertheless, he had got the message from her comments.

His face changed, not to anger but to something akin to despair. 'You've seen the ghost, haven't you?'

'*Ghost?*'

'Murderer lived upstairs once, and now he blooming well comes back and haunts the place.'

'When was this?' she asked faintly.

'No idea. It was years ago. Why does he want to keep coming back, that's what I want to know. A man's got a living to make.'

By years ago, did he mean three hundred years or nearer three, she wondered? Was it clad in doublet and hose or flower-power gear? 'Have you seen the ghost yourself?' she asked.

She and Peter were wary of claims about ghosts. Headless horsemen and the like were not part of their approach to their work, even though she realized that many so-called ghosts might in fact be what they called 'fingerprints' rather than wailing phantoms.

'Well, no. Nor has anyone, so far as I know. But he's there all right. Heard him stalking up and down the steps and thumping over the floorboards. And a mate of mine heard him crying one night.'

'Who was the murderer?'

'Some clown or other. I've only been here a year or two.'

She gave up. She wasn't going to get any further with him, and there can't have been much local sympathy for this killer or Gary would have been making the most of his unwelcome apparition – if any. 'Do you live upstairs?' she asked.

'No way. Use the flat for storage, that's all.'

She wondered whether she should ask if she could look round but managed to convince herself that that would achieve nothing. The sooner she and Peter were out of there, the better. They could return another day *if* their interest lasted. After all, this afternoon they would need all their strength to lay an emotional ghost of their own. Nevertheless, as they left Gary's Fish Bar, Georgia was uneasily aware that those thumbs of hers were still pricking.

Christine Reynolds lived further along the same road as Gary's Fish Bar. Number twenty-four Jameston Avenue, off the High Street, was in a terrace of Victorian or Edwardian houses, shouting of seaside architecture. Uniform gables, white-painted balconies and solid red-brick provided an aura of turn-of-the-nineteenth-century comfort, and as time passed they must have proved ideal for boarding houses.

The fish and chips lay uncomfortably in Georgia's

stomach as she walked beside Peter to the front door. Her tension was increasing, and a quick glance at her father reassured her that she was not alone in this. Now that the time had come, she realized just how much she – and she was sure Peter too – was relying on this meeting to settle their private unfinished business.

At last there was a chink of light in the shadow that had lain over them both for the past fourteen years: her brother Rick's disappearance. The nearer they had approached the Reynoldses' house, the more the ghost at the fish and chip shop was receding in her mind, and with ample reason.

Rick had vanished while on holiday in Brittany, and before this fragile lifeline had been thrown to them in the form of Christine Reynolds, his family had had no information on what had happened to him. Neither the police investigations nor their own had revealed any clue to his fate. Living with the lack of knowledge still had its effect, particularly on Peter, bringing nightmares and sleepless nights to them both. Since she had been living with Luke Frost, Georgia had mercifully had fewer, but that didn't mean the constant tug was not still there in the background. Now there was hope at last.

Georgia could hear her heart beating as they waited for the door to open, and she had a sudden impulse to turn and run, in the hope of returning to the grey no-man's-land they had lived in for so many years. Surely that would be better than reaching yet another dead end and facing that inevitable blow of disappointment? Suppose – but Peter thankfully cut short her train of thought.

'*Que sera, sera,*' he muttered as she heard footsteps approaching the door from inside. He had been a Doris Day fan in his youth, and his singing of her hit song 'Whatever Will Be, Will Be' had driven both Elena, his now divorced wife, and Georgia crazy over the years. The platitude had irritated her then, but now it seemed a relief.

The door opened, and the die was cast. No turning back now. Christine Reynolds looked about thirty-five – the same age as Rick would have been now. She was fair-haired dulling to brown, looked somewhat harassed and was very obviously pregnant. Practical loose trousers were offset by a jaunty tank top and an overblouse with penguins on it. Georgia rather liked the look of Christine, and her hopes rose.

'My first baby,' Christine announced with pride. 'Due in August.' She had explained on the phone that she was a teacher but would be at home that day, where it was easier to talk than at the school.

'I hope you're not expecting too much,' she continued worriedly as she led them through the house to the rear. Peter's wheelchair only just made it along the passageway, which had obstacles in the form of a table and two chairs. More concern, more reassurance from them.

'Expecting no, hoping yes,' Georgia replied. 'It's good of you to see us. We wanted to meet you rather than just talk on the phone. We've waited a long time for any news at all, and it will seem more real this way.'

Last year her mother, Elena, had come over from her home in France and thrown a bombshell at them – or life-line, whichever way one looked at it. She had learned that a year or so after Rick had disappeared a girl had called at the farm where he had been staying in Brittany to ask if anyone knew where he could be contacted. The farmer could not help, and all he remembered about the girl was that she had lived on or near the Kentish coast. In the slight hope that even all these years later this mysterious girl might be able to provide a fragment of a clue to Rick's disappearance, Peter had advertised in every local news-paper in Kent, not to mention Internet sources.

For months there had been no reply, and he had all but given up. Then something – perhaps Georgia's marriage to Luke at Easter two months ago – had sparked a new hope in him, and Peter had tried one last round of advertise-ments. And this time Christine Reynolds had replied. She had just returned to Kent to live nearer her father in Broadstairs and had seen the curious advertisement.

Georgia went to help Christine make tea in the kitchen, disciplining herself not to burst out with the questions she longed to ask, until Peter could hear the answers too.

But as soon as the tray was put down in the living room, she began nervously:

'Did you know Rick before Brittany?' Oh, the relief of simply being able to speak about him to anyone other than Luke and Peter.

'No. I met him there. We were both staying at the same farmhouse. I was backpacking my way round the world on a gap year – I'd just graduated. That's why I didn't know he was missing.' Christine looked worried again. 'I'd come to Brittany to see the Carnac megaliths, but I was really on my way south. I went to Marseille and on from there, ending up in Australia. I wasn't back for ten months or so, and by then I suppose the publicity about his disappearance had died down. I had no reason to contact Rick – didn't even know his surname, though I remembered he mentioned living in Kent.'

Georgia's hopes plummeted. She had hoped for a brief summer romance, but this had obviously been a much more casual relationship.

Peter wasn't giving up so soon. 'So what made you call at the farmhouse again?'

'It was just a whim. I was in Brittany again, a year or so after my return. I was doing a PhD in archaeology, and Rick had some interesting ideas that might have been useful if I could get in touch with him again. I thought he might have left his address in the farmhouse visitors' book.' She caught Georgia's eye. 'Nothing sexy about it,' she added. 'I only knew him for a few days, but we got on well – we both wanted to change the world, of course, or failing that just help it along a bit. We'd a lot in common. As well as archaeology we both had a passion for music.'

'*Music*?' Peter asked, looking as surprised as Georgia felt. 'What in particular? I know he played the clarinet at one time, but I thought he'd dropped that by the time he reached university. Languages were his forte.'

'Scarborough Fair' – that was all Georgia could think of. It was Rick's favourite song as a child. Had that led Rick on to something that his family hadn't known about? She felt her stomach lurch at the thought of all the untaken opportunities to know him better. And yet . . . and yet . . . she had thought it impossible that anyone, even Peter or Elena, could have known him better than she did.

Christine looked equally astonished. 'He talked about music all the time. It was his passion, whereas archaeology was only an interest.'

Georgia was still incredulous. The words 'Are you sure?' came to her lips but she suppressed them. Of course Christine was sure. This was the Rick she had known, albeit probably for only a few days. Rick had had many passions during his short life, most of which he had dropped after a month or two. Perhaps music was one of them and Christine had hit a particular moment when it was top of the list.

'Mozart was his particular idol,' Christine continued. 'He talked endlessly about him. That might just have been because of Miss Blondie, of course.'

'Who was she?' Peter picked up sharply.

Christine looked taken aback. 'I'd forgotten about her,' she said in astonishment. 'You've just brought it back to me.'

Thank goodness they had come in person, Georgia rejoiced. The telephone could never have brought this un-expected revelation – if that's what it was. Please . . . please . . . let it be, she prayed.

'I suppose I was very single-minded then,' Christine added apologetically. 'I was so intent on my PhD, I must have put her to the back of my mind.'

'Who? What?' Georgia tried to control her excitement, and she could see Peter trying to do the same. Every vein in his hands stood out in tension as he clutched the arms of the wheelchair.

'He told me –' Christine frowned in concentration – 'about this girl he'd met the previous week. She'd been staying in Carnac-Plage, the resort part of Carnac. She was a singer – a *real* singer, I understood. That's where the Mozart came in, of course. Rick had stars in his eyes about her. He insisted on showing me a picture of her – well, I might not have been interested in Rick that way, but I was hardly going to be bowled over at another girl's photo, so

I didn't take much notice. I began to call her Miss Blondie to tease him. She was fair-haired obviously, and he talked of her as if she was a sort of fairy princess. I had this fellow of my own, so no problem there. Rick used to retort by teasing me about Colin. I'm married to him now, but that summer I was planning to meet him in Cape Town for the great romantic world trip.'

'Did you meet this princess?' Georgia asked hopefully.

'No. She'd just left when I met Rick.'

'Do you remember her name?'

Christine looked doubtful. 'Pamela, or something like that? No, it was something to do with Mozart—'

'Pamina?' Peter asked quickly.

'Could have been. Yes, I think it was.'

Georgia could read the disappointment on Peter's face – indeed it must have been mirrored on her own. Pamina could just have been a nickname if she and Rick were devotees of *The Magic Flute*.

'What was Pamina doing in Brittany?' Peter prompted, as Christine seemed to have come to a halt. 'Giving a concert, or on holiday?'

'No idea. Probably holiday, because so far as I recall Rick didn't mention having been to any musical events. Though I could well have forgotten, of course,' she added apologetically.

That wouldn't be surprising, Georgia thought, given that it was fourteen years earlier, and in fact, Christine was doing brilliantly in remembering even this.

'But there was something else,' Christine added, just as Georgia was giving up hope. 'I got the impression it was an ongoing thing – that she had left Brittany but not vanished from the scene, if you see what I mean. I think Rick said she was on her way to some Mozart do and had asked why didn't he come too. I've no idea where. It could have been nearby or in Timbuctoo.'

Christine looked from one to the other, obviously still worried that they were disappointed. But Georgia couldn't speak for fear that Peter was not thinking as she was. Suppose it wasn't a local event. Suppose it was somewhere else entirely – and *suppose that's why the police could get no lead on Rick?*

'How long were you with him?' Peter sounded as if he were trying desperately to seem normal, but he wasn't. Georgia could see that now. He was trying not to get too hopeful.

'A few days longer. Then I left and he stayed on – I don't remember how long he intended to do so. This was all within the time span of four or five days, as far as I remember.' She still looked apologetic. 'I'm sorry you've had this long hunt for me. I've only been back in Broadstairs six months. My dad lives here, my mum's dead, and it seemed a good plan to return to the ancestral hometown. My dad's a journalist,' she chatted on. 'He enjoys it – I think he reckons he's another Charles Dickens. There's not much excitement round here though. That's what Colin and I like about it.'

'No excitement? We ran into a murderer at lunchtime,' Georgia tried to joke for politeness' sake, surprised that the fish-bar ghost was lingering so close to Rick in her mind.

'What?' Christine looked startled.

'The ghost at Gary's Fish Bar at the corner of this road. You must know it.'

Christine didn't answer for a moment, but then she replied awkwardly, 'Yes, you're right. They do say it's haunted.'

'Do you know the story?' Peter asked. It was obvious that she did, but he was clearly too far back in the past with Rick to have his usual alertness in working order.

'His name was Tom Watson. He was a clown.' Christine looked almost defiant.

'Oh, a real one?' Georgia exclaimed. She had assumed Gary had been using the word in a general sense. With the thought of a real clown, in hat, paint and white Pierrot's costume, the ghost began to take the stage in her mind. Ghosts traditionally appeared where there was unfinished business, and perhaps this was true of the clown. Clowns wore effective masks with their painted faces, and who could tell what the real face beneath portrayed? Had this clown been a vicious killer, or as jolly as his painted public face, or had he wept underneath that concealing paint?

'Very real indeed. The Three Joeys they called themselves. They were one of the resident acts in the summer show at the end of the pier. Those were the days, of course,' Christine added, 'when Broadstairs was very much top of the list for exclusive summer holidays in the late nineteen forties and fifties, after the war.'

'Who was Tom Watson's victim?' Peter asked with every sign of great interest, although Georgia could see this was still an effort with Rick's shadow very much present.

'The usual. His wife, Joan. She was murdered in the early fifties.'

'So he was hung then?' Peter asked. 'Or did he escape that?' The death penalty had not been abolished until the nineteen sixties, but there must have been a changeover period, Georgia thought, when capital punishment was on hold.

'He did. In fact he was acquitted, although everyone was sure he did it. Except his girlfriend, but then she wouldn't believe it, would she?'

'What happened to Tom Watson after that?' Georgia persevered, trying to concentrate on what Christine was saying. Poor man. Assumed guilty despite the verdict.

'He stayed on in the flat for a while, and then he disappeared. No one heard from him again, and it was generally reckoned he killed himself. Probably walked out into the sea and drowned himself one night.'

'But the body has never been found?'

'No, but Tom hasn't reappeared alive in all these years, and he'd be a fair age now.'

'I suppose there's little doubt he killed her?' Peter asked.

'None at all, apparently. His wife was a flighty lady, so I gather, and he killed her out of jealousy. *Crime passionnel*, as they say.'

Peter glanced at Georgia, and she knew that he was thinking as she did: why the fingerprints on time if he had been acquitted? There seemed no unfinished business about that. Not like Rick . . . Unfinished business often dovetailed with injustice, but did being deemed guilty without proof add up to injustice?

'Have you ever seen this ghost?' she asked Christine.

'No, and I don't know anyone who has. It's just a load of crap, I reckon. Keeps the story going, that's all.'

'Who would want to keep the story going?' If the Watsons had children, Georgia reasoned, they would surely want the story forgotten.

Christine smiled. 'Well, my dad has a go at it every now and then.'

'A murder fifty years ago? There can't be much to find out now,' Peter said, clearly hoping there was.

'Dad says there's always something if you look hard enough. But he has a special interest,' Christine added. 'My grandad was one of the other Joeys. They were Tom, Sandy Smith and Micky Winton – Micky's gone now, but Sandy is still going strong. My dad is Ken Winton, Micky's son. Oh, and there's Cherry Harding, of course.'

'Who's that?' Georgia's interest was growing.

'Tom's girlfriend. She still lives in hope that one day Tom will come marching back, poor old soul.'

Georgia understood all too well. She and Peter both secretly hoped that Rick would come marching in through the door again, even though rationally they knew he must be dead. She suspected that was one reason her father had stayed in the same house in Haden Shaw in which he had lived with Elena, Rick and herself for many years. It was Rick's home when he disappeared, despite his university years, and to Peter it still was. She knew the hope that Rick was alive was illogical, but if one lived by logic alone, life could be unbearable. Some people coped one way, some another. If and when Peter found out what had happened to Rick, the pain might eventually heal, however. Is that how Cherry felt? Christine had spoken of her in the present tense. She'd therefore been hoping for well over fifty years, poor woman.

'If we wanted to find out more about Tom Watson, could we talk to your father?' Where had that come from? Georgia had surprised even herself by the question.

'Go round whenever you like. He's at number fifty-nine. You should find him home at this hour; if not, he's probably in a pub somewhere,' Christine said drily, then quickly added, 'Not that he's a soak, but they're a good source of information.'

'Which way?' Peter asked as they left the house.

'Literally?' she asked as she unlatched the gate. Her mind was still reeling both from the unexpected lead on Rick – if lead it could be called – and from the coincidence of Christine's family being associated with Tom Watson. It was a push in the direction of further investigation into the ghostly clown – if only to keep their minds from too much hope about Rick. Nevertheless she was not at all sure whether Peter was going to be of the same mind.

'Yes, literally,' he answered. 'One way leads to the car, the other to the home of Christine's dad.'

'We can't do anything here and now about Rick, so—'

A look halted her. 'Would you prefer to go haring off after this Miss Blondie right away?'

'Of course,' she admitted. 'But we can't expect a crock of gold at the rainbow's end, and meanwhile—'

'We can try.'

'Certainly. But we might need another Marsh & Daughter enterprise to keep us sane while we do so.'

'That's not a good enough reason to take one on,' he objected at once, 'let alone with a story like that of Tom Watson and sweetheart Cherry at stake. The case has to stand on its own feet, not simply be a diversion from thinking about Rick. And we don't know if the Watson story is strong enough, or even if there is one. We've a shelf full of cases at home that it would be interesting to follow up. What's the motivation for choosing this one?'

'We're here, and we don't know how strong it is until we look a little further,' Georgia retorted, defending her uncertain wicket. 'Like Rick, Tom Watson disappeared. Unlike Rick, he probably committed suicide, but there's no proof. We don't know whether there were other suspects for the murder of his wife, but we could find out right now.'

'Most people thought he did it.'

'Most people can be awfully wrong.'

'We should do more work on it,' Peter objected, 'before we talk to this journalist.'

She knew he was right. Background research was usually the first essential in order not to plant possibly biased viewpoints in their minds by speaking prematurely to interested parties. Marsh & Daughter not only investigated such cold cases, but they also wrote books about them afterwards, which meant they had to be full of fact, not fingerprints. Moreover, these books were published by Frost & Co, the owner of which, Luke Frost, was now her husband, and he was a stickler for fact being sacred: facts, all the facts and nothing but the facts, was his dictum, as well as an insistence on a good writing style.

Nevertheless, a decision about Marsh & Daughter's next book subject was overdue. Georgia's honeymoon, which had delayed the decision, was over, however – and a good one it had been. Rome, Venice, Tuscany in spring had been a marvellous antidote to work, but when she and Luke had returned they had found Peter champing at the bit with impatience, longing to share the news of the answer to his advertisement about Rick.

Now the danger was that the harder they threw themselves into the hunt for Rick, the greater the disappointment if it failed. Surely Peter could see that the sooner they started on a case such as Tom Watson's the better? It seemed as if for the survivors it carried all the same sense of wasted life and anguish at lack of resolution as Rick's disappearance did. What she and Peter might not be able to do for themselves, they might achieve for Cherry. Why could Peter not see that?

'We're right here on his doorstep,' she said firmly, 'and we have the relevant facts already. Tom Watson disappeared – and one person at least believes him to be innocent. No body has ever been found. Basic questions: did he flee because he was unable to take the pressure of most people believing him to be guilty? Did he commit suicide? Or was he guilty all along? How does Cherry feel about it?'

'Or felt about it,' Peter amended. 'We don't know that Christine is right in saying that she still feels the same way.'

'But perhaps she does. That's just what we're doing with Rick. Let's take a risk and visit Ken Winton right now. At least we'll have made one positive move towards solving Tom Watson's fingerprints, even if we never track down this elusive Miss Blondie of Rick's. If we give up other work while we're waiting, we could be shutting our eyes to helping other people solve their own problems – such as Cherry Harding.'

Peter considered this for a moment and surrendered. 'Agreed. We break our usual rules. Onward, Georgia, to number fifty-nine and Tom Watson.'

TWO

Ken Winton, to Georgia's relief, was at home. She hadn't fancied trying to communicate about relatively delicate matters in a pub. He appeared to be a casual sort of man – perhaps that was why Christine looked so worried about him – and seemed to think it quite natural that two people, one in a wheelchair, should turn up at his door asking for information about a murder case over fifty years old.

In fact far from looking annoyed, he looked pleased. 'Come in,' he said.

You could tell a lot from two words, Georgia thought: did Ken's really mean 'Go away, but I can't say so with politeness', or did they stem from loneliness or was it a straightforward 'that rings a bell. I'll see if I can help'? She thought the last of them in Ken's case.

'On second thoughts, don't come in,' Ken promptly added. 'We'll make for the garden. Easier for the wheelchair.' He was right. The wheelchair would not have passed easily through the house, as his hallway looked even more clogged with furniture than Christine's had been.

The house was a lookalike for Christine's, at least structurally, and with seagulls calling overhead and the freshness of the sea breeze, there seemed to be a slight air of unreality hanging over this visit. It was almost as though she and Peter had stepped temporarily into the world of Narnia, Georgia thought. Perhaps, however, that was less due to Ken's home than to the fact that her surge of hope over Rick's disappearance was insidiously draining away. They would almost certainly be on another hiding to nothing if they pursued this, and perhaps the same would be true of the fish-bar clown.

Ken Winton was about sixty or perhaps in his late fifties, and his pleasant, rather insipid face and blue eyes seemed to look trustfully out upon a world that had failed to offer him his big scoop but might remedy that at any moment.

Where had that thought come from? Georgia was amused as she and Peter followed him through the side entrance into the garden at the rear. Much nicer to be outside on a reasonably nice day such as this. One look around her told her that Ken was a keen gardener. Pots of flowers were dotted at strategic intervals and different heights for maximum effect, and what bulb leaves could still be seen blended happily into the new greenery of May leaves and the army of blooms preparing its march to blossom.

'We visited your daughter,' Peter explained, after Ken had established Georgia and himself in garden chairs, 'about another matter, and we got to talking about Tom Watson. She said you had written about his case. The nineteen fifties, wasn't it?'

Ken had no hesitation in replying. 'Nineteen fifty-two was the murder. Trial the next year. It doesn't get as much coverage as some other cases because it ended in acquittal. Less scope for lurid speculation, even though poor old Tom did himself in. Disappeared in autumn 1953, officially presumed dead in 1963. No libel risk therefore, but his case still gets overlooked. Not by me though. Chris probably told you my dad worked with Tom.'

'She did. The Three Joeys.'

'Right. My dad doesn't bother to pop back to see me, like Tom's ghost. I take it that's what you're after? The ghost story? We have lots of you folks down here from time to time. Lunch at the haunted house, that sort of thing. You'd think Gary would make a fortune, but he just doesn't get it. Make a feature of it, old boy, I tell him, but will he? He will not. So it's ghosts that you're after?'

'No,' Peter said. 'We leave that to the Society for Psychical Research. We're interested in the murder case itself.'

Ken looked taken aback. 'Who did you say you were?'

'Georgia and Peter Marsh.'

He reacted with some alarm. 'You write true crime books, don't you? I read the one about the Goblet. So that's why

you're interested in old Tom? Well . . .' He was backing off
fast and the situation had to be remedied.

'Not necessarily,' Georgia said hastily, afraid that he
foresaw a conflict of interest as the journalist in him began
to hear alarm bells. 'We listen to a lot of interesting stories,
but we can't look into them all. Only a few make that
stage.'

'How long does it take you to write up the cases?'

This was a familiar question to Georgia, but it seemed
an odd one, coming from a journalist. 'About nine months,
once all the evidence is in place.'

'Right,' he said slowly. The matter seemed to have been
settled to his satisfaction, because he added, 'Don't see why
I shouldn't help you then.' He gave a nervous laugh. 'Just
in case Tom gets to be one of your few. Sounds like the
Battle of Britain, doesn't it?' Another laugh. 'You wrote
one on that too, didn't you?'

'Something like that,' Peter said politely. 'We'd appreciate anything you could tell us about the case, even at this
early stage.'

Georgia was beginning to warm to Ken. He might appear
to ramble on, heading nowhere in particular, but she thought
there was more to him than that. He seemed a kindly man
but not one to whom life would offer many unexpected
boosts in his career, or one with the power to fight his way
to success. As a result, however, he seemed far more
contented than many journalists she had met.

'Local stories are my cup of tea.' He chuckled. 'I can
reel them off till the cows come home. How about this for
an idea? I'll give you the background to Tom's story, every
blinking detail you want, but not my pet angle. Not till it's
published. If you do decide to take the story on after I've
had my scoop, we can pool resources. It will be in the
Broadstairs Chronicle very shortly.'

'That sounds good,' Peter agreed. A white lie, if ever she
had heard one, Georgia thought, even if in a good cause.
Peter wouldn't be against sharing information, but he would
think long and hard before working with a third party on
a book project. Such an arrangement was too open to

conflict. A big thank you in the acknowledgements was more usual for Marsh & Daughter.

'I need to get my story out on the street quickly.' Ken gave a nervous laugh.

'The enemy on your trail?' Peter joked.

It didn't go down too well. 'You never know,' Ken muttered, and Georgia was afraid he would clam up just as she had hoped they were getting somewhere. Did he really fear retribution?

She held her breath as Peter tried to rescue the situation. 'You're right. All we'd like from you today is the basic story.'

'Nineteen fifty-two then,' Ken began, settling back in his garden chair like an ombudsman now that the situation was clarified to his satisfaction. 'Night of Saturday the sixteenth of August, when Joan Watson was found murdered. Stabbed with a kitchen knife.'

'Did you know her?' Georgia could have kicked herself for asking such a stupid question.

Ken grinned. 'Do you mind? I was two years old then, and didn't have my future profession in mind; otherwise I'd have taken notes. Most of what I know about Joan, I've learnt from my dad Micky, or from the press – and of course there's Sandy; he was the third Joey. And Cherry. Know about her, do you?'

'Yes. Christine mentioned her. It must have been very hard for her.'

'She was a nice kid, Dad said. Still is, though not a kid any more. She was over the shock by the time I got to know her, though she's never got over Tom. She stayed on here for a year or two after Tom's trial, so Dad said, then married Harold Staines, the producer of the show, went up to London with him and disappeared off the radar. Then the marriage vanished too, and back she came. No kids. Never had much luck, did Cherry. Got a job as a dancer at the Margate Lido for a year or two, then married again. Then *he* died. Anyway, best start at the beginning,' he said guiltily. 'I always put my big feet in before my head, so my dad always said.'

'First,' Peter said quickly, 'could you tell us whether there was any doubt over who murdered Joan? Any suspects other than Tom?'

'Plenty of them, but Tom never denied killing her.'

'Did he *admit* it though?' Georgia asked. This did not add up with the fingerprints at the cafe being Tom's; where was the unfinished business?

'Ah-ha,' Ken said maddeningly. 'Like I said, let's start at the beginning. With the show itself. *Waves Ahoy!* it was called. It began in Ramsgate just after the war, then moved here. Know Broadstairs, do you?'

'Slightly,' Peter said ambiguously. In fact Georgia remembered it from seaside visits when she and Rick were young, and Peter knew it even better, but it would be good to have Ken's take on it.

'The show was at the end of the pier. Heard of Uncle Mack, have you?'

'Yes, a *Children's Hour* presenter on the radio,' Peter said promptly.

'Not that one. The *really* famous one, here in Broadstairs, who put on minstrel shows right from the year dot, round about 1900, I think; they were on the sands in the daytime and in the evenings under the shelter on the pier. I never saw it, of course – too young – but I heard so much about it, I felt as if I had. He was an institution was Uncle Mack. Went right on until he died in the late forties. Then Harold Staines brought over *Waves Ahoy!* from Ramsgate and the show ran for three or four years in a temporary canvas-enclosed theatre on the pier.

'We had other theatres in the town too,' Ken continued proudly. 'One in the High Street, the Bohemia, the Playhouse in Westcliff Avenue and the famous Garden on the Sands – that's still there. *Waves Ahoy!* was more downmarket, catering only for holidaymakers, day-trippers and kids for the summer season, but that's where the Three Joeys came in. Clowns for the kids, cancan dancers for the dads, and comedy sketches to keep grandma rolling in the aisles.'

'And for the mums?' Georgia enquired, amused.

'David Maclyn,' Ken replied promptly, to her astonishment. It was a name she knew well, even though it predated the age of the Beatles. He was a crooner who had hit the big time in the fifties. What had happened to him? She racked her memory and decided he must have lost his popularity after Elvis, rock and roll and the Beatles supplanted fifties' melodies.

'He sang here regularly?' she asked.

'Sure did, before he made it big time. After the murder, he left here pretty quickly.' Ken hesitated. 'Not that he'd any reason to *kill* Joan, of course. He died of drink years ago, when his career and voice ran out of steam. Anyway,' he added before Georgia could leap in with another question, 'you need to know about the Three Joeys first. None of them really called Joe, of course.'

'Could we take Tom first?' Peter asked firmly.

Ken still came at this obliquely, to Georgia's amusement. Peter always liked firming up on the central characters before he broadened his approach. Perhaps Ken sensed this – there might be more steel to him than she had realized. 'You need to understand the trio to see Tom's place. There were Sandy Smith, Micky and Tom. Sandy was the frontman, the conjurer and comedian, Dad was the acrobat and Tom was the general knockabout and, it has to be said, stooge.'

'Did Tom mind that?'

'Not a bit. It wasn't in Tom's nature, Micky said, to want to stand out; he liked being one of the trio and was only too happy to play wimp – both in his career *and* marriage.'

'Joan ruled the roost?' Georgia asked. Was this a case of worms turning? Had Tom been guilty after all? As he had never denied it, it looked at least possible at this early stage.

'She wasn't the nagging kind, but she did what she pretty well liked, and Tom had to put up with it. She was a cracking dancer, Micky said. There has to be a pivot in any group, and Joan was to the chorus line what Sandy was to the Three Joeys.'

'Does Sandy still live in Broadstairs?'

'Very much so. He's over eighty now, so he's not as active as he was, but he's still in reasonably good nick. His daughter looks after him. They live out on the cliffs towards Kingsgate.'

'What happened to the Three Joeys after the murder? Did the show go on during the trial and after the acquittal?' Peter asked.

'The show went on for another year or two without Tom, both before and after his acquittal. Then Harold Staines married Cherry Harding and left for more profitable fields. No one had the heart to find a permanent replacement for Tom after he was acquitted, so Dad and Sandy carried on the act alone. When Harold left they split up. Sandy said he was leaving Broadstairs to travel the country; he did that for fifteen years or so, then decided to return to his roots. Micky was more sensible. He just stayed put, like me. When you find a good place, stick to it.'

'I've heard of Harold Staines,' Peter commented. 'West End producer? Highly acclaimed musicals and so on?'

'Right. He's retired now, but he went on to fame and fortune in London. Not straight away though. David Maclyn hit the top quicker, but only Harold lasted the course. He worked his way up. *Waves Ahoy!* wasn't a bad show, so Micky said. After it folded, Dad got regular work in Margate or Ramsgate or here in Broadstairs on the strength of it. He'd built up a bit of a reputation with the kids here, he said, and that stood him in good stead.'

'Was Cherry in the show too?' Georgia asked. Cherry was the marker with whom she could identify. The one who waited.

'Sure. She was in the chorus line, so Joan could keep a beady eye on her when she realized Tom was having it off with her.'

Peter pounced on this. 'Was his affair the reason for the murder? Was his wife standing in the way?' He was beginning to get hooked, Georgia thought.

Ken looked smug. 'You've got it all wrong. My fault. It wasn't only Joan who was the victim of this marriage. Tom was too. The prosecution case was that Tom discovered Joan was having an affair. In fact it was affairs in the plural. She liked to spread her favours around, did Joan. Cherry and Tom just held hands, Micky said. She was an innocent, and so was Tom, till he got driven mad by Joan.'

'So Tom was jealous, but what was she like? You're not giving her a good press so far,' Peter pointed out.

'On the contrary, Micky liked her a lot,' Ken said. '*Everyone* liked her, that was the problem. Dad said she was one of those beautiful, warm-hearted women who believed in having a good time but not in hurting people.'

'She presumably didn't mind hurting Tom,' Georgia pointed out.

'Micky didn't think she meant to. To her sex was natural, he said, and she couldn't understand why Tom was so mean-spirited about it.'

Unusual, to say the least. Georgia wasn't convinced by Ken's endorsement of Joan. Maybe his father had been one of those who fancied her.

'Did Tom only find out about her lifestyle on the night of the murder?'

'So the prosecution suggested, but who knows what goes on in a marriage?'

The way Ken looked at them made Georgia suspect they were getting rather less than the full story here, but that was to be expected after the 'rules' he had laid down. 'Was this public knowledge?' she asked.

'You know what showbiz is like. Hotbeds of little intrigues while the show's on. When it's over, everyone goes his own way. The jigsaw pieces are shaken up, and next season you begin again.'

Rather glib? Georgia wondered. Surely some little intrigues got taken further, as Tom Watson's certainly had. 'Presumably there was a performance on the night the murder took place?'

'Yup. The season began in June and went on until the end of September. It might have been only a tuppenny ha'penny pier show, Micky said, but there were some good acts in it.'

'About the murder itself. I assume it took place in the flat over the fish and chip shop. Was that there then?'

'No. It was an old-fashioned dress shop run by two elderly ladies, and the Watsons lived in the flat above. Tom's story was that he came home and found Joan dead. She'd come straight home after the performance because she was tired, but he'd been to the pub first. Only trouble is no one could be found to back him up in this, except for Cherry, but no one believed her, of course. Their regular was the Black Lion in the High Street, but no one had seen him there. Unfortunate for him. Dad told me the flat was a mess, as though there'd been a struggle, although I don't suppose he saw it for himself. It was a knife attack. One vicious deep stab to the heart, which managed to strike lucky – or unlucky if you were Joan – first go.'

'Forensic evidence?' Peter asked.

'His prints on the knife – that do for you?'

'Was the knife left in the wound?'

'No, but there wasn't much blood around.'

That might be one point in Tom's favour, Georgia thought. It would suggest Joan was dead when he pulled it out. If he had found her like that, it was just possible he might instinctively have removed the knife immediately. On the other hand, he could have been overcome at the horror of what he had done and waited some time until he pulled it out. Ken obviously had plenty of facts at his fingertips, which meant he had been into the subject thoroughly. She longed to ask what his pet angle was, but there wasn't a hope he would spill the beans on that. She wouldn't, if she were in his shoes.

'Was the knife from their own kitchen?'

'Not known. No one could or would identify it.'

'So why was Tom acquitted?' Peter asked. 'The evidence you've cited so far seems pretty damning.'

'One member of the jury couldn't be bullied into agreeing on a guilty verdict and talked all the rest round. And before you ask, that's privileged information, not generally known. Don't ask me how Micky found out, I've no idea, but the good lady's been dead many a long year. It was a shock verdict, Dad told me.'

'Did anyone else other than Cherry and the jury member think he was really innocent?'

After what she'd heard, she expected the answer to be no, and so was surprised when Ken said, 'Dad always

thought he was. Said Tom hadn't the strength to do it.'
Christine had not mentioned this, Georgia thought. Did she
just forget, or had Ken only just found that out? Was this
part of his scoop? she wondered.

'But Tom was a clown – a general knockabout, you said,'
Peter immediately objected. 'He must have been fairly
strong.'

'I reckon Dad meant mental strength. Tom adored Joan
– or he'd never have put up with her fancy men.'

'Assuming he knew. Was the prosecution case challenged
at the time? It could be – sorry – hearsay, Ken.'

Ken didn't take offence. 'Fair enough. Reckon I could
find out if we needed to. The kid won't like it, but—'

'What kid? Did they have a child?' Peter interrupted.

'Sorry. Should have said earlier,' Ken replied airily. 'Yes.
Pamela Trent she is now. Married to Matthew Trent, local
tycoon. Joan and Tom had been married in the late forties,
and Pamela was only three or so when this happened, so
you won't get much from her.'

'Except presumably she'd like to knock the rumour that
she was a murderer's daughter on the head once and for
all,' Georgia said. Ken was just a mite too casual about this
daughter. 'Is she still in Broadstairs?'

'Nearby.'

'Could we have her address?' she persisted, but was
hardly surprised when he replied:

'Best not at this stage. Take it slowly, eh?'

Georgia could see Peter's increasing interest. He liked
facing challenges such as this, and Ken's reply suggested
there might be something juicy to discover.

'Do you have any photos we could look at?' she asked
hopefully, with the daughter avenue at least temporarily
closed.

Ken, as she had hoped, seized on this as a diversion from
Pamela Trent. 'Sure. Mostly of Micky but some group
pictures. There's a couple of Joan. Snapshots – you know
the sort of thing.'

Georgia did. Fuzzy black and white jobs, although they
were often better at conveying atmosphere than colour.

Ken disappeared indoors and reappeared with a box file, which he proceeded to empty on the garden table. Fortunately there was no wind, but even so Georgia found herself scrabbling on the grass for stray photos that had slipped off.

'Not sorted,' he told them unnecessarily. He made up for it by searching through the pile and picking out some, which he thrust under their noses one after the other. 'Here we are. The Joeys. That's Tom.'

Georgia had a brief glimpse of three men in street clothes, arms round one another's shoulders, standing on what was clearly Broadstairs pier. Tom was the one in the middle, the shortest of the three, which made him look the stooge straight away. The one in the middle of the sandwich, the fall guy. Or was she reading too much into the situation, given what Ken had told them? Certainly he looked like Mr Ordinary Man in the Street, but then it was hard to tell from such an old snapshot. Sandy Smith was the one with the sleeked-back – Brylcreemed? – hair and Micky the one with the happy grin.

'Where's Joan?' Peter asked. Ken whisked through the pile and pulled one photo out. This was a studio picture, head and shoulders, Hollywood forties style, and it instantly brought her to life for Georgia. She looked a typical pin-up girl.

She recognized David Maclyn without Ken's help. No studio picture, this. He was snapped strolling along the promenade with his arm round a short, energetic-looking girl who looked as if she was about to leap at the camera.

'Mavis,' Ken said briefly. 'Married her just after the war, 1947, I think.' He took the photo from her to pass on to Peter. 'Look happy, don't they? I tell you, there's a story there. And that's not the only one, believe me.'

'Your scoop?' Peter asked, not exactly in a loaded voice but hardly innocently. Obviously Ken picked up on this, because he began to gather up the photos. At the bottom of the empty box Georgia glimpsed a white envelope, but if there was anything interesting inside it, they clearly weren't going to get the opportunity to see it, as the photos were being heaped on top of it.

'Do you have one of Tom on your computer?' Peter asked. He was clearly trying not to sound too eager, and Georgia guessed he wanted one for their website.

'Might have,' Ken said. He was fencing, Georgia realized.

'I wonder if you could send me one. I like having relevant photos pinned up in the office. It helps us to focus better.'

'I'll see what I have.' Ken sounded ungracious, to say the least. 'Fancy a stroll down to the pier where it all began?' he then asked heartily.

'Why not?' Peter said agreeably.

Georgia could think of plenty of reasons, like spending more time with these photos, but Ken was already putting the lid on the box.

'Will that – er – ?' Ken pointed at the wheelchair.

'It will get me there OK. Any reasonable request fulfilled,' Peter said, sounding remarkably cheerful.

Why was that? Georgia wondered. Had he spotted something she had not? Or was it that Ken so obviously wasn't telling them everything?

Broadstairs was not crowded that afternoon, and the paved walk along the seafront to the pier was a pleasant stroll and must always have been so, Georgia thought, with the cliffs ahead of them and Dickens's Bleak House overlooking the town and pier. She knew it wasn't called Bleak House in his time, and that its provenance as the inspiration of the novel was disputed, but nevertheless today it made a fine and convincing picture. In the mid nineteenth century Dickens, whose favourite resort had been Broadstairs, had come flying down that hillside to sit by the pier and chat to the fishermen. Now, senior citizens were flocking to the pier benches, but it was still possible, Georgia thought, to imagine these sands packed with children listening to Uncle Mack or other entertainers in Victorian and Edwardian times.

As Ken led them past the old boat house and on to the pier, she could see there were still a few fishermen and moored boats, but cars had now come to join them on the pier's far side. The familiar image of a pier was of a long, slender construction reaching far out into the water, but Broadstairs' pier was short and stubby, a working pier – and she liked it the more for it. Ships' figureheads on the boat house and a plaque commemorating a lifeboat from the doomed *Lusitania* that had once been there were but two of the pier's connections to history, but the modern age had its say too. At its end, where *Waves Ahoy!* must have taken place, there was now a cafe.

'To me the theatre – as we called it – is still there,' Ken said ruefully. 'I never come here without seeing it there, and Dad and the others all playing their socks off, even sometimes when the waves came right over the pier and soaked the lot of them. The show packed up when I was four or five, so I can't have seen it often, if at all, but it's so vivid that Dad must have talked about it a lot. I can hear the laughter, see the chorus girls – and then I look again and there's nothing there. I hear the singing too. And that's without nipping into the Tartar Frigate.'

The pub at the shore end of the pier was an ancient establishment. Given its name, it must be crawling with ghosts from the past, of whom Dickens was probably one, Georgia thought. Nice to think of him propping up the bar.

'If your father believed Tom was innocent, who did he think was guilty?' Georgia seized this opportunity.

'No idea,' Ken said promptly. He looked distinctly uneasy now. 'Facts, I said. You're asking for hearsay. And my scoop comes first.'

An awkward silence followed, which Georgia had to break. 'Sit down and I'll buy three ice creams,' she offered. When she returned from the kiosk, Ken was sitting in silence on a bench while Peter chatted away about the view in front of them.

The gift mollified him. 'I haven't eaten one of these for many a long year,' Ken said in surprise as she handed him the ice cream cone. 'Looks daft eating it though.'

'Not if you like them,' Georgia said, licking her own and hoping Ken's might lubricate his tongue again.

'Would we trespass on your scoop if we talk to the people you've mentioned, other than Pamela?' Georgia asked.

Ken shifted uneasily. 'Depends, doesn't it? Never know whether it's best to speak out or keep mum. It needs to be published soon. The more people know the better it is, I suppose.'

'Could you let us have Cherry and Sandy's addresses then?'

Ken still hesitated. 'Sure, but take care. And we've got a bargain, right? My scoop first.'

'If anything was needed to make me curious about Tom Watson, that was it.' Georgia was determined to keep off the subject of Rick as long as possible. At the moment that lay in her stomach like an undigested meal. 'I saw one big chicken sitting on some lovely eggs about to hatch.'

'Your chicken seemed very uneasy about giving birth to any eggs at all. Did you note his "need" to publish soon?'

'I did. I took that to mean that there were others after the story.' Had she misread that? 'Or do you think it was because someone might try to stop him publishing it?'

'Could well be the latter. He was nervous about something, and it wasn't us. Tom's daughter perhaps. He was very cagey about her. And to be fair, Georgia,' Peter added, 'we didn't have that much time with him, and nor were we in our best interrogation mode.'

'No,' she agreed as Rick's shadow danced before her. 'Shall we —'

'No,' Peter almost barked at her. 'Let's keep away from Rick till we get home. Then you can dig Luke out of his office and we'll mull the whole thing over with him. OK?'

'Yes.' Georgia felt her tension subside. Luke would be umpire, Luke could give his judgement on how and indeed whether this lead should be followed up – and on whether they should hope or treat it as just one more possible line that would peter out.

'Back to Tom Watson,' Peter said firmly. 'One factor seems very odd indeed.'

'Cherry?' She glanced at him.

'Right. If she believed him innocent, why —'

She finished it for him. 'Didn't they marry when he was

acquitted?' So that's why he had been so cheerful earlier. He'd spotted a loophole.

Peter sighed with relief. 'We make a good partnership, don't we?'

She laughed. Peter had obviously decided he could see this as a Marsh & Daughter venture. 'On the whole. Is that where Ken's scoop lies – the Tom and Cherry angle?'

'I doubt it. That's a basic question he'd have dealt with long ago. His dad probably knew the answer. There was another interesting line though. Did you note the emphasis on "kill" when he talked about Maclyn's relationship with Joan?'

'No,' she admitted guiltily. 'What's the inference from that?'

Peter nobly did not reproach her. 'That there was a relationship *other* than motive for murder.'

'Ah.' She turned this over in her mind. 'Maclyn was one of Joan's lovers?'

'Highly possible, I suppose.'

'Ken's scoop?'

'Could be. Who knows?'

'We certainly don't. We're starting from scratch.'

Peter agreed. 'Much better. Tom Watson was acquitted, but was he really guilty? Disappeared, but no body was ever found.'

'Like Rick.' Georgia could not stop herself and immediately regretted it. 'Sorry, Peter. I suppose I'm beginning to see too many similarities. Poor Cherry still waiting, still drifting along on a cloud of hope and irresolution.'

Peter gave in. Rick obviously wasn't going to wait. 'We're not drifting. Not now. Do you want to go ahead with this Tom Watson case – if case it is – side by side with Rick?'

It was her own fault. She saw the quests side by side. She had a terrifying fantasy of a long road stretching ahead, with Rick strolling along it into the distance with a golden-haired girl and a clown trotting behind them. Although his back was to her, she knew that clown was still wearing his painted face. Suppose they all vanished into the distance without once turning to wave goodbye?

Nonsense perhaps, but the image would not go; she had

to force it to disappear. 'We might succeed in finding the answers to both.'

Peter did not reply, and she had to continue jerkily, 'We can't turn back now. We'd always wonder whether we should have gone on.'

This time he did reply, with a surprisingly resilient, 'You're right.'

'But that's really a hopeful lead,' Luke said immediately, when Georgia told him of their modest breakthrough over Rick. 'Do you agree, Peter?'

Luke must have been able to tell from her expression that it was important, as he'd made surprisingly little protest at being hauled out of his office in the oast house and into Medlars' living room.

Medlars was only a mile or two from Haden Shaw where Peter lived, and its adjacent oast house housed the Frost & Co offices, which (as Georgia worked in Peter's office in Haden Shaw) distanced their home and working lives admirably.

Medlars was a ramshackle and comfortable house, and she knew Peter felt almost as at home there as she and Luke. Its wisteria-covered walls, old terrace and multi-period additions and restorations gave it the air of having solved problems far worse than theirs for a great many centuries, and today he needed such relaxation. He rarely came to the house in the evenings, however, and had paid even less frequent visits in recent months, now that he spent a lot of his spare time with Janie Gale, whom he had met during their previous case.

'Yes,' Peter agreed, to Georgia's relief. 'But it's a pretty daunting task, you must admit. A nameless singer, an un-identified event and venue.'

'Not that daunting,' Georgia said stoutly, in the interests of spurring Peter onwards. 'We've got the date, after all. We can check what Mozart events were on at that time. With her nickname, it could even have been *The Magic Flute* – that would explain the something-really-special element.'

'How do we know if this Miss Blondie was persuading him to come to an opera, a concert or just a general local knees-up? Or even whether this girl was singing herself or only in the audience?' Luke asked.

'We don't. But she was a professional singer, so that could suggest an opera.' Peter was beginning to fasten on to the problem now, Georgia realized thankfully. She had been worried that he would stay outside the discussion, afraid even to hope that it might lead somewhere.

'Does her being a professional make a difference?' she asked.

'Yes. As a professional, even if she were in the audience, it's unlikely to have been a village-hall concert if she had persuaded Rick to go with her.'

'Possibly,' Luke didn't seem too convinced. 'It depends on your definition of professional. Miss Blondie could simply have had a few singing lessons and a date in the local pub for which she was paid a fiver.'

Georgia was thrown by this dose of cold water. 'That's pretty pessimistic, Luke.'

'He's right, Georgia,' Peter said gently. 'That's why we're here, to come down to earth and start seeing the situation for real.'

'At least you have a trail to follow,' Luke said placatingly.

Georgia glared at him. 'You mean a straw to clutch at.'

'Yes, but a straw might turn into a stick, and then a branch.'

'But we shouldn't get our hopes up.'

'Nonsense,' Luke said in genuine surprise. 'This is something you've been hoping to find for years. So go for it.'

He was right. Why not? Now they had the lead, they had no choice. Leaving it to lie fallow was not an option. And neither, perhaps, was Tom Watson.

'We've heard of someone else in roughly the same boat,' Georgia told Luke, 'in that there's nothing tangible, just an unfinished story and a missing person. There's a murder involved, so it might make a case for us.'

'A publishable case?' Luke looked interested. 'I was beginning to think Marsh & Daughter had found another publisher.'

'We'll be in touch in due course,' Georgia said grandly.
'After we've met the person in the same situation as us.'

'Who is it?'

'An old lady called Cherry Harding. She believed in her
lover's innocence over the murder of his wife. He was
acquitted of murder but condemned by his fellow towns-
folk by word of mouth. Then he disappeared – and probably killed himself.'

Luke looked dubious. 'Remember the Luard case, near
Sevenoaks, where the husband was thought to have
murdered his wife? She was found dead in their summer
chalet in woodland. He was never charged with murder,
and yet there was a witch-hunt against him, and he
committed suicide probably for that reason. The case was
never solved. What's the situation with your man?'

'Again never cleared up. Tom Watson apparently adored
his wife.'

'Then why,' Luke threw over his shoulder as he headed
to the kitchen to cook the spaghetti, 'did he need a
sweetheart?'

THREE

Why did he need a sweetheart? For the umpteenth time, Georgia turned the question over in her mind. Lots of reasons surely presented themselves. For instance: Tom could have been a womanizer, or Cherry a fantasist, or their love was not mutual, or his relationship with Joan was not as Ken had made it out to be. Was Tom's daughter a factor? Ken's reluctance to provide contact details suggested she might be.

She longed to get started on the case, both for its own sake and because it might help the nagging ache that came from thinking about Rick. Despite the endless Internet work, endless press reports, endless speculation, she and Peter were moving forward on neither mission. This Tuesday morning, arriving at the office she shared with Peter on the ground floor of his home, she decided enough was enough. It had been nearly two weeks since their visit to Broadstairs. Yesterday had been a bank holiday, which Peter had spent at the Fernbourne Museum with Janie, and she and Luke had wrestled with the garden when the weather permitted.

Pulling up ground elder was a satisfactory way of getting rid of frustration, but today, back in the office, the latter returned with as much force as no doubt the former would. She and Peter had been holding back from contacting anyone until the spadework had been done, and until they knew when Ken's scoop would appear. That didn't prevent images of a clown removing his painted face to reveal – what? Nor did it remove that even more poignant image of Rick on his long road to eternity with a fair-haired girl at his side.

'Don't you think we've given Ken enough time? Let's ask him what's happening,' Georgia pleaded as soon as she had flung off her jacket, greeted Margaret, Peter's carer, who was busy in the kitchen, and cast one scathing look

over the piles of catalogues, bills and other inessentials that
had constituted post.

Until recently she had owned the house next door, where
she had worked and lived until she moved to Medlars with
Luke eighteen months ago. Her own house had now been
sold, but just at the moment she could have done with its
solitude to work off her grumpiness.

'Your patience is rewarded, child,' Peter said smugly.
'Ken's emailed to say it will be in next week's issue of the
Broadstairs Chronicle. It comes out on a Friday.'

'More waiting!'

'They also serve . . .' Peter murmured maddeningly. 'If
it cheers you up, Mike's come up with the name of a chap
who worked on the Tom Watson case.'

'Really?' It did cheer her up. Mike Gilroy had been Peter's
sergeant during his police career, before the accident that
forced his retirement – if Peter's life today could be called
that. Peter still treated him as his private number two, which
Detective Superintendent Mike Gilroy permitted, although
he had his own ways of gently saying enough is enough.

'He claims he can't get at the records of the investigation,' Peter said scathingly. 'Claims he's Downs Area and
this case was under Thanet, and then some rubbish about
the Data Protection Act. Tom Watson, although officially
declared dead in 1963, might still pop up and threaten to
sue the almighty Kent Police. Anyway, Mike's chap lives
in Tenterden now. His name's Brian James, and he was a
PC wet behind the ears in 1952.'

'What about Cherry Harding?' Georgia demanded. She
was impatient to put her image of Tom's sweetheart out of
her mind and firmly implant the real woman, because she
was surely at the centre of this case. 'Shouldn't we see her
first?'

'Police first. Cherry Harding will be prejudiced,' Peter
pointed out.

'And the police never are?'

A withering glance. 'Less likely, let's say. We're all
human. Besides,' he added, 'I'd like to see James before I
read Ken's scoop. He was nervous about it, either through

excitement or because it was going to stir up the case again, and so we need to know the police's angle on it first.'

'The murder was well over fifty years ago,' Georgia pointed out. 'It's ancient history to the vast majority of *Chronicle* readers.'

'It's the minority Ken might be worried about,' Peter said darkly. 'Ten to one it will pass unnoticed, but just in case it arouses slumbering passions, I'd like to have more than the basics. It's possible our ex-Chief Inspector Brian James will add some colour.'

'Possibly over-lurid. Time adds rose-coloured spectacles but sometimes darkens them instead.'

'Very poetic, but I'm going even if you don't want to.'

Georgia knew when she was beaten. 'OK. Let's book it.'

'I have, darling. We're off on Friday afternoon – provided you've no more important engagement like a hair appointment.'

'My hair,' Georgia retorted, restored to good humour, 'knows when to lie low.'

Fingers were drummed on the table. 'There's something else too, Georgia.'

She was immediately alert. 'Rick?' Peter was avoiding her eye, so it almost certainly was.

'All thanks to Google. I scrolled through another thousand or so entries. Have you heard of Guidel?'

'No.' Her heart seemed to be beating painfully.

'Or the Festival des Sept Chapelles?'

'No.'

'Janie says it was inaugurated in 1986 by the Duc de Polignac with the help of Dame Moura Lympany. A music festival, of course, not opera, but it would include Mozart. It's now the Festival de Polignac.'

'Janie?' Georgia was taken aback. 'You've told her about Rick?'

Peter looked at her steadily. 'You have Luke, Georgia.'

'And you have us both.'

'Sometimes, just sometimes, that's not enough.'

'No, I see that.' She did. She liked Janie, but there was no real rapport between them, probably, she thought fairly, because they'd not yet been close enough to develop one. But it was Rick who was important today, not Janie. 'What about the festival?' she asked.

'In 1994 it took place in July.'

The month Rick disappeared. Hope flared immediately. Could this really be a lead? Could they have hit gold so soon?

'And it's remarkably near Carnac,' Peter continued.

So why wasn't Peter cock-a-hoop at this discovery? Surely it must mean a positive line of investigation at the very least? Georgia's head began to spin with ideas and 'what ifs'.

Peter was watching her. 'Darling,' he said gently, 'think.'

She couldn't, and Peter had to do it for her. 'Why, if Guidel was their destination, did Miss Blondie go there so much earlier than Rick?'

'Maybe the festival went on for quite a time. Maybe he just went only on the day she was singing or just for one particular concert.'

'It did go on for some time. Two weeks I think.' He was still avoiding her eye, not sharing her flame of hope. 'There's a big hitch, Georgia,' he said at last.

Too late she realized what it was, and the let-down was all the harder to bear. If Guidel was near Carnac, the French police would have tracked down any accidents or deaths there. There had been a thorough search for Rick after his disappearance had become apparent. As far as she could recall, he had given no fixed time when he expected to be back; she remembered only the uneasy two or three weeks as her parents and she had increasingly tried to believe that Rick was simply somewhere so fascinating or remote that he had no access to a phone or even postbox. No universal mobiles or email then.

'The police,' she said miserably. 'Perhaps they overlooked something?'

She thought back to that terrible time when she and Peter had travelled to Brittany; he had not yet been confined to a wheelchair by that botched raid and was still in the Kent police force. The French police had pulled out all the stops, as for one of their own. Every line that Peter could suggest had been followed. Nevertheless, by the time the family had realized he was missing, the trail was cooling. She remembered that nice young inspector, François Décourt, who'd looked after her on the one occasion she had broken down, and had treated them so sympathetically when he told them the search had to be called off.

'Perhaps Rick went to this festival and then on to somewhere else,' she said desperately, making an effort to recapture lost hope.

'A blonde girl and an Englishman in the audience of a music festival nearly fifteen years ago, or even singing in it? It's not much to go on, is it?'

'It's something,' she forced herself to say. 'If she sang, there would be a programme, a name. Just something to take us forward.'

At least with Tom Watson there was a certain path ahead, she thought. With Rick, there was no known way. She thought of Minnie Haskins' poem made famous by the king's Christmas broadcast in 1939 about the man who stood at the gate of the year: faith was needed to face the darkness to come. Did she have faith now? Cherry Harding still did.

The drive to Tenterden, once Ashford's ring roads had been negotiated, was a pleasant one, despite the rain. Georgia had always liked the town, whose wide streets spoke of another more elegant and prosperous age, despite the infiltration of supermarkets and other modern necessities. Brian James lived on the road to Appledore on the ground floor of an old Edwardian house.

To Georgia, ex-Chief Inspector James still appeared the energetic and energizing leader he must have been during his working life. Upright, tall and with a mop of grey hair, he did a fine impression of a jolly uncle – until one saw the way his sharp eyes were summing you up.

'Are you still involved with police work?' she asked as he ushered them into a conservatory despite some difficulty with the wheelchair.

'I tried not to be,' he said ruefully, bustling around with

cups, saucers and a teapot. 'Couldn't resist, of course.
Promised them not to dabble in matters no longer my
concern, so I'm involved with a police charity. Keeps my
hand in together with the odd lunch and reunion. I'm still
part of the machine, even if I'm winding down. Amazing
the way that work expands to fill the time available.
Parkinson's law, isn't it?'

Peter laughed. 'We've met before, haven't we?'

James looked pleased. 'Good memory. Yes, I remember
you. The curse of the force, I recall. Just as they'd got a
case all straight and tidied up you'd throw a spanner in the
works.'

'Only if it tightened the right nuts and bolts.'

'It didn't always, if I recall rightly. Remember the case
of the woman who—'

'Water under the bridge,' Peter said firmly. 'Now, about
Tom Watson . . .'

'Ah, yes, my first murder case. I was sick on the way
out. Made to clear it up.'

'Always tough, the first,' Peter sympathized. 'Mine was
an easier run. A disputed suicide out of the river. About
Tom Watson: he was acquitted, but general opinion seems
to be that he was guilty. Where do you stand?'

'Speaking as a policeman in the force or as an individual?
In fact, the answer's guilty in both cases. It worried me
when he was arrested, but when he was acquitted, I was
still worried – only the other way round. I put it down to
first-murder-case nerves, but doubt seemed to go on past
that stage.'

'You didn't think he was guilty?'

He hesitated. 'I wouldn't go as far as that. It was just
that his reactions were odd when we took him in.'

'How could you tell if it was your first murder case?'
Georgia asked.

He looked startled, as if surprised that she too was questioning him, not merely the note taker. In his day even
women PCs were probably seen and not heard, she thought.

'That's why I didn't push it. But maybe it's also why
it's stayed in my mind so clearly. Not all the whys and

wherefores afterwards, but that first scene. It was he who made the call, you see. A flat "My wife's been murdered." I didn't hear it myself, but that's what the record said. Straightforward enough, if a bit cool. Two of us went along, me and the sergeant, in case it was just a nutter anxious to shoot a policeman. That didn't happen too much in the nineteen fifties but it was always on the cards. That was still the world of *The Blue Lamp,* the Dirk Bogarde and Jack Warner film, which shockingly suggested for the first time that out in the real world nice policemen could be shot by nasty villains. Relatively speaking, the murder rate was low, but petty crime was soaring after the war. They were hard times, and once you got past the image of brave citizens struggling with shortages and rationing – some was still in force in 1952 – there was a lot of petty theft, black-market spivs and so on. Anyway, back to Tom Watson. He was living in a flat above a dress shop.'

'We saw it,' Peter told him. 'Flight of steps at the rear. Entry at the side of the shop.'

'Right. We both went up, the sergeant first, then me. Watson opened the door to us, blood on his clothes and hands. "My wife's been murdered," he said again. Very flat, very conversational, as if he'd told us he'd had a bad day at the office. That struck me as strange, and still does.'

'Because he was so calm?' Georgia asked.

'No. You often get that. The shock hasn't struck home yet, and they go on automatic pilot. I suppose it was the choice of words, exactly the same as on the phone. Don't know why that struck me as odd, but it did.'

'Did he continue in that way?' Peter took over.

'He didn't lose his cool, if that's what you mean.'

'*Was* it cool?'

James shot a look of respect at Peter. 'I heard you were sharp. No, in fact, cool isn't the right word. It was as though he didn't care.'

'About his wife or his situation?'

'Can't tell you. The latter probably. We went into the living room – parlour, I suppose you'd have called it then – and there she was. Sprawled on the floor on her back, surprisingly little blood, but the knife lying at her side was covered in it.'

That confirmed what Ken had told them, Georgia remembered.

'We asked him if he'd done it,' Brian James continued, 'but he didn't reply. Not a word. Not even a shake of the head. He just stayed sitting on the sofa watching us while we called the station to get the inspector over there. We didn't have all this crime-scene stuff in those days, but the principles were the same: the doc, the photographer and so on. What we didn't realize at first was that there was a kiddie on the next floor. I was sent upstairs to see if anyone was up there and found this toddler. She was still sound asleep. She woke up then, of course. There weren't many women PCs in those days, and one of the neighbours took her in. She told us her daughter had been in there babysitting earlier that evening, so the kid was well used to them. The daughter had gone home after Joan came back – alone, incidentally,' he added.

'And the corpse – Joan. Anything odd about that?'

'Not particularly. She was all dressed up, I remember. Buxom figure, I suppose we'd have called it then. Too old for me, but I could see she was a looker. Long dark hair, English-rose complexion. Blouse, skirt and great platform soles and heels on her shoes.'

'She'd been dancing in the show earlier,' Georgia commented. 'She'd come straight home, so why dress up?'

'You ladies always come back to clothes,' he joked.

Georgia cringed.

'She has a point,' Peter said fairly, leaping in before Georgia could get her retort out.

'But it could be that what was "dressed up" for you was her everyday garb. Or that she'd intended to go to the pub and changed her mind. Or—'

'Don't tell me. She was expecting her lover for a quick one.' James laughed again, but Georgia controlled herself. 'Risky with husband Tom expected home at any moment, don't you think?' he added.

'The prosecution case,' Georgia said icily, 'was that Tom had discovered she was having at least one affair.'

'Maybe. But that doesn't mean the lover popped in that night, does it? Nor was there any evidence to that effect at the trial, from what I heard.'

'He would hardly be likely to step forward voluntarily,' Georgia whipped back.

The jolly glare was turned on her. 'Miss Marsh, if you knew my old governor, DI Tim Wilson, any such assignation would have been winkled out quicker than a rabbit by a ferret.'

'Were there any signs of sex?'

'Not that I heard of. Never saw the PM report, of course, but I don't remember it coming out at the trial. She was fully clothed anyway. No. Tom Watson had a row with his wife and killed her. That's what it looked like, and that's what must have happened. When the inspector came, we marched Watson out into the other room and grilled him. He wouldn't say anything. Nothing, except a shake of the head. Later at the station after he was charged, he had his story ready though. He was at the pub until closing time and when he got home, he found her dead.'

'Did Tom have any previous history of violence?'

'We didn't do official domestics in those days. A bit of wife-beating was OK.' He looked sideways at Georgia. 'The neighbours said it wasn't exactly a happy marriage. Joan Watson was a forceful sort of woman, always shouting the odds – he was much quieter.'

'Did you follow up other suspects?' Georgia asked. This had hardly been Micky Winton's view of Joan Watson.

'Well, now, I can't answer that, for the simple reason that I was only a copper on the beat and not privy to my lords' and masters' deliberations.'

'The press reports mentioned a few witnesses,' Peter pointed out hastily, perhaps having sensed her reaction to his patronage. 'David Maclyn was one, the singer. Was there any suggestion he or any other witnesses were her lovers?'

'No idea. Joan Watson put herself around a bit, but as I said, I was only a PC – politically correct that stands for.' Another smirk at Georgia. 'What happened that night never fully emerged. The prosecution went for a row over her having lovers, but it could equally well have been that Tom was having it off with someone else.'

'Cherry Harding?' Peter asked.

'Who? Thing is, Watson didn't deny he was guilty. We followed up his story, talked to the folk in the show he was in and found his alibi didn't hold up, so that was that. He was right there with his fingerprints on the knife.'

'Anyone else's?'

A glare. 'Can't remember everything.'

'Cherry Harding was Tom's sweetheart. Did she give evidence in Tom's defence? I couldn't find any reference to her in the press reports,' Peter said.

James thought for a moment. 'Don't know about giving evidence. I think I remember her though. She was down the station the next day. There was some girl sitting there on a bench, scared out her wits, hanging on to her handbag like grim death and asking what was happening. Looking back, I guess she had a crush – or pash as we used to call it, didn't we, Peter? – on him. Big eyes, I recall. Too young for Tom Watson. She was out of her depth, she was. Burbling on about Tom being with her at the pub. The gov said she'd be a liability as a witness, as so many others could testify he wasn't.'

'After he was acquitted, was there an investigation as to who else might have done it?' Peter asked, nobly not objecting to being lumped in the same age group as James.

'No idea. I wasn't involved if so, but I don't recall talk of it. There would have been an hour before Joan Watson could expect Tom home from the pub, and I suppose someone else could in theory have nipped in, but pretty unlikely, eh?'

'Why do you think he was acquitted?'

'Hell knows. The gov was hopping mad. The judge looked flabbergasted, so the gov said, when the verdict was given.'

'It seems it didn't do Tom Watson any good.'

James shrugged. 'So what? We all knew he did it.'

'I do not love thee, Dr Fell, The reason why I know full well,' Georgia misquoted savagely as they left Tenterden.

'You don't have to love him to take note of what he says,' Peter pointed out.

'I noticed no signs of a wife around.'

'He could be a widower.'

'It was worthwhile going to see him,' she conceded. 'Does that satisfy you?'

'Cherry clutching her handbag on the seat waiting? It does,' Peter replied. 'And on Tuesday you too can be satisfied. We'll go to Broadstairs to see the little sweetheart. Happy? Or would you rather go alone?'

Georgia was torn. Usually she did most of the interviewing while Peter did the Internet work. Although she would dearly love to meet Cherry Harding in a one-to-one interview, perhaps this early in the case, Peter should be there too. Cherry was a key witness. And, Georgia admitted with a struggle, it was just possible that she might be prejudiced in Cherry's favour. Peter's presence would keep her within limits.

When they reached Broadstairs on the following Tuesday, the public gardens on the seafront were crowded. The town seemed to have launched itself into the new summer season, and there was a general air of expectation. Cherry lived in a flat set back from the seafront at the western end of the town, and as they approached the apartment block, there were many elderly residents to be seen. Not that the town had the atmosphere of a retirement resort; far from it. The generational range seemed much broader judging by the mothers out with children and groups of schoolchildren gathering in the gardens.

Cherry lived in a first-floor apartment, but there was a lift to accommodate the wheelchair. She was almost the frail, white-haired, rosy-cheeked lady Georgia had pictured in her imagination. She was of medium height, perhaps five foot five, with silver grey curly hair framing her face, and she did indeed have rosy cheeks. She looked rather more robust than the stereotype Georgia had conjured up, however – perhaps the result of the sea air. She clearly lived an independent life of her own choosing – if the beaming smile and general air of serene confidence were anything to go by. An obviously home-made iced walnut cream cake made its appearance on the tea table, set amidst a bone-china tea set. Georgia thanked her for going to so much trouble, and Peter joined in enthusiastically. Excellent carer Margaret might be, but she believed in healthy apples, not cakes.

'Nothing's too much trouble for anyone interested in my Tom,' Cherry answered matter-of-factly.

'Will it be painful for you to talk about him?' Georgia asked gently, the girl at the police station still fixed in her mind.

'Not a bit, if it helps.' Cherry sat to attention in her chair, almost as if she too remembered her younger self's long, anxious wait.

'You always believed him innocent of killing his wife, didn't you?' Georgia asked.

'Of course,' came the surprised reply. 'My Tom couldn't have murdered anyone.'

'But someone did. Do you know who that might have been or why?'

'No, my dear. I've been asking myself that for over fifty years. I told the police Tom couldn't have done it, but it didn't make any difference. I told them he was at the Black Lion with me until closing time, but they didn't call me as a witness. They must have thought I would be lying to protect him. But I wasn't. He was there all right. He was with me in a small bar at the back, not in the public where the rest of them were. Tom wouldn't have got home until about eleven thirty, and the police said he called them at eleven forty. Not much time to have a fight, kill her and then straight away ring the police. It isn't a natural way of going on, is it?' She began to look distressed, and Georgia hastened to calm her down.

'He was acquitted,' Georgia said soothingly. 'Did the police come to see you after that?'

'No. No one did. Only Harold, and Micky and Sandy, of course. Everyone still seemed to think he was guilty.'

'What did you think of Joan? Did you like her?'

Cherry giggled – like a schoolgirl, Georgia thought, caught out saying something naughty. 'No, I didn't. I was eighteen, my dear. I was in love with this older man, so of course I didn't like his wife. I thought Tom was the cat's whiskers. So funny, so gentle, and I had not had much fun and gentleness in my life up till then. I thought Joan was all right too, till she found out about me and Tom. She was a stunner and a lovely dancer. All the men fell for her, but she was a holy terror to Tom *and* to me when she found out.'

'When was that?' Peter asked. 'The prosecution thought it was the night of the murder.'

Cherry looked surprised. 'Oh, no. Tom told her some days before that. He was going to leave her and marry me.'

Georgia's heart sank. This was a different picture to the one they had been given by Ken, and it was not a good one. Why hadn't the prosecution pounced on this? Tom would have had a motive, if Joan had refused to let him go. Divorce laws were far from lenient then. Either he would have to sue on grounds of her infidelity or persuade her to divorce him on those grounds – and from what Georgia had gathered about Tom, he was hardly likely to have let Cherry's name be used.

'I wasn't there, of course,' Cherry continued. 'Tom just told me they'd had a row.'

Georgia guessed what Peter was thinking. It was looking worse for Tom, and Cherry must have realized it, because she looked anxiously from one to the other. 'But he would never have *killed* her over it. Tom wasn't like that.'

'Why did Joan pick Tom to marry? From what you say he wasn't the type to fit her lifestyle, and in the photos we've seen so far he doesn't look particularly handsome. Was she on the rebound from someone else?'

'I mustn't spread stories,' Cherry began maddeningly.

'But you need to clear Tom if you can,' Georgia pressed her.

'He *was* cleared,' Cherry said stoutly. 'I know people still said he did it, but he didn't. I wanted to tell everybody that at the trial, but I wasn't called. They thought I'd be prejudiced – and so I was. But because I knew it was true. He was with me.'

'There's still a chance to establish the truth. The *Chronicle* is to publish another article about it soon, so everyone will be talking about the case again.' Peter was embroidering somewhat. 'You would want to know what really happened, wouldn't you? The real killer has never been found.'

Cherry still looked undecided, and sitting here eating her walnut sponge it was easy for Georgia to believe she was still living in a world of over fifty years ago.

'Ah, well, David's long dead, so I suppose it won't hurt,' she said at last. 'David Maclyn and Joan had an affair. He was married to Mavis, and Joan was single when it began. Something went wrong – Mavis, probably – and Joan jumped into marriage with Tom. She treated him worse than a faithful puppy. I'd only just joined the show that season, but I could see what was happening.'

'So it was love at first sight for you and Tom,' Georgia said encouragingly.

Cherry looked pleased. 'It was. He said he'd never been so happy as that summer.'

'But he had a baby at home,' Peter pointed out. 'That must have worried him if he was about to leave Joan.' Georgia froze in case he had gone too far.

'No,' Cherry shook her head vigorously. 'It didn't. Mind you, he was fond of baby Pamela. Very fond.'

For the first time Georgia began to have doubts about Cherry's memory. Had she convinced herself that it was true that Tom would leave Joan regardless of his child?

'What went so wrong that could have driven Tom to murder as the police believed?'

'Her lovers, dear. Not just David. There were others. There was an American sergeant at Manston. That was the wartime RAF station near here. The Americans had taken it over, and this sergeant and Joan hit it off. Tom hoped Joan would want to get spliced to him, if they split up.'

'And there were others too?' Georgia asked. Was this another example of Cherry convincing herself that Joan was unworthy of her beloved Tom?

'Yes, but I don't like to spread tales.' Cherry sounded very determined, and Georgia decided not to press the point.
'Could she have been pregnant when she died?'
Cherry looked shocked. 'I don't know. Tom never said.'
'When he came home again after the trial, what happened then?' Peter moved to safer ground, helping himself to more walnut cake – which pleased Cherry.
'It was terrible. Me being so young, I couldn't handle it. He was in a daze, didn't know what to do with himself. He told me he'd get through it alone, and then we'd be wed. My parents were dead against it, of course, and I needed their consent, so he said we'd wait until I was twenty-one, and then we'd marry and get away from Broadstairs.'
'But something made him change his mind and kill himself. What was that? Did the show not want him back?'
'He didn't kill himself.' Cherry glared at her, and Georgia was instantly contrite. 'Harold – he was the producer – said it was too much of a risk to have Tom back in a family show even though he was acquitted. Perhaps he was right. Harold usually is. But poor Tom! It was hard on him because Harold was looking for someone else for the Three Joeys, not expecting him to be back.'
This didn't tie in with what Ken had told them. Harold was obviously still alive, and Georgia wondered what his side of the story would be.
'What happened to the little girl?' Peter enquired. 'Didn't she give him a reason for living?'
'Joan's parents took Pamela. They wouldn't give her back even when Tom was acquitted. He was unemployed, so he couldn't insist.'
'How did you know Tom had disappeared?' Peter's voice was quiet, and Georgia realized Rick was on his mind as well as on hers. They had had an illogical but never-ending niggle of guilt that they had reported Rick's disappearance too late.
'Tom said he'd got the offer of a job in Eastbourne. That would have been about October or November in 1953. It was a job in pantomime, he said. Off he went, but he never came back.'

Georgia saw her lips tremble again. 'You must have been broken-hearted for the second time. It was hard on you.'

'It was. I married Harold a year or two later – I did it only to get over Tom's going. It was worse than the case itself for me. He just walked out, without telling me or even leaving a note behind him. That's why I know he's not dead, you see,' she added confidently.

That happy smile wasn't assumed, Georgia thought uneasily – Cherry really did believe this.

'He would have told me, you see, or left a note. Tom loved me,' Cherry continued serenely. 'I've got a lock of his hair on my dressing table. I look at it every day, so I know he'll be back.'

'But where has he been in the meantime?' Peter asked.

'He made a new life for himself, that's what happened. For my sake, or so he thought. But now we're older – he'd be eighty-six – he'll come back. He always said we'd die in old age in each other's arms. So I know he will come back soon. It's just . . .' Her voice faltered. 'I'd like to know when. And where he is.'

Like Rick, Georgia thought dully. Like Rick. Before they had set out, Peter had broken the news to her that the 1994 festival programme at Guidel had no singers in it. That did not mean Rick and Miss Blondie had not been present, but as the police had covered that area in their search, they had agreed to discount Guidel as a lead. She and Peter were no further forward, and Rick became a smaller and smaller figure as he walked away briskly from them along that country road. Her nightmare.

Talk of work was banned from Medlars itself, except on rare occasions sanctioned by both parties. Unfortunately Georgia could dream up no way of keeping *thoughts* of work out of her mind. Family talk either of Luke's relations or of Peter's sister Gwen, who now lived at Wymbourne between Canterbury and Dover with her second husband Terry, or of Gwen's son by her first marriage, Charlie Bone, only took so much time, and setting the world to rights was too tough a task for evenings after a day's work. Usually, the boundary was respected, but when Georgia returned from Broadstairs she found Luke in the Medlars' living room engrossed with sales figures.

As a result, vague worries about Tom Watson refused to disappear. The meeting with Cherry had both helped and hindered her. Cherry was a dear but unfortunately so fixed in her own prejudices over Tom that her contribution to the investigation was not going to be as significant as she and Peter had hoped. On the other hand, the meeting had brought the case to life in a different way. Cherry had been there at the time, and therefore what had been history could now be brought alive in a way that even Brian James could not achieve. But where next?

'Supper might help,' she said aloud, breaking the silence.

Startled, Luke looked up from his laptop, caught her look of reproof and laughed. 'Sorry. We could talk about redecorating the bathrooms, if you like.'

'Great idea,' she agreed as the phone rang. It was Peter, which caused instant alarm. He so rarely rang that she knew something must be wrong.

'Have you seen the regional news this evening?'

'No.' A terrible foreboding shot through her.

'A man was found knifed on the seafront path at Broadstairs early this morning.'

'Who?' Her voice sounded strangled.

'I'm afraid it was Ken Winton.'

FOUR

Coincidence – or did Ken's horrible death have some connection with their visit or his scoop? Georgia's sleep had been punctuated by long periods of thrashing over this unanswerable question. Had he been the random victim of a drunk? Possibly. The use of a knife suggested that, and it would be all too easy to assume that because Tom Watson was occupying her mind, Ken's death must somehow involve him. The restless night meant she was early at work the next morning, but when she arrived in the office, Peter was already engrossed in the computer screen, regardless of an apple and plateful of toast at his side. Margaret was obviously failing in her familiar task of coaxing Peter into eating some kind of breakfast.

'Your turn,' came a call from the kitchen. Margaret had obviously heard her enter and was passing on responsibility for Peter's breakfast to her.

'Ah, Georgia.' Peter swung round from his desk, sending the toast flying and Georgia diving for it.

Margaret must have heard the noise from the kitchen, as there was a grim call of 'I'll bring you some more.' When Georgia went to fetch it, she added, 'And you look as if you could do with some yourself.'

Georgia sensed that Margaret was becoming proprietorial about her role in the household, probably due to Janie's frequent presence here, although she had never dared to raise the subject. Although Margaret graciously accepted Georgia's help in what she saw as 'her job', Georgia had the impression that Janie's was a different matter, and sometimes, if Janie was free of museum responsibilities, she would come over during the day as well as the evenings.

Toast might comfort, but it couldn't cure, alas. Peter did deign to have half a slice, but his mind was on other matters, and Georgia could not blame him. 'I've been on to Mike again,' he told her.

'It's not his area.'

Peter looked surprised. 'So? He has staff, who are presumably capable of emailing Thanet?'

As usual, Peter was supremely confident that Mike was waiting at the end of a phone, eager to help him. Perhaps his blithe assumption worked, for the phone rang and, judging by Peter's look of triumph, it was Mike.

'Thanet said my contribution confirms what Christine told them,' Peter said, as at last he finished the call. 'Ken was probably killed late on Monday night. Not too many strollers along the seafront at that time, and even if he were seen slumped on a bench, he could have been taken for a drunk or assumed to be sleeping rough, which is why it was discovered only early yesterday morning.'

'No arrests yet?' she asked, expecting the answer she received.

Georgia was sickened that they had both been in Broadstairs yesterday, but unaware of Ken's murder. It must have taken place much nearer the pier than where she and Peter had parked.

'No. Keeping mum about lines of enquiry, if any.' He glanced at her. 'We can't blame ourselves, Georgia. It wasn't us who stirred up the story. It was Ken himself, and his blessed scoop.'

Georgia voiced her fear. 'Suppose he was thinking twice about something or someone and we galvanized him into publishing too soon?'

Peter sighed. 'Joan Watson's murder took place fifty years ago. The probability of anyone caring enough to *kill* over it now has to be so remote that we could hardly be blamed for not thinking it might present any physical risk.'

'If it does . . .' Georgia decided not to take her unwelcome thought any further, but Peter finished it for her.

'Then there's a chance it's also a risk to us, if Ken's killer knows we're sniffing around too. That being the case, do we continue with Tom Watson or keep our powder dry for Rick?'

Georgia struggled with the answer, longing to say yes to

the latter. But she could not do it. It would seem a betrayal of Ken – and indeed of Cherry. 'Continue with both?'

'I agree, of course,' Peter said. 'But if – and it is still *if* – Ken's death should by any chance be connected to Tom Watson, it would suggest that there's a lot more to the story than he told us.'

'Agreed, but in what way?'

'Anyone directly connected with Joan's murder – Cherry, Sandy, Harold Staines or Joan's lovers – is going to be in his or her late seventies at least, and probably older. Agreed again?'

'Yes.'

'Whatever we uncovered, we would be unlikely to be able to *prove* conclusively, and mere allegations are going to be defamatory and therefore unpublishable. Agreed?'

'Yes, but that's often the case.'

Peter impatiently waved this aside. 'Due to age, it's unlikely any of these people would kill again, especially with the obvious risk of discovery. If by any chance one of them is guilty, it implies there's an angle to this case that we don't know about. After all, look at the inconsistencies even in the story as we know it so far. There are plenty of them, and they're remarkable, even given the passage of time. Joan Watson was warm-hearted, a bitch of the first order, promiscuous, devoted, all at the same time. Tom was guilty, not guilty, devoted to Joan, devoted to Cherry; he committed suicide, would never have done such a thing . . . No, there's more to this, and since I think it unlikely that an octogenarian would be knifetoting around on the seafront at midnight, a wider range of interested parties could well be involved.'

'What about Ken's scoop?' Georgia asked, leaping ahead. 'That was to be published on Friday, and Ken might have handed in his copy already. If stopping the scoop was the murderer's aim, there would not be much point in killing Ken – the article and his notes would have to go too. Was his home broken into?'

'Full marks. I'm afraid it was. No info on what was taken. It's the *Chronicle* for you, Georgia. Right now.'

*   *   *

Georgia found the *Chronicle* office easily enough, having parked near Broadstairs High Street. It was tucked in a side road opposite Jameston Avenue and was hardly flaunting itself. With so much media competition its circulation was unlikely to be large, she realized, although for local communication it must be invaluable.

The office promised more from its outside appearance than it did inside. A back room was obviously given over to technology, and the front office into which Georgia walked straight from the street had three desks set close together, although only one was occupied. There was also a small glassed-off partitioned area for, presumably, the editor.

As she entered, she saw a head glued to a computer as earnestly as if it provided the answer to the Big Bang all by itself. Fortunately its owner, an attractive tall blonde girl in her twenties, leapt up to greet her after a moment or two. Trousers, tank top and the kind of face that could launch a thousand ships, Georgia thought. She had the brightness and confidence of a girl who knew where she was going in life and why. Today the *Chronicle*, tomorrow *The Times*. 'Sorry. We're all pretty busy today,' the girl apologized.

'With Ken Winton's death, I expect. That's why I'm here.'

The girl grimaced. 'You're right. It's not good having to report the murder of one of our own, especially Ken.'

'I can imagine just how much,' Georgia said sympathetically, and then explained who she was and why she was here.

The girl considered this. 'You'd better talk to Will Foster. He's the editor. I'm only Number Two, limping in a long way behind. Cath Dillon,' she introduced herself.

She led the way through the glass door to where Will, who looked scarcely older than Cath, was at his desk staring gloomily at his screen. 'Georgia Marsh is here about Ken. She met him a few days ago.'

Will looked interested. He waved her to a fold-up seat that just fitted in between his desk and the partition wall, and Cath took another to complete the cosy threesome as Georgia repeated her story.

'Ken told us about his scoop,' she ended hopefully. 'He said it would be out on Friday.'

'Would have been,' Will said gloomily. 'He was going to send it over today. We weren't expecting much. We've heard the story before. Always the big one next time. The lion roars, but out trots a pussycat.'

That was a blow. 'He seemed sure enough,' Georgia nevertheless persisted.

'I wasn't holding the front page.'

A setback this might be, but it was also a relief. If the scoop had been only in Ken's mind, it could hardly have been the reason for his death, and some of the turmoil inside her relaxed.

'He must have meant it this time,' Georgia replied. 'My father and I were considering the Watson case as our next full-length book project, and Ken was eager to help. *After* he'd published his scoop. It was in his interests to publish quickly, and he was keen to get involved.' Was that true? She had a sudden doubt. Could Will Foster be right? Ken had been eager, but in hindsight it had been a nervous excitement, suggesting what he'd *like* to be doing rather than what he could do. 'He'd never let you down on producing copy, had he? Did he email his copy in?'

'No to the first; he was reliable at least. Yes to the second.'

'But obviously he didn't this time. Could he have typed the story on the computers here?'

'Nope. I checked,' Cath said. 'We're doing a big feature on him, of course, and it would have been good to use his story, scoop or no scoop. But I can't get at his home computer – even if it's still there. It's an official crime scene, because of the break-in. I'm waiting for his daughter to give me the all-clear.'

'I've met Christine. It must be very tough for her.'

'She's a trouper though. She'll help if she can,' Cath said. 'We're going to make a big thing of Ken having been Micky Winton's son, and the Watson murder.'

Georgia felt more hopeful. This could spark public interest back to the point where interesting details might emerge from the woodwork. Would that make or mar the case for Marsh & Daughter entering the scene? She had a stab of guilt at this self-interest when Ken's death was so recent and could have been due to the same cause.

'I suppose he gave you no idea of what the scoop might have been? Though I realize,' Georgia added hastily, 'that you couldn't tell me what it is.'

Will grinned. 'No. But I can tell you his pet theory was that Tom Watson did not commit suicide. He just disappeared off the radar and created another life somewhere.'

'Is that really possible?' Even if it was, it seemed low-key, and only reproduced what Cherry Harding believed. Unless, of course, Ken had actually discovered a line on what that other life had been. 'Did he have evidence for that?'

'Not to my knowledge. That's the problem.' Will leaned back in his chair. 'You say you met Christine Reynolds, Georgia. She's writing a piece about Ken to go with Cath's feature on the family, and bringing in the Watson murder. How about adding a bit from your professional standpoint? Interesting case and all that. Might do a book on it, etcetera.'

'You're on,' Georgia agreed promptly. 'But would Christine be up to it?'

'She sounds as if she'd be glad of anything and anyone to occupy her mind,' Cath said. 'Let's go.'

Cath was right. Georgia had been ready to back out, if Christine could not take both her and Cath arriving together. As Cath had predicted, however, she seemed eager to see them both, even though her face looked as if she had not slept since the news of her father's death had been broken to her.

'Colin's in France,' Christine explained, 'and can't get back until tomorrow. I'm going quietly spare here on my own. At least this gives me something to do. I'm going crazy telephoning people with the news, unable to say anything about the funeral or what's going to happen, and just going over the details time and time again either with the police or to myself. That's the worst bit.'

'Would you like to get out of the house?' Georgia suggested, knowing all too well how four walls could so easily close in at such a time. 'We could do the feature story later.'

'Yes, I would. That's why I particularly wanted to see you. The police have rung. I can go round to the house, but I didn't feel like going alone. I went to see them there yesterday to see if anything had been taken, but today I'd be alone. So I need company – and the more professional, the better, so I can pretend it isn't happening.'

Georgia knew how that felt. She'd often done that herself, and sometimes it helped. Sometimes, however, it just put off the evil moment when the situation had to be faced. As they walked out of Christine's home, the sun came out as if in encouragement. Christine looked even more heavily pregnant now than when she had seen her three weeks earlier, and perhaps the sun would help to raise her spirits just a little. Not only did Christine have to deal with the death of a father she had clearly been devoted to, but now she had to cope with the aftermath.

Number 59 struck a sombre note even from the outside, although no police were present, as Christine had predicted. 'The police think that whoever killed my father took his keys and then helped himself,' she explained. 'That included Dad's computer, I'm afraid, which would tie in with a random killing and a follow-up burglary, or I suppose the computer could have been the real target.'

This was no more than Georgia had expected, but even so it was a hard blow. Nevertheless, there might be *something* here to help. She steeled herself to enter the house; it was hard enough for her, after having visited Ken so recently, so she could imagine how terrible Christine must be feeling. An empty house has an atmosphere all its own, and one with a story such as this was even more depressing, with all the signs of life suddenly interrupted, the unwashed mug and glass, the supper plate not yet consigned to the dishwasher. There were no signs of upheaval in the kitchen, however, unlike Ken's office, which was a mess. Georgia could see files and drawers emptied on to the floor in heaps, which would make it difficult to tell what was missing.

'Did Ken have a backup for his computer?' Georgia asked. It was a forlorn hope that whoever had done this had not thought of this obvious possibility. If it was a chance burglary, however, it would have been the laptop that would be marginally worth pinching.

'He had a backup hard disk. I don't see that either.'

Only the printer remained on Ken's desk, and helped by Cath, Georgia began to tidy up the mess on the floor, though with little chance of finding anything of interest. The papers seemed to be all tax and bill related, not work notes.

'Were any other rooms raided?' she asked Christine.

'The bedrooms. Look at them if you like.'

They too presented a depressing scene. It persuaded Georgia, however, that it was Ken's work the thief was after, not valuables. Drawers had been emptied, and yet a gold watch had been ignored.

'The photos,' Georgia remembered. 'Ken showed a box of them – have they gone too?'

Christine's face lit up. 'I know the one you mean. I didn't check. He kept it in the living room, not his office – don't know why, except that there were family photos in it.'

Georgia followed Christine downstairs, hardly daring to hope.

'They were kept in here.' Christine opened up a box chest that doubled as a stool and could therefore have escaped the intruder's notice. Inside was the box Georgia recognized, and she was conscious that Cath was peering over her shoulder and equally excited. Christine looked from one to the other and managed a grin. 'Let's take these back to my home. You can fight over them in comfort. Besides, I need to get out of here.'

'This should stir something up.' As Georgia arrived on Friday morning, Peter was scanning the *Broadstairs Chronicle*, which she had asked the Haden Shaw newsagent to order for them. 'Well done. You come over as quite an authority on Tom Watson.'

The newspaper had not only devoted its front page to the murder but also included a double-page feature on Ken written by Cath. Another whole page was devoted to his obituary, and facing that was Christine's tribute, plus an article focusing on the interest still felt in the Watson murder, together with her own contribution.

'Georgia Marsh,' she read, 'of the Marsh & Daughter partnership, well known for its true-crime studies, spoke to our reporter Cath Dillon: "The trial of Tom Watson for murdering his wife, which ended in his acquittal, is an interesting one. I am sure there are still avenues to be explored. According to Ken Winton, there are unanswered questions, and that always attracts Marsh & Daughter. Tom Watson's ghost is popularly thought to haunt his former residence – could it be that he too thinks that justice has not yet been done? After all, the true murderer of Joan Watson was never found."'

'That might bring a few creepy-crawlies out of the woodwork,' Peter said with satisfaction.

'Perhaps too many.' Georgia was uneasily aware that now the die was cast. Marsh & Daughter had firmly nailed their colours to the Tom Watson mast and now needed to set sail in earnest. Ken had not sent them any photos by email, as Peter had asked, but she had now had time to look far more carefully at the box of photos than Ken's rushed overview had provided. It had convinced her that Marsh & Daughter could not abandon ship on this case, which now included not only Tom but possibly Ken.

Some of the photos of the groups of young men and women in the fifties had been identified on the back, but many were not. There were a lot of family photos, of a smiling Micky, wife and son. Some of these had been taken much later than the fifties, judging by the use of colour and the clothes. Christine had looked equally at a loss when asked to identify the fifties photos. But then Georgia had discovered the white envelope she had noticed while the box was open in Ken's garden. These photos were a mixture, and one in particular had struck her. It was of Tom and Cherry together, taken on the pier, and just seeing their

obvious happiness had convinced Georgia that the fingerprints at Gary's Fish Bar had not lied. There was a story
there, which needed to be followed up.

Christine had been reluctant to let the photos out of her
possession, and no wonder at such a time, but she offered
to scan those that Georgia was interested in and send them
with their captions by email – and to do the same for Cath.
Full marks: she had done so right away, and Peter had
pounced on them, not least with the Marsh & Daughter
website in mind.

The publicity in the *Chronicle* brought quick results, in
the form of a phone call from Fenella Dale on behalf of
her father, Sandy Smith.

'My father,' Fenella said, 'would greatly like to meet
you. Would you be free to visit him next Tuesday, the tenth?'

Georgia could see Peter nodding vigorously as she agreed.
'She made it sound like an imperial summons,' she
commented uneasily as she put the phone down. Hadn't
this response been just a little *too* prompt?

'Carers,' remarked Peter, somewhat bitterly. 'They're all
like that.'

Sandy Smith's house was along the North Foreland Road
on the way to Kingsgate. Set well back from the sea and
high above it, it was the sort of home that a retired naval
man might choose, rather than a conjurer. Plenty of sea air
and open space around. The grounds of the house were
large, and parking was easy, which pleased Georgia, as
Peter had been particularly keen to come on this visit.

As Fenella Dale had not sounded overfriendly on the
phone, Peter could well be right that she was a protective
carer, especially as she had warned them that her father
was very upset over Ken's death. She had made it sound
as though it were their fault, and pray heaven she wasn't
right, Georgia had thought. Had Sandy Smith been outraged
at the *Chronicle* story's implication that there was more to
be discovered about the Watson murder? She braced herself
for a difficult time.

Sea View – the house's anodyne name – was a relatively

modern house, nineteen sixties perhaps, with bland white-painted woodwork. There was a double garage to one side, with an old Bentley parked outside. The car was being washed by a tall, heavily built middle-aged man, perhaps Fenella's husband, with such pride that he must have been either the owner or the chauffeur, or both.

Fenella, who opened the door, looked about fifty and a late flowering product of the sixties or seventies, as she was clad in flowing Indian robes, making her a majestic figure. In that way she reminded Georgia of Janie, who also had a penchant for such flowing garments, although Janie had a much gentler, softer face and was younger and slimmer.

Fenella seemed to be sizing them both up keenly as she offered them coffee, indicating that Sandy was to be found in his study to the left of the front door. 'Don't upset him,' she barked ominously.

It was more likely to be the other way round at this rate, Georgia thought crossly as they made their way in. The sight of the room startled her so much that the old man sitting in the wing armchair by the window went unnoticed for a moment. This was both a clown's room and a magician's. Puppets in clown costumes, blown-up photos of the Three Joeys, boxes of conjurer's gear, colourful scarves swathed round a magician's recess – it was an Aladdin's cave, so stuffed with memorabilia that Georgia expected a genie to loom up any moment. There were framed programmes on the walls, and more photos of the Three Joeys, like the ones she had seen in Ken's box. There were others in magician's gear, indicating, she guessed, Sandy's career post-Broadstairs while travelling round the country with his show. It was the clowns who drew her attention most, however. Distance of time had bestowed sadness on those supposedly merry faces, especially considering how they had ended. There was also a clown's outfit displayed in one corner, as though Sandy were about to leap into it. A top hat and wand lay by its side, and a large picture of the entire cast of *Waves Ahoy!* took pride of place on one wall.

'I've got a war record, you know.' The voice from the armchair startled her into awareness that Sandy Smith had been watching their reactions to his room.

'That's a fine thing,' Peter said politely.

'Yeah. Vera Lynn's. Get it?' A cackle, and Sandy Smith stretched out a hand that could have been a claw. 'Sandy Smith, late of the Three Joeys. And the three Cs. Conjurer, Clown, Comedian.'

'The Two Ms,' Peter responded, wheeling the chair up to him. 'Georgia Marsh and Peter Marsh.'

'Of Mystery and Murder?' Sandy chuckled.

'Strictly in written form,'

'Glad to hear it. Hear that, Fen?'

Fenella had brought four mugs on a tray into the room, cleared a space on a table for it, and sat down to superintend proceedings. Oh yes, the perfect carer, Georgia thought. Sandy had a blanket over his knees, but his face and eyes were as alert as a man half his age. It was easy to see that this man had been the leader of the Three Joeys. He had the energy and verve that the others – probably nicer men – lacked, if their photos were anything to go by.

'Now, what's all this about Tom?' Sandy asked. 'Bad do about Ken being killed. Micky Winton was a nice chap, and so was his son. Who did it? Do they know yet?'

'No arrests yet.'

'Not the same thing.'

Peter grinned. 'No, but it's the only news we're getting ourselves. We're on the periphery of the case.'

'But you're thinking of writing up old Tom's case though?'

'If there's more to find out, it's possible.'

'Always more to find out. It's whether it's worth doing is the point.'

'Would you be against it?'

'Why should I be? Ken used to rattle on about Tom and how his dad thought he was innocent, but I couldn't see the attraction of the theory myself. Tom killed himself, and that was that. It's over. History.'

'According to Ken, you couldn't back up Tom's claim that he'd been in the pub with you.'

'No, and you know why not? Because he wasn't in the Black Lion that night.'

'Could it just be that you didn't see him there? Cherry says they were in one of the smaller bars.'

He snorted in disgust. 'Cherry would. Believe me, we'd have seen them. It's not that big a place.'

'Did you see her there?'

'Yeah, I think she popped in, and so did Micky and Harold, but I do know Tom wasn't there. And you know why? I still reckon he put the knife in Joan. I'm soon joining the vast majority up above, and so I'll cast my vote with the majority here on earth too.'

'Micky didn't think he did it.'

'Didn't he? He talked as if he did, until after the verdict. He was a softie was Micky. No one spoke out in public. But Micky and me, we talked it over.'

'Tom didn't admit to the murder to the police.'

'Why would he?'

'My guess is,' Peter said, 'that Ken didn't think he was guilty either. He had fresh evidence.'

Sandy cackled. 'Poor old Ken. He wanted his scoop. So first Tom was guilty, then he wasn't. Then he decided Tom was still alive – Cherry liked that one – then he wasn't. No use going by what Ken thought. It changed every few weeks.'

'Why,' Georgia persisted, 'are you so sure Tom was guilty?'

'Joan was a real corker, that's why. Treated Tom like dirt. She left him to look after the kid, while she flung her legs around wherever she liked. Tom got tired of it, that's all.'

'And that evening, he snapped?'

'We'd had a bad performance. Nothing special, but flat. Everyone was off-colour. We said we'd go the pub to cheer up, but I reckon Joan had other ideas. Tired, she said. That woman was never tired. Not of sex, anyway. I should know. She made big eyes at me, and I wasn't married, so I thought why not?'

A step forward? If Sandy was on Joan's list, it certainly was.

Sandy must have noted her sudden interest. 'Not on the cards that night, ducky. Me and my Jeannie were going steady then, married a year or two later, so I was on my best behaviour. We were both in the Black Lion.'

'If Joan was expecting company, it must have been with someone else in the show or she couldn't have been sure that she would be going home alone,' Peter pointed out.

Sandy's eyes shifted slightly. 'No names, no pack drill, but she'd plenty to choose from,' he told them nonchalantly.

'Did you notice anyone else's absence from the pub? I realize,' Georgia added hastily, 'that it's over half a century ago now, but you must all have discussed it at the time.'

'Likely we did, but then we all thought Tom was guilty, so we weren't doing any Hercule Poirot stuff.' There was an edge to his voice, which suggested the barriers were going up, and Georgia hastily changed tack. 'And his suicide? Do you believe he could still be alive?'

Fenella intervened quickly. 'You've been talking to Cherry Harding, haven't you? From what I gather, Tom wasn't what I'd call a survivor. He's gone, and that's for sure.'

Sandy nodded, looking at them with the hooded eyes of age. 'I reckon he meant to go to the pub but changed his mind. He walked home and scotched Joan's plans.' A pause.

'But what about Cherry?' Georgia asked. 'If Tom loved her, why be so bothered over Joan?'

'Psychology ain't my forte. I may be a magician, but I'm not a trick cyclist.' After a tired guffaw he added, 'There was a spat between Mavis and Joan at the show that night, and Tom joined in.'

'Mavis Maclyn?' Could Sandy be relied on after all this time? she wondered.

'Right. Very possessive was Mavis. Thought her husband was hers alone, but Joan thought very differently. Tom must have heard it going on.' Sandy was definitely flagging now, but then he suddenly perked up. 'Of course there was that sergeant. A real bruiser that one. Tom didn't get on with him. Not his sort. Dillon, his name was. Buck Dillon.'

Dillon? Georgia took a wild guess. 'Any relation to Cath Dillon at the *Chronicle*?'

'Granddaughter.' Another guffaw. 'Go on. Ask me what you like. I'm always helping with enquiries, as the old lag said.'

FIVE

'Will the real Joan Watson please stand up?' Peter looked despairingly at the photos that Christine had sent. He was having second thoughts after his first enthusiasm. 'I see what you mean about them. The ones marked "white envelope" which have no identification aren't going to tell us a lot; the ones that are identified are similar to those we've already seen. As for the others, we only have the Hollywood starlet offerings, which don't get us any further forward on Joan. I suppose . . .' He looked at her hopefully.

'Christine's got enough on her plate. It will have to wait until after the funeral.' Official permission for this had now been given, and Colin had, so Georgia gathered on the telephone, taken all the stress of arranging it off her shoulders.

'I suppose this one would do for the website.' Peter pointed to one of Tom with a grin on his face. Some personality came through in this photo, not aggressive or otherwise remarkable, but that of a man who had a life of his own and was not just the victim – or perpetrator – of tragedy. 'I'll put it in Suspects Anonymous too.' He cocked an eye at her to see how she took this.

Badly. Georgia was not impressed. She had never been a fan of Suspects Anonymous, despite the fact that this software was the brainchild of her cousin Charlie Bone and intended to assist Marsh & Daughter in their work. Unfortunately Peter had more faith in it than she did. It was all very well seeing icons of little men in striped jerseys dashing across the screen, Georgia thought, but translated into harsh real terms the software couldn't work unless there was input from their all-too-human brains and hands.

At the moment this was sadly lacking. As regards suspects for Joan Watson's murder, Tom stood very firmly at the top of a list of one. Witnesses yes, but no suspects. She and

Peter had fed the times, names, alibis, recollections in so far as they could, but nothing shot up as a warning flag to indicate there was any clash or discrepancy, although in other areas the software came to abundant life, notably over the golden-hearted Joan versus the first class bitch.

Marsh & Daughter's website was far more productive as an aid. There, nets could be cast upon the water and the results carefully trawled. Now that Tom's photo had been put up on their website, there was a faint chance that it might strike a chord in someone's memory, either from his younger days up to 1953 or, if she and Peter were really lucky, later than that. Cherry's fairy-tale hope that Tom had survived might just prove not to be fantasy.

It took only two days before precious metal, if not gold, was struck, but it was not the website that produced it. To her chagrin, it was Suspects Anonymous. Instead of Peter's usual frustrated shout of 'I don't know why I bother with this rubbish', she was surprised to hear him call out, 'Hey, Georgia, look at this.'

There was a note of real interest in his voice, and so she hurried to peer over his shoulder. On the Forgotten Elements screen, designed to pick up statements that didn't connect with anything else on the site, there was usually only a long list of drivel. Today – perhaps it was something to do with its being Friday the thirteenth – it contained something that had caught Peter's eye, and no wonder.

'. . . her daughter had been in there babysitting that evening.'

'The babysitter!' she exclaimed. 'We'd forgotten her.'

'And the neighbour,' Peter cried in unison with her. A few moments of rapid mutual congratulations, and then, 'How do we find them, or at least the daughter?' Georgia asked.

'Elementary, my dear Georgia. We can try Gary's Fish Bar or—'

'Pamela Trent.'

'Who was three years old at the time.'

'But might have known who they were.'

'Accepted.'

'I'll write to the Trents. I winkled out their address from Christine. They're not in the phone book.'

'No telephone number?'

'No, and it's too chancy. Gives them no time for reflection.'

'That might be just as well,' Peter muttered. 'Gwen's asked us over to lunch on Sunday, by the way. Luke too, of course, if you can prise him away from his desk. Apparently, Charlie's got a girlfriend, and Gwen wants support when she meets her.'

'*Charlie?*' She was flabbergasted.

This must be serious. Charlie seemed the eternal bachelor, more dedicated to roaming cyberspace than searching for a girlfriend. Not that he locked himself up in a room with a screen that passed for life. Far from it. He dashed here, there and everywhere, solving abstruse problems and enjoying the life o'Reilly on his travels. Travels, song and different ways of life were his métier, with a huge circle of friends of both sexes worldwide. Girlfriends had come and gone; he wasn't gay, he wasn't asexual, so far as she could tell, but nothing ever seemed to happen. Gwen was despairing, so bringing a girlfriend to Sunday lunch with Mum and Stepdad was a big advance.

'Who is she?' she asked.

'No idea. Not sure Gwen knows either. You know what Charlie's like.'

She did. This girl must be spectacular to have managed to pin Charlie down to any date, let alone this one. 'Casual,' she replied.

'Not this time, apparently. Anyway, it sounds like a good opportunity to slip something in about Rick without making a point of it through a special visit or phone call. Gwen and Terry might have some ideas. We won't broadcast the news to Charlie and lady-friend yet though.' A pause, then an airy, 'Janie's coming too, by the way.'

'To a family gathering?' Georgia was taken aback. Was Peter making a statement by carting Janie along too? She'd no objection, but if Peter specifically wanted to talk to Gwen about Rick, Janie's presence was going to make an awkward addition. True, Terry was relatively new to the family too. He and Gwen had been married two years, but Janie was surely a somewhat different case.

'Why not?' Peter answered, somewhat defensively. 'Anyway, I've nothing dramatic to report on Rick. Have you?'

'No,' she was forced to admit. The fact that their enquiries were going nowhere was tearing at both herself and Peter, however much they tried to conceal it.

'Then it will only be a negative situation report to Gwen.'

'Did you check Glyndebourne?'

'Yes. They were presenting *The Marriage of Figaro* that season.'

Georgia wrestled hard to believe that a possibility but had to face defeat. 'No good, is it? Rick would have let us know he was back in England, even if he wasn't staying in Haden Shaw, and,' she added bravely, since it was better to get it in the open, 'we don't *know* it was Mozart he and Miss Blondie were going to hear. Even less that it would have been *The Magic Flute*, even if it were an opera.'

'No, but we have to narrow the search down little by little.'

'What about Salzburg?'

'No to that as well. Their Mozart week was in the winter of 1994, and the only Mozart opera I can trace is *La Clemenza di Tito*, which was during their Easter Festival, not the July one. So if Rick and lady friend were heading for Salzburg, it can't have been for a Mozart opera. There was a major event with Carreras in the Requiem in Sarajevo, which would have had Rick scurrying off to hear it, but that was in April. But we can't ignore the big obstacle. Even if he was rushing off to a special do, why not telephone us?'

She had to say it. 'Perhaps he was madly in love and everything else went out of his head?' Love, marriage, grand-children – they were all left to her and Luke now, and time was rapidly passing. If Rick had lived, how different it might have been. No, don't think that way, Georgia disciplined herself. Think forward. Think positive leads.

Peter seemed to be thinking the same, for all he said was, 'So it's back to the drawing board.'

'Phone call for you,' Luke said, coming with Medlars to summon her. 'On my office phone. One Matthew Trent. Mean anything to you?'

So her letter had done the trick. Georgia had only posted it to Pamela Trent on Saturday, and this was Monday. A very prompt reply. But why to Frost & Co's phone and not her own? This did not bode well.

'I told him you would call him back,' Luke continued. 'He doesn't sound a happy gentleman.'

Georgia debated whether to leave it until she was in the office the next day, thus making a point, but on the whole decided it was best to face dragons as soon as they started breathing fire. Turn your back on the problem and the heat would grow.

Deep breath, and she rang the number. 'Mr Trent? Georgia Marsh.'

She could sense the atmosphere at the end of the line without a word being spoken in reply.

'You wrote to my wife asking whether she would be prepared to give you information pertaining to her father. The answer is no.' Neutral voice. Icy edge. 'Our view is that the case was over fifty years ago, and there is no point in raking over old coals.'

'I can understand that point of view, particularly when your wife's mother was the victim. I hoped to be able to explain face to face why my father and I are investigating it.'

'That would be pointless, as she has no interest in discussing the matter.'

'The subject is hardly dead. It comes up regularly in the *Chronicle*.'

'No one who knows anything about the case would take Ken Winton seriously.'

'And yet Ken was murdered.' She had crossed the Rubicon now, but she was not going to achieve anything by dithering about on the riverbank.

The ether almost crackled in fury. 'Do you have any proof that Mr Winton's death is connected with Joan Watson's?'

'His laptop was stolen.' Was that privileged information? She couldn't remember, but it was out now.

'Laptops are often stolen,' came the sharp response – too sharp, too quickly? 'But rarely for information inside them.'

'Forgive me, but your wife's father was acquitted, so you must both wonder who *did* kill her mother?'

'If we do, Miss Marsh, it is in the privacy of our family, not for public muckraking.'

'The public is already involved as the trial was a public one. But,' she hastened to add, 'I do understand it's upsetting for your wife even though she was only a toddler at the time.'

'Quite. She was a child and has no recollection of this neighbour or the babysitter. Is that clear? And whatever rumours might be flying around, she is in no position to comment on them.'

'Would your wife not want them scotched by an outside examination of the facts?'

'That rather depends on what your line would be.'

'The truth, so far as we can establish it.'

'I doubt if you could. And I have to add, Miss Marsh, I doubt if you *should*.'

He rang off abruptly, and Georgia put the receiver down, shaken. She was being warned off, and this must be why Ken had hesitated over putting her in contact with the Trents. But why the need for secrecy on Matthew's part? Devotion to his wife? His reaction was excessive, if so. Knowledge of what really happened? That would depend on his age. If he was roughly the same age as Pamela, his knowledge would be second-hand. To have first-hand knowledge, he would have to be about fifteen years older and his voice did not sound like that of a man in his seventies.

Gwen and Terry's home, Badon Lodge, set under the North Downs, was an ancient house built on an even more ancient site. The house was of never-ending interest to Terry, who dug for archaeological artefacts and fossils happily in the cellar and garden and spent much of his time striding the hills with a resistivity machine in search of clues, while Gwen battled with keeping the lawn borders and vegetable garden in order, and preserving the resulting produce. Housewife at heart she was not, however. In her younger days she had been as much of a traveller as Terry, perhaps greater, but now she pursued this interest through books and the Internet.

Georgia had thought that Charlie, her only child, lived in London, but now it appeared from what Gwen told Luke and herself on arrival that he had bought a house near Whitstable. Peter and Janie had already arrived, and Georgia found her father in the kitchen getting Rick's story off his chest, while Gwen flew around checking last-minute details of the lunch and Terry looked after Peter and the drinks. Luke, seeing Janie on her own in the living room, had tactfully gone in to talk to her.

The reaction to the news about Rick was unexpected, at least by Georgia.

'Full marks, Peter,' Terry commented. 'Question is: suppose you do work out which concert or opera Rick might have gone to, what then?'

Peter looked taken aback. 'We take it further.'

'How, darling?' Gwen asked, bestowing a kiss on Peter's bald patch as she passed by with a tray of potatoes for the oven.

Time to step in, Georgia realized. Peter looked upset at what he probably saw as a negative rather than practical comment. 'We can check the local police for unidentified deaths.'

'But if he was with this girl,' Terry said, 'he wouldn't have been unidentified. I don't want to be pessimistic, but she would have reported his name and details. Very unlikely for them *both* to die in the middle of a concert.'

Put that way, it sounded dismal, and for a moment Georgia too was thrown. This was the problem about sharing news; one threw the dice, but they could come up with unhelpful instead of helpful comments.

Providentially, at that moment Luke came in with Janie. 'You're right, of course,' he said, 'but I disagree with your conclusions, Terry. Once Peter and Georgia know *where* Rick was, a whole new scenario opens up.'

'That's how I see it too,' Janie said firmly.

Georgia struggled between gratitude for her support and a desperate but illogical feeling that Rick was somehow moving further away from them with this spotlight on their fragile lead.

'Don't you see,' Luke continued. 'Once there's a pinpoint, we can advertise. Offer a reward. Check hotel registers, someone might remember, we might even find the girl herself.'

It sounded good, it sounded hopeful, but was Luke just saying that or did he really mean it? He must have sensed Georgia's doubt, for he squeezed her hand.

'Trust me,' he said blithely. 'I'm a publisher.' As she laughed, he added, 'But I did mean it. After all, what have you two got on the Tom Watson case? Not one firm foot further forward, and yet you're both still sure there's a story there. So push on with Rick.'

Georgia heard the sound of a car pulling up, and one that could only be Charlie's. (The silencer needed attention.) Now the moment was upon her, Gwen looked panic-stricken, so Terry rushed over to kiss her, then seized her by the arm and led the way outside, with Luke following. Peter took himself as near as he possibly could to the doorway, thought better of it and remained in the living room to meet the new arrivals. Janie inevitably stayed with him, and feeling ridiculously anxious about the coming meeting, Georgia did too. She longed to peer through the windows but resisted temptation. Janie caught her eye and laughed, obviously reading her reaction correctly.

'I'm glad I'm not the only nervous one,' she said.

'Daft, isn't it?' Georgia said amiably. 'I can't get used to the idea that Charlie has a real girlfriend.' Too late she realized that this was hardly tactful, as Janie did not comment and looked away.

Something sounded familiar about the girlfriend's voice

as Georgia listened to the chatter outside, but she couldn't place it. Not, that is, until the girl came into the room with Charlie behind her and stopped short. It was Cath Dillon.

'Georgia Marsh!' She looked totally bemused. 'Why didn't you tell me, Charlie?'

'Didn't know you knew each other.' Charlie grinned, coming over and giving Georgia a kiss.

'We met over a case,' she replied. Now was not the time to mention which one. This was a time to be delighted for Charlie. Don't muck it up this time, Charlie, she thought. If she could have chosen someone for him, she couldn't have done better than Cath – so far as her limited knowledge of her went, of course. 'Where did you two meet?'

'Over what I thought was going to be a boring piece about new businesses in Thanet,' Cath joked. 'It wasn't that boring.'

'Damned with faint praise.' Charlie threw an arm round her shoulders.

From that moment everything went with a swing, to Georgia's relief. Terry and Gwen happily chatted to Cath, and Luke and Peter seemed to be thoroughly enjoying themselves, as indeed she was. Janie was joining in well and looked much more relaxed than Georgia had ever seen her. The whole lunch passed happily, and only when it was over and they gathered in the garden did Georgia remember with a sickening jab who Cath's grandfather was – if Sandy Smith had been right.

Janie was firmly at the wheelchair's side, but Luke, ever adept at sensing what was needed, steered her away. Peter looked relieved and manoeuvred himself close to Georgia. 'I take it this is Buck Dillon's granddaughter?' he whispered to her, and when she nodded, added, 'Let's pull out all the stops. Don't hold back the horses, because we'll never get another chance like this.'

Luckily, the horses didn't need holding, as Cath herself came over to them, looking anxious. 'Sandy Smith told me you've been chatting him up over the Tom Watson case.'

'Of course. He's a central plank, as one of the Three Joeys,' Georgia replied.

'And that you asked him about my grandfather.'

'No. He told us.' Was Sandy Smith making mischief or was this a misunderstanding?

'Whatever,' Cath said impatiently. 'What's Grandpops got to do with the Watson case? His name's Bill, anyway, not Buck.'

'There was a US sergeant at RAF Manston during the 1950's who was a friend of the Watsons.'

Cath frowned. 'My grandfather was in the USAF Europe here, but I never heard him talk about the Watsons. For heaven's sake, he wouldn't have had time to fraternize with the natives.'

'Yet he seems to have settled here,' Peter pointed out.

She glared at him. 'That's true, I suppose. He married Gran in the mid fifties. But what's that got to do with Tom Watson? If Grandpops is this Buck, how would he be mixed up with the murder?'

'Just as a friend of Tom's or Joan's, or both,' Georgia said. 'That's why Peter and I would like to talk to him.'

Cath shot a journalist's appraising glance at her. 'Just how would he fit in to the Watsons' life as a friend? I don't see Grandpops getting chummy with a clown and his wife. He'd only have been about my age, or even younger. If he was in Broadstairs, he'd be into dating the local girls—' She broke off. 'Ah, I see,' she said furiously, 'you have him lined up as dating Joan.'

'We don't have him down as anything,' Georgia said evenly. 'We'd just like to meet him.'

'Now that,' Cath said, 'would not be wise. Because I can tell you now, if you put Grandpops in the frame for Suspect Number One for Joan Watson's murder, instead of Tom, you can forget it. He's too old and too happy to have muck raked up when it's not true. Subject closed. Clear about that?'

'Clear about your opinion, Cath,' Peter took the situation on, and it was high time to stop it in its tracks. Georgia could see Gwen and Terry looking aghast at this exchange, and Charlie – as usual – was nowhere to be seen. 'It's possible, however, for someone to be old and so appear to

have buried the past so completely it's forgotten. But sometimes it isn't. Your grandfather should judge that for himself,
not you, unless of course he's mentally or physically ill. I
give you my word that we won't upset him.'

Cath set her mouth in an obstinate line. 'You don't have
to. You won't be meeting him, if I have anything to do with
it. And believe me, I will.'

'That,' Georgia remarked, 'is the second threat I've had
in a few days. Why is everyone so eager for us not to reopen
the Tom Watson case? There must be some reason.' And
before Cath could answer, she added, 'Look, I'm really
happy you're with Charlie. Let's drop the subject of Tom
Watson and enjoy the rest of today.'

'Suits me,' Cath said neutrally. 'Just don't go anywhere
near Grandpops.'

'Yet another protective carer,' Georgia remarked ruefully
to Luke. 'First we have Janie, then Fenella, now Cath.' The
afternoon had been a reasonably successful one after the
storm had died down.

'Don't lump them all in the same category. It won't help.
They're all different people, different personalities, different
needs.'

Georgia felt rebuked. She tried hard to tell herself that
Luke too was falling under Janie's spell but failed. He
wasn't. He was just *right,* damn him. It didn't help to admit
this. Anyway, Monday morning in the office would be the
time to discuss Cath, not here.

When Monday came, however, Peter had more news from
Mike to relate to her. 'Thanet police have arrested a local
fellow who'd been acting suspiciously, but he's been
released without charge.'

'Nothing more?' she asked.

'No. The official view given the time and place is that
it was a random attacker, one of those nutters who decide
to murder the first person they come across.'

'Unlikely for Ken to go down to the seafront at that time
of night, and unlikely for a random attacker to search for
a key and follow up with a burglary.'

'I agree, but I did say "official view", and it's still a possible theory. Now what do you want to do about Buck Dillon? I think we should leave him until we know more about his relationship with the Watsons. Then we'll have firmer ground to move on.'

That seemed sensible, Georgia agreed, even though it went against the grain to appear to give in to Cath. That just added to her frustration. They weren't making headway either on Tom Watson or on Rick. There were so many musical events in the capitals of Europe, especially Prague and Vienna, that it was like searching in the proverbial haystack for a single straw worth clutching. She was beginning to lose faith in the idea anyway. It would have been unlike Rick to have hitch-hiked on a relative whim to far-off cities, unless, of course, the girl lived in one of them. Was she even British, or had they just rashly assumed that? The Iron Curtain was well and truly raised by the time Rick disappeared, but it must have been a very special occasion or singer to make Rick travel so far without a word to them. Or, she acknowledged dolefully, a very special woman.

Think about Tom, not Rick, she told herself. Avenues still existed where Tom was concerned and she and Peter might actually achieve something. 'Anything on our website yet?' she asked.

'Someone who thought she saw Tom in a supermarket last week.'

Georgia sighed. 'Not very likely. Have you got details?'

'Of course,' Peter replied crossly. 'What do you suggest? That we haunt every supermarket in Kingston until he comes back to do another shop-up?'

Silence. Even Luke's well-intended softeners did not break the gloom that evening, which persisted overnight. When she reached the office next day, she was relieved to find that Peter looked brighter. 'A call from Christine. The funeral's next Monday, June twenty-third. She'd like us to go. She's a game lass, Georgia. She says everyone might be there.'

'Of course we'll go. Who's everyone though?'

'Sandy Smith, at least. She thinks Harold Staines may be there too.'

'We can't use a funeral blatantly for our own purposes.'

'Give me some credit, Georgia.' Peter looked offended. 'I'm always tactful.'

She decided discretion was the better part of valour and bit back a reply. Fortunately her mobile rang, which distracted her. At first there was a silence, then a heavy accented:

'Georgia Marsh?' And when she confirmed it, 'Buck Dillon. More officially, William J. Dillon, Junior. I'm told you wanted to speak to me.'

She brightened up. Had Cath relented? She felt it was only fair to say, 'Cath was against it, Mr Dillon.'

'But I, Miss Marsh, am for it. When might you be able to come over? I regret I'm not driving any more. Not my choice, but the fat lady has to sing sometime.'

Buck Dillon lived at Sandwich, and his home was on the outskirts of the town, a post-war house, but not that recent, judging by the size of the forecourt and garden. He obviously went in for style combined with comfort, Georgia thought. No stinting here. She had come alone today, as Peter deemed this her domain. She could charm him, Peter had said airily, to her annoyance. In theory, charm should not be a factor, yet facing the realities of life, she could see his point.

Buck answered the door himself. 'Morning, Miss Marsh.' His accent was still marked. Keen eyes took in every detail of her appearance, and, she was sure, he would remember them.

He did not look like a man in need of the protection his grandchild was so eager to give. Buck Dillon was massive, tall and stalwart. As a sergeant he must have put the fear of God into his men, with this air of calm confidence in himself and his powers. He was still good-looking too, although he must be rising eighty. The shock of white hair and lined, tanned face helped rather than detracted from this image.

'Have you lived here since your air-force days?' she asked as they reached an airy and comfortable conservatory.

'Ask the lady out there.' He waved a hand towards the kitchen, where Georgia had glimpsed a slim and nimble elderly lady of roughly the same age as he was. 'She's the reason I stayed,' Buck said. 'Went back for a year, but then I heard the seagulls calling – not to mention Mary.'

'Does Cath live here too?' It didn't seem likely, as Sandwich was a long way from Thanet.

'No, she's an independent lady, is Cath. Tells me Charlie is your cousin.'

As the talk continued, Georgia decided she liked Buck Dillon. He seemed straightforward and there was no beating about the bush for him.

'What's your interest in Tom Watson, Miss Marsh?' he asked her matter-of-factly, and then listened in silence as she explained what Marsh & Daughter's plans were.

'Do you mind talking about the case?' she asked.

'I guess that depends. Just why does the murder of Joan Watson interest you?'

This was a man who needed the right answer, she realized. That could only be the truth or he would instantly recognize it for what it was.

'We – that's my father and I – feel there are unanswered questions about it.'

'Because no one was ever convicted?'

'That, of course, but there are others as important to us. Why, if Tom was innocent, did his alibi not stand up? Why didn't he fight for himself? Why did he disappear without trace?'

'I guess there are easy answers, but you must have ruled them out already. Tom was unlucky no one could or would support his alibi. He wasn't a fighter by nature, and the woman he loved was dead. He just couldn't take the blame he read in everyone's eyes after he was acquitted.'

'Do you believe those answers yourself? If so, there are counter-arguments to all of them. That's the reason we think it interesting,' Georgia replied swiftly. 'And of course, for Cherry's sake, it would be good to find out the truth.'

He looked at her steadily. 'Would it? Cherry's a fantasist.

Suppose you could prove Tom guilty? How would she – and you – feel then? It might kill her.'

Georgia swallowed. He was fencing, keeping her at a distance, but yet he had to be answered. 'Can you be sure of that? Unanswered questions stick around. We can't just say it's the past and therefore it doesn't matter; it might matter very much to someone else.' Rick was beating at her mind for entrance, but she gently pushed him away. She needed to concentrate on Buck, who had a plan in this battle of wits.

'I can't be sure, but I don't have to be. You do.'

'If I needed any proof that Joan's murder needed investigating, Ken Winton's death has provided it. It's at least possible that was connected with his articles about the murder. He had fresh evidence.'

Buck regarded her steadily and impassively. 'Ken Winton was another fantasist. Cath brought me all the *Chronicle* material, but Ken was the type who thinks Elvis and JFK are sitting side by side on a Greek island. OK, Georgia,' he said shrugging, 'we'll agree to differ, but I'll talk. You want to know how I was involved, eh?'

'Yes, please. Do you mind if I take notes?'

'Go ahead. And here goes. In July 1952 I became part of the 406th Fighter Bomber Wing. We Yanks were sharing Manston with the RAF. There'd been a bad series of crashes that summer, accidents, one after another. One of them was at St Peter's at the back of Broadstairs, with civilians killed, so all round morale was pretty low. We were a long way from home, so we got off the camp as often as we could in search of entertainment. The chief of which, not unnaturally, was women. Margate's Dreamland entertainment hall rated highly because one of its attractions was that dances were held there. It was at one of them that I met Joan Watson.'

'Although she was a professional dancer in the pier show at Broadstairs?'

'For her, that was business. Dreamland was fun, and anyway, forget the dancing. Joan had different ideas. Invited me back for tea, all very decorous, but she had more energy in the sex department than sense. She left her kid with Tom or at her parents' home whenever she had a free afternoon and got the bus or train to Margate. Anyway, I met Tom, liked him, went to the pier show and joined their circle. I had my own wheels, so coming and going from Manston was easy enough. I was twenty-two that year, and it all seemed a barrel of laughs – when we weren't working. That was war in Korea time, and we were always waiting and practising for the off. For your ears only, I slept with Joan once or twice. I knew I wasn't the only one, though she never gave me names. Nothing serious on either side.'

Or if it was, Georgia thought, he wasn't going to come clean on that.

'I reckon it was Sandy Smith told you about me, eh?' Buck added.

'Yes, and Cherry Harding.'

'Yeah? Sandy liked to know what's going on. Cherry too.'

'What did you think when you heard about Joan's murder? Did you assume Tom was guilty?'

'I guess that's an oblique way of asking whether I was there that evening. No, I was on duty at the stores. Heard about it next day, but by that time Tom was under arrest. From what I'd seen, it didn't seem unlikely he'd killed her.'

'And when he was acquitted?' Georgia privately pondered the chances of there being any proof of his being safely at Manston that evening. Nil now, she imagined, although perhaps he had given a police statement at the time.

'It was getting on for a year later. I'd moved on.'

'So you weren't a witness at the trial?'

'Nope.' He grinned. 'Reckon that makes my story mighty damning.'

'Could be,' she answered lightly. 'Did you go to see Tom while he was awaiting trial?'

'Yeah, I did. Kinda awkward. He was a sad fella by then. I couldn't do much, and Sandy and Micky said they were looking after him – so I guess I left it at that.'

'Do you believe that he killed himself?'

She thought he wasn't going to reply, but he did. 'As I said, I'd moved on. I'd left Manston and the UK. By the time I was back to marry Mary, it had all died down.'

He'd replied, but he hadn't answered the question.

SIX

'This isn't really what my father would have liked,' Christine said ruefully, 'but we couldn't all squeeze into a pub bar.' The crematorium was in the countryside near Margate, but the party had returned to the Shore Hotel on the outskirts of Broadstairs for a buffet lunch.

Georgia looked around her. The hotel seemed ideal to her now that the rain had at last relented, especially as the private room that Colin had booked gave on to an open terrace and gardens. With the sun continuing to shine, the mixed gathering was beginning to divide into its various groupings of work colleagues, family connections, neighbours – and those present because Ken had been Micky Winton's son.

In the latter group Georgia could recognize Cherry Harding and a couple who might possibly be Matthew and Pamela Trent; with them was a tall elderly man with his arm round Cherry whom Peter identified as Harold Staines. Sandy Smith was also here somewhere. She'd noticed him draw up in the Bentley driven by the same man she had seen valeting it at Sandy's home, Fenella's husband, Vic. He was in charge of Sandy and his wheelchair, while Fenella marched purposefully at their side, clad in long black skirt and shawl.

No sign of Buck Dillon, however. Georgia had seen him at the service with his wife, but they had obviously gone straight home. Significant? It could have some simple explanation, she speculated; it did not necessarily mean that he wanted to avoid the Tom Watson circle – or possibly even Marsh & Daughter.

'Harold holds the reunions in this hotel,' Colin Reynolds told them. Georgia had glimpsed him at the service, and he looked a good partner for Christine, in his thirties, rather retiring and non-aggressive.

'Reunions?' Peter pricked up his ears.

'Harold gathers as many as possible from the old *Waves Ahoy!* show once a year. Nowadays it has to include the next generation, and chums and supporters too. Cherry usually warbles a song and does a sort of dance, and Sandy puts on a terrific conjuring show. Mavis—'

'Mavis?' Georgia queried, unable to place her immediately.

'David Maclyn's widow, and another chorus-line veteran. She's over there.'

Colin pointed, and Georgia glanced over to the elderly, stout, pleasant-looking woman in her late seventies or maybe early eighties standing by the drinks table; she was beaming away with a glass in her hand and did not look anxious to join the *Waves Ahoy!* group.

'My father used to do some of Micky's old patter and put his clown's outfit on,' Christine told them, 'but now Sandy is the only one to represent the Three Joeys' act. Some of the others are still going – a couple of comedians and singers, and Mavis does a bit of a song and dance – if she's having a good day. Harold runs some home-movie footage to pad out the material. It's a good show – invitation only, but I'll invite you, so do come along. It's in August, so Colin and I might not be there.' She patted her stomach affectionately.

The service at the crematorium had been a moving one, evoking both the Ken Winton whom Georgia and Peter had briefly met and the one who belonged to many other worlds. Will Foster had given a short address on behalf of the *Chronicle* and a cousin had put Ken into a family context. The highlight for Georgia, however, had been a girl of about twenty singing 'I Know that My Redeemer Liveth' from the *Messiah*. Her voice was trained and had a fresh, light quality that Georgia took to immediately. Now *there* was a Mozart voice, she thought – and immediately wished she hadn't. This was a sad enough day without dwelling on Rick. She could see the girl a short way away talking to a young man about her own age, and asked Christine who they were.

Christine glanced round. 'That's Gemma Trent – Pam

and Matthew's daughter. And she's being chatted up by Greg Dale, who's Sandy's grandson courtesy of Fenella and Vic. Vic works for Matthew in the car business, so that's why you can see him buttering up Pamela over there. Greg is OK, but he fancies himself more than a little.'

'Gemma sings wonderfully well,' Georgia said. She was trying to concentrate on the Trents, but it was difficult. Rick, Miss Blondie and Mozart were still singing their way through her mind, and she had to steady herself for a moment.

'Are you OK?' Christine asked, concerned.

'Sorry. It's you who's entitled to dizzy spells, not me.'

'I've been having them too all this week. Clearing the house is no fun at all. Look, why don't you come back to our house for a while after we've finished here? You might like to look through some of the stuff – a lot of it is Micky's.'

'Yes, please,' Georgia said promptly. 'But won't you be tied up with family duties?'

'No. It will give me a good excuse to avoid it, believe me. I'm knackered. I could take you, but not everyone else. Understand?'

Georgia smiled. 'I do.'

'I'll do my family bit now, if you'll excuse me.' Christine moved off, leaving Georgia to join Colin and Peter.

'I thought you'd be making for the Tom Watson circle,' Colin said.

'It looks like a circle that is pretty unbreakable, with everyone mentally gripping their neighbours' hands.'

'Right first time,' Colin agreed.

'Didn't Ken manage to break into it?' Georgia asked.

'I don't think so. He was scuttling round the periphery for years. He really thought he'd found a way in this time though. I doubt if he did. He never seemed to get enough central players on his side to take the story further.'

'And that circle knows the identity of Joan's real killer?'

'Wish I knew,' Colin said. 'Or maybe I don't. They're a creepy lot. Maybe each of them is busy sheltering his or her own wounds and not caring about the others. Much better to let the past lie buried. That's what I told Ken.'

But he had ignored it, and the result might well have led to this funeral, Georgia thought with a shiver.

'Unless one takes Ken's murder as coincidence,' Peter said, 'someone must have broken out of that circle to kill him. Question is: do the remainder know who it is?'

'If I were in their shoes, I'd be playing ostrich,' Colin said matter-of-factly.

Georgia could see his point, but she and Peter were past that stage. As she studied the group's body language she decided that Harold Staines was indeed the pivot of the circle and should be their next target. Cherry was deep in conversation with him and the Trents, but Harold was glancing round as if planning his escape. She was right, for as Colin moved away, he came ambling across. He was still a commanding and robust man and even now had an air of leadership about him.

'You must be Georgia and Peter Marsh. Cherry had been telling me about your project.' He made it sound like a schoolroom module, Georgia thought with amusement.

'I'm afraid she'll still be expecting us to produce him alive,' Peter said ruefully.

'No disagreement there, but I don't see what you two can do after all these years,' Harold commented. 'Not much forensic stuff for your magnifying glasses to pick up, is there?' A hearty laugh might have been meant to indicate that no offence was intended – although of course he was using the art of gentle put-down.

'Fortunately people remain much the same over the years. Only the lines on our faces get deeper,' Peter retaliated, equally jovially. 'Where do you stand on Tom Watson?'

'He was a dear chap,' Harold replied promptly.

'Who committed a murder? Or was innocent as the jury decided?'

Harold studied him for a moment. 'I remember only a man who was broken,' he replied quietly.

An act? Perhaps not, Georgia thought. 'The jury acquitted him.'

'You were there that night,' Peter said. 'Was there no sign that you later wished you'd picked up on?'

'He was no different then than on any other night.'

'We were told there was an argument between Mavis and Joan, which he joined in.'

Harold laughed. 'My dear chap, have you ever had anything to do with theatre? There are always temper tantrums. It's one way of getting rid of the tension.'

'In high drama perhaps, but in a variety show?'

'It's still performance,' Harold said shortly. 'Just offstage. Joan was the kind of woman who attracted trouble, and that depressed Tom. That's all.'

'Were you in the Black Lion that night?'

'Not for long. Fifteen minutes or so. Look, there really seemed nothing different about the performance that night.' Harold began to look his age. 'Joan would arrive vibrant, enthusiastic and conscious of her looks. She lit up the room, you know. She really did. Tom would always be in her wake, the quiet kind. He was also genuinely pleased to see you, but he never showed anger, or jealousy. Even so, they had plenty of spats offstage, as with all the rest of the cast. We were all squashed together, so it was to be expected that tempers would flare. I wasn't surprised when Tom went over the top. It was all boiling up inside him, with no outlet.'

'But you didn't want him back in the show after he walked free?'

'I can see I'm already down as chief villain in your script.' Harold pulled a face. 'Tom didn't want to rejoin the show, in fact. I did offer – and meant it – but he said no.'

'Cherry said you were looking for a replacement for him after his arrest and acquittal.'

'Not guilty.' Harold looked annoyed. 'Tom was in prison, not on bail. We all had livings to earn, including Sandy and Micky. We got a replacement immediately after the murder until the end of the season – only a month or so. We did without one for the following season, and when he was acquitted, I told Tom he could come back for the 1954 season.'

'Did Tom accept?' Georgia was inclined to believe him, for this sounded a reasonable story, even if it did slightly contradict what they had been told.

'A bit of humming and hawing for pride, and then he said yes. I asked him how he'd get through the winter and spring, and he said he'd had one or two offers.'

'Did you believe him?'

'Frankly, no, but I couldn't tell him that. I thought I'd keep an eye on him through the winter to make sure he wasn't starving to death. And I tried. Before you ask me, no, I didn't think he would ever walk away and kill himself. It was hard to tell what he wanted to do. It wasn't a case of "shall I do this or shall I do that?" but sheer apathy.'

'Can you define the reason for that?'

'No. Maybe he'd thought he was in for the big jump and was so surprised at being let off that he didn't know what to do next. Maybe it was just losing Joan – and the kid. He adored Pamela, but Joan's parents were a cussed, obstinate couple; he hadn't a regular job and they weren't giving her back. It was the last straw in my opinion.'

'You kept in touch with him?'

'After his release I used to pop round on a Sunday during the season. Then I got a bit erratic because I was trying to cast a pantomime in Margate and not doing well. I saw him one Saturday night in September, and he seemed much the same as usual, quiet and depressed. The following Saturday there was no reply, and no one had seen him during that week. He'd vanished.'

'With or without his possessions?'

'Hard to tell. I gather he left the flat just as it was when he was with Joan, but there was no one, not even Micky and Sandy, who could tell whether he'd taken *some* of his stuff.'

'Had Cherry seen him that week?'

'You'll have to ask her that,' he answered shortly, looking across to where his former wife was talking to Sandy. The look, Georgia thought, was far from loving. She wondered what kind of marriage they had had: with Cherry on the twittery side and Harold verging on the pompous, it seemed an awkward fit, which perhaps accounted for the marriage's brevity, once the first ardour was over. 'I doubt if you'll get much more information from her though. No one has yet,' Harold continued. 'Some people are against raising the matter again,' he said.

'To the extent of murdering Ken?'

'*What*?' Harold looked as if he had been caught completely off guard. 'Is that some kind of joke?'

'No.'

Harold sat down heavily on one of the terrace chairs. He was very pale. 'Sorry,' he said. 'Bit of a shock. Is this your theory or the police's?'

'More than just ours, and the police are considering it.' A slight exaggeration, but it was technically true. Peter was in touch with both Mike and the Thanet Area force.

'I'd no idea. No idea at all.' He looked up as Cherry came to join them and rose to his feet with some difficulty, still looking uncertain of his balance.

'Darling Harold, are you telling Peter and Georgia all about the old days?' Cherry said cheerfully. Without waiting for his reply, she rushed on, 'We are having our reunion this year, aren't we?'

'Of course,' Harold replied, though Georgia could detect little enthusiasm in his voice.

'It will be Ken's memorial,' Cherry said. 'He did so much for Tom.'

'You mean Micky did?' Georgia asked.

'No, Ken,' Cherry corrected her indignantly. 'He came to see me after your visit, Georgia, and do you know what he told me? He knew exactly what had happened, and my Tom really was still alive.'

'Cherry,' Harold said sharply, 'Tom would be in his mid to late eighties now. There would be over fifty years of his life that didn't include me or you. You're living in dreamland as usual.'

She looked at him with hurt eyes. 'He wouldn't die without coming to see me.'

'Unless—' Harold began, but he must have thought better of it. Unless what? Georgia wondered. Unless Tom had found another woman?

'You'll go on trying to find him, Georgia, won't you?' Cherry pleaded anxiously.

Find Tom himself? It was very unlikely. Fortunately a smile sufficed in answer as Cath Dillon came over to them. Georgia separated herself from the group, braced for the inevitable reproaches over her grandfather.

'Grandpops told me you visited,' Cath began, though to Georgia's relief she seemed far more sanguine than she had expected.

'I enjoyed meeting him.'

Cath shrugged. 'I did my best, but I reckoned without him. Did you grill him like a sardine?'

'We prefer our sardines to speak for themselves.' Peter joined them as Harold and Cherry moved away. 'Georgia tells me he's the sort to do his own grilling.'

'That's true.' Cath smiled. 'It worries me,' she added more seriously, 'that he was involved with the Watsons. I didn't know that – but why not? I'd talked to him often enough about the case. Isn't that weird?' She looked anxious.

'Not necessarily.' Georgia felt she could hardly shout out *yes*.

Cath's eyes gleamed. 'No need for fence-sitting. Do you think Grandpops is hiding something, or did he tell you all his little secrets?'

Georgia hesitated. 'At present I prefer to think he's not telling me everything.'

Cath dismissed this. 'Because if so, I agree.'

One hurdle overcome, and with Cath on the same side as her, Georgia thought with relief, Charlie might continue to regard her as his cousin.

'So,' Cath continued, 'can we call it quits and work together?'

Georgia hesitated. 'Supposing we find out something hurtful to you?'

'That's a risk I have to take. I put my faith in Grandpops.'

'Then yes, provisionally.' Georgia had one eye on Peter, who was nodding. 'You might feel differently if push comes to shove.'

'And for starters,' Peter said, 'any hope of getting us near the Trents?' Obviously he had overcome any prejudice against information sharing, Georgia thought. 'We don't seem to be their favourite people.'

'Then you're in the vast majority. Look at them.' Cath waved a hand in their direction. 'What do they look like to you?'

'Rich fat cats?' Georgia looked at the exquisitely suited couple in late middle age. Matthew was holding forth, taking centre stage, while Pamela's face looked blank. She was a striking woman though, and in her youth must have been a stunner. But now? The face said nothing to her – yet. Matthew looked in his mid sixties and his wife in her late fifties, so as she had thought, first-hand knowledge was unlikely for both of them.

'That's a stereotype,' Peter observed.

'When they open their mouths to us, they'll be people,' Georgia shot back.

Cath smiled. 'I can see why Charlie is so fond of you both. You'd better meet Gemma first.'

'Are she and Greg Dale an item?'

'Don't know. Childhood friends at least.'

Gemma's headed for the bright lights, Georgia thought as Cath marched them over to the couple. Greg, however, struck her as the sort of lad who would think his own great talents were being belittled if his companion's were extolled, and his arrogant stance diminished the effect of his good looks.

'Are you training professionally, Gemma?' Georgia asked, having praised her singing. With her fair hair and wonderful voice, it was hard to keep Miss Blondie out of her mind.

'No. I'm reading maths at uni.'

'Maths and music often go together.'

Gemma grinned. 'Maths are more useful.'

The sight of Marsh & Daughter chatting to Gemma brought her parents quickly over to them, as it must have been obvious who they were.

'I believe we've spoken on the telephone, Miss Marsh.'

To Georgia's surprise, Matthew's tone suggested it had been the jolliest chat ever, which was useful as it paved the way for Peter to engage him in light conversation while

Cath, with practised ease, took Gemma away. Once alone with Pamela, Georgia was relieved to find that she was a great deal more approachable than her husband.

'I'm sorry we had to be so firm,' Pamela said immediately. 'Ken was really going over the top with one theory after another, and we had to call a halt. We've had quite a few such approaches over the years.'

'Theories about the trial or about what happened to your father later?' Georgia tried to look concerned solely on Pamela's account.

Pamela looked ill at ease, however, and Georgia regretted she had rushed in so quickly. 'All sorts,' Pamela answered vaguely. 'Mostly just rehashes of the same old story, trying to get my angle for a quote. Of course, Tom wasn't my real father. My mother was married twice and my real father died before I was born.'

Georgia tried not to look as stunned as she felt. Tom *not* her father? That had been blindingly obvious, she supposed, if they'd thought about it – but no mention had been made of it by anyone else. Was it publicly known, she wondered? She was so busy working out the ramifications that she jumped in shock at a loud guffaw behind her – not from Pamela, but from Mavis, who had crept up without Georgia being aware of it.

'Come off it, Pam darling. Of course Daddy didn't die. Not then anyway.' Mavis lurched forward and wagged her finger in Pamela's face. 'Naughty, naughty. Second marriage indeed.'

In a trice Matthew was back with them, trying to lead Mavis away from an appalled Pamela, who was staring at Mavis as though she couldn't even remember who she was.

Mavis promptly threw his restraining arm off. 'Keep out of it, Matthew. Get a drink for your dear old mother-in-law.'

It took a moment or two for Georgia to work this out, but when she did the answer to Pamela's parentage was clear. David Maclyn had been her father – if Mavis had it right, of course.

'That's not true, Mavis,' Pamela managed to whisper.

'My father's name was Sidney Wilson and he died of war wounds.'

'Quite right, dear.' Mavis nodded vigorously. 'Let's all be posh and pretend it didn't happen.'

Pamela was so white Georgia thought she might be about to faint. 'Let's think of Ken, shall we?' she said, with the only intervention she could think of.

Mavis took a caustic look at her. 'Pardon me for asking, but who the hell are you?'

'Georgia Marsh.'

This met with Mavis's favour, surprisingly. 'Oh yeah. Ken told me. You and the chap in the wheelchair are writing that book. Well, well, what a brave couple to walk into the lions' den. And you're quite right, of course. Frightfully bad form to chat about adultery at a funeral.'

'Mavis . . .' Cath tried to help, but was faced down as Mavis simply handed her the empty glass that Matthew had not rushed to refill.

'Kindly look after this, my dear. I want a few words with Sherlock and Watson here.'

Pamela was trembling with what seemed genuine shock as Mavis planted herself firmly in their path. 'You just come to see me, ducky,' she crooned to Pamela. 'I'll tell you all about your daddy.'

'More lies?' Matthew shouted at her.

'And more truth about darling Joan, of course. Pamela's lovely mummy, who drove my husband to his death.'

After that it was a race between Cath and Georgia as to who would distract Mavis first, and Georgia won. 'Why don't we get another drink, Mavis?' she suggested, slipping an arm round her. 'Then you can chat to Cherry.'

Mavis beamed at her. 'Lovely idea, darling. Do I know you?'

'You will, Mavis,' Georgia assured her, acquiring an orange juice for her at the bar. Mavis looked at it, turned it upside down, flooding herself and Georgia with juice, then handed the empty glass back with great aplomb. The ploy – if it was – worked, Georgia thought ruefully, as when she'd finished mopping herself down, she saw Mavis chatting to Cherry. They looked as if they were the best of friends – perhaps because Joan had been the bête noire of both ladies.

'Ring a ring o'roses, all fall down,' Peter mused on the way home. Georgia had offered to drive Mavis home too, and she was now sound asleep on the rear seat, together with a box of Micky's diaries, a treasure trove from the pile that Christine had just shown them. Georgia had made her apologies for not staying longer and explained about Peter and Mavis awaiting her outside. Christine had seemed relieved, in fact, which was hardly surprising. 'Which of the ladies falls down?' Peter finished. 'No contest. The one on our back seat.'

A voice from behind startled her. Trust Mavis to wake up at that moment.

'I shouldn't have done that,' Mavis observed. 'I can't help pushing it when I see that lot together. But they can't keep me away from a funeral, can they?'

'Why would anyone want to keep you away?' Peter asked, tongue very obviously firmly in cheek.

'They're scared of what I'll say.'

'With reason it seems,' Peter commented. 'Got any more fireworks like that one?'

'About time the old trout knew,' Mavis muttered sullenly. 'Her mum seduced more men than that woman who sat on an island.'

'Circe?' Georgia asked, amused.

'Maybe. There's lots more about that crowd waiting to be spat out.'

'Such as?' Georgia asked lightly.

'I don't know. That's the trouble,' Mavis wailed unexpectedly. 'But my David always said don't get mixed up with that lot, Mave. Funny things going on there.'

SEVEN

'**N**othing heading nowhere,' Peter declared, waving a hand round the office.

Georgia did look and was forced to agree, although Peter seemed remarkably sanguine about it. The office was not shouting a triumphant progress towards success but presenting a dismal picture of loose ends. Copies of photos were posted on the walls and the contents of the box she had brought back from Christine's home were piled on the desk. So far the expected treasure trove from Micky's diaries had not materialized.

The word diary, she thought crossly, implied long entries revealing not only the writer's exact state of mind but every detail of daily life in case it was of interest to someone coming across it in the year 4000. Micky's diaries were not in that class, at least if the volumes she had chosen from the stack Christine showed her were anything to go by. They were for the years 1948 to 1953 but chiefly contained only jotted notes of appointments to come or cryptic comments whose meanings would be clear only to the writer. There was little that expressed the thoughts and emotions of the happy-looking man in the photo stuck on the cork board in the Marsh & Daughter office. Sandy the leader, Micky the acrobat, Tom the stooge.

Even the entry for the sixteenth of August 1952 was disappointing, recording only, 'The day it happened'. It was nevertheless possible to infer that Micky had been hit hard by the murder, as Ken had implied. He thought Joan was the cat's whiskers, even if others thought of her only as the cat. The ink looked heavier for these words, as though Micky's pent-up emotions had transferred themselves to his pen nib.

For the week that followed there were just a bitter 'the

show must go on' and a plain 'her funeral'. His wife, Muriel, was often mentioned and also Ken, or as he appeared here, Kennie. The only later entry that displayed personal bias was 'bloody show a sell-out'. Did that indicate Micky's bitterness that Joan was no longer in it, or that Tom was in prison awaiting trial for her murder?

'Might be something here.' Peter was holding a few photos. 'I kept these back. They were in a pocket pasted at the back of the 1952 diary.'

'What are they?' Georgia asked hopefully, swivelling her chair round from her own desk as Peter spread them out on his. The most interesting showed Joan in the middle of a group. One of her arms was round Sandy, the other round Buck Dillon. There were two others in the photo, neither of whom she could identify with certainty, as their faces were fuzzy. 'That one –' she pointed to one of the fuzzy-faced men – 'looks as if he might be David Maclyn; the other is too blurred.'

'Micky himself? It's captioned "The Crew", but not in Micky's handwriting. Perhaps Joan was lining up all her lovers? Perhaps Micky drooled once too often over Joan Watson, and his wife objected.'

'No, it's too tall for Micky, or for Tom,' Georgia countered.

'Harold?' Peter suggested.

'Could be. The height would fit, but not the theory about the lovers. No one's suggested Harold was one of Joan's circle.'

'Anyway, if these were Joan's paramours, why doesn't jealousy come into the picture? Buck seemed happy to be one of several, David probably knew all about Joan's flings and so did Sandy.'

'Joan was used to getting her own way, using sex as a magnet as well as a charm weapon,' Georgia pointed out. 'If it amused her to get all her current extramaritals together, no one would say no. But it's a wobbly thesis.'

'I'll stick it up on the wall. It might remind us that the focus of the case could be Joan, not Tom.'

'It won't do any good,' she said despondently, swinging

back to her own desk. 'We're taking a suggestion here, an idea there, lurching forward and then falling back. Just like Rick. The real story seems to float further away whenever it seems just within reach.'

There was a silence that made her glance at Peter – *still* looking cheerful. 'No luck on Mozart?' she asked.

'Now you mention it,' he replied airily, 'yes, there is. I was keeping it back to cheer you up. Mind you –' he must have seen her instant reaction '– don't pin too much on it.'

'*What?*'

'Forget Salzburg and Prague. Think Aix-en-Provence. They have a summer festival in July. There was one in 1994, of course, and it lasted three weeks. Operas are put on in the courtyard of the Archbishop's Palace. And guess what?'

She hardly dared breathe. '*The Magic Flute?*'

'Got it in one. A fabulous performance, especially good because Natalie Dessay was singing the Queen of the Night. Worth Rick and Miss Blondie Pamina travelling all the way from Brittany for?'

'Yes.' It came out as a croak. 'There must be a drawback.'

'Let's hope not. But the drawback could be that the French police sent details about Rick all round France.'

He was right. She remembered Inspector Décourt telling them so. And yet . . . and yet . . . Aix was the obvious place they might have gone to.

'I'll get on to them,' Peter added.

Despite the warning, Georgia's hopes were racing ahead. Surely in this lead Rick had left some kind of fingerprints – just as Tom had?

There seemed an air of holiday in Broadstairs. It was only late June but the town – or perhaps more accurately the tourist face of the town – looked proudly ready for the main season, and the general spirit helped Georgia to feel better about facing the Watson flat again. Gary, when she accosted him in the fish bar, had been mournfully accepting of her quaint wish to revisit the scene of the crime.

'Put a quid or two in the charity box,' he suggested. 'Can't guarantee a ghost though, so no money back.'

'Thanks. I don't need a ghost.' Those fingerprints Tom had left were all too clear without the need for a phantom to come gliding through a wall. She passed the ordeal of the steps up to the Watson flat as quickly as possible, breathing a sigh of relief as she reached the top. Wasn't it odd, it occurred to her, that the fingerprints were at the foot of the steps, not up there inside the flat where the violence had taken place?

The key turned easily in the lock, naturally enough, as Gary had told her he kept stores there. It was clear, however, that the flat hadn't been lived in for some time. Although there were radiators in the rooms, the damp atmosphere and smell indicated they had not been operated regularly. It didn't help her instinctive reaction to the place. No fingerprints perhaps, but a general sense of waste and decay.

The walls were still covered in nineteen fifties wallpaper, and open, tiled fireplaces made it seem as though she had taken a step back in time. The living room was to the left and the kitchen to the right. A staircase went up to the bedrooms and presumably a bathroom. Georgia pictured Brian James running up it that night and finding Pamela peacefully sleeping through the nightmare of what lay below her.

The flat was still carpeted but no longer furnished. Boxes of cafe supplies were piled high in the living room, although to one side of the room was an old and very dusty sofa, which looked as if it might have been here in the Watsons' time. It must have been here that Joan's body had been found, and Tom had perhaps been sitting on that very sofa when the police arrived. It was easy, now that she was in the actual room, to conjure up the scene. Saying nothing, doing nothing, he was just looking at the corpse, all passion spent. Georgia shivered. Those three words were from Milton's *Samson Agonistes*. Joan had been a Delilah, but Tom was no Samson. Not physically anyway, although perhaps mentally he had been driven beyond his normal limits to kill the woman he loved. No, she corrected herself, it was Cherry he loved. That meant Joan could have been standing in his way. Even in those days, however, one could divorce wives for adultery, so why turn to murder? Georgia swallowed. Whichever way one looked at it, Tom Watson still retained his secrets.

How about Pamela Trent? she wondered as she went upstairs. Was she the key to the situation that had led to murder? Perhaps Tom only found out that night that she was David's child, not his? He had almost certainly been present at the row between Mavis and Joan that night, and yet if Tom had killed Joan for that reason, there would have been no unfinished business or injustice, as the fingerprints on time still suggested, when she had walked up the outside steps. Or, it occurred to her, were they Joan's fingerprints, not Tom's? Whatever Ken might have said, it was Joan who had been the major victim.

Slowly Georgia went back downstairs, aware that she now had to run the gauntlet of those fingerprints again. She forced herself to open the front door, lock it behind her and then face the steps again. The fingerprints met her in full force as she walked down to the yard. Worse, there was someone lounging against the back gate, who in that scaring instant seemed to reinforce the threat that the fingerprints were making. She had seen him before. It was Greg Dale.

'Hello,' she made herself call out as normally as possible. 'We've met, haven't we?' She tried to conquer the shakiness in her voice as he detached himself from the support of the gate and stood astride at the foot of the steps, hands in his pockets.

'Yes,' he answered in a polite voice that did not fit his stance. 'I believe we did.'

She forced herself into a normality she didn't feel. What was he doing here? Watching her? *Following* her? 'Here for some fish and chips, are you?' she asked nonsensically.

'Not really.' He was grinning now, as if he felt he had the upper hand. 'Did you happen to find anything up there?' To pass him she would have to push past him. Was he really a threat, or was this just the fingerprints having their effect on her?

'Only a couple of ghosts,' she replied lightly.

He stared at her, the grin vanished. 'Nothing else?'

'What would you expect?'

'What did you go for?' he countered lazily. 'The Trents don't like anyone poking around up there.'

'The flat belongs to the fish bar, not the Trents.'

'They still don't like people nosing around. Just thought I'd mention it.'

'Nothing moves on in this world if no one is prepared to nose around.'

'Then no one would come to any harm, would they?' That oh-so-polite voice gave this a creepier edge than she could deal with. Whether it was intended or the result of the fingerprints, she longed to wipe the smile off his smug face. She pushed him aside so forcefully and unexpectedly that he stepped back, leaving her enough room to get by to return the keys to Gary. Should she go out through the front entrance of the cafe? No, she wouldn't give Greg Dale the satisfaction of retreat. She would go back through the yard. When she did so, there was no sign of him, but as she reached the corner of Jameston Avenue, there he was, watching her from a doorway. Just watching.

Mavis lived in a sheltered home on the outskirts of Canterbury. Today it looked just as sedate and anonymous as it had when she had driven her home from the funeral. What did the other residents make of her? Georgia wondered. Perhaps Mavis kept her wilder side for her jaunts out, rather than playing the enfant terrible on her own home turf. Once the door had opened, however, it was clear that Mavis would be Mavis wherever she was. The flowing purple print and the challenging body language assured her of that. In a way, Georgia was relieved. Much easier to deal with the Mavis she had already met. After yesterday's encounter with Greg Dale, it would be a doddle.

'It's good of you to see me,' she began politely.

'I don't do good.' Mavis grinned. 'I only do *want* at my age. Come in.'

Georgia followed her as she half waddled, half floated

down the hallway to a living room overlooking a small patio and pocket handkerchief of a garden. 'Drink?' Mavis offered.

'No thank you.' Georgia could see the wine bottles lined up on the dresser. 'Tea?' she asked hopefully.

'If you must.' Sigh. 'I blame David for this lot.' Mavis waved a hand at the dresser's display. 'I was a tea girl myself when we met, but once he hit the jackpot, teapots flew out of the window. Those were the days, eh? The bottles got him in the end though, and now they're after me.'

'At the funeral you said it was Joan who got him,' Georgia reminded her.

'Joan led him to the drink. That who you want to talk about?'

'Can you bear it?'

'I think about it all the time, so why not have a nice chat too?'

As Mavis made tea, Georgia looked at the photos of David crowding the room, including some of him with the younger Mavis she had seen in Ken's photos. She was recognizable today only through her energy and general vitality. No wine or spirits appeared, in fact, as Mavis opted for tea too. Perhaps her relapse at the funeral had been brought on by the strain of facing the event rather than habitual drinking.

'Did you mean what you said about David being Pamela's father?'

'Of course,' Mavis answered readily, and with dignity. 'You don't think I'd have said it otherwise, do you? That's why Joan married poor old Tom in such a hurry.'

'Did Tom know she was pregnant when they married?'

'What you mean is: did David know and is that why he dropped her?' Mavis said calmly.

'Both,' Georgia admitted. 'Unless . . .'

Mavis took a long, noisy sip of tea. 'Unless it's embarrassing, eh? Well, it doesn't say much for my sex appeal, does it, that David wandered off to so many fresh fields? We'd only been married two years when little Pam appeared. Trouble is, I was up the spout with my first when she was conceived. I couldn't provide any action for David, and darling Joan guessed it. She'd always been hanging around, but he gave her up to marry me, and she saw her chance of revenge when I was laid up with David junior. Rest on your back, said the good old doc. Reckon he gave her the same advice, only not for the same reasons. She spent more time on her back than on her dancing feet, that's for sure. That do you, darling?'

'I think I get the general picture,' Georgia replied. 'Not much fun for you though, feeling rotten and knowing David was with her.'

'You can say that again with knobs on.' Mavis pulled a face. 'Then Joan did her usual trick. Told David she was preggers, and he told me. Poor chap, wasn't his fault. These women threw themselves at him.'

Georgia wondered just how hard they'd had to work. David had certainly been lucky in his wife, and she seemed to bear no grudge.

'I was all for her getting rid of it, but Madame Joan says no she won't. She had a better idea. Before we knew it, she was spliced with Tom and had the cheek to give David the bill for the wedding.'

Georgia blinked. This tallied with the Joan of 'The Crew' photograph. 'Tom didn't realize she was pregnant when they married?'

'Not that I know of. There was a lot of talk, of course, but we all liked Tom, so there was none when he was around.'

'Did he ever find out?'

'I don't know, dear. I'm not a fly on the wall. But if you're thinking it was that evening – well, it could have been. We none of us said anything to the police for the kiddie's sake, as well as Tom's.'

'Did it come up during your spat with Joan on the night of the murder?'

'Might have done,' Mavis replied airily. 'Tom muscled in on it halfway through, so he could have overheard. She'd been mocking me as he arrived because she was having it off with David again, so I told her that was nothing. Four other women could say the same. She didn't know whether to believe me or not, so we had a right set-to, and I told her the next time she came near David she'd have me to reckon with. I'd get her thrown out of the show.'

'Could you have done that?'

'You bet I could. If I'd told Haughty Harold that she was upsetting his prize star, he'd have sacked her, even though she was sleeping with him too. All good for Madame's CV.'

Harold? So he could have been in that photo, Georgia thought. 'In that case, wasn't he more likely to sack David?'

'You don't know Harold. The show first, which meant career and money. Sex second. After Joan tired of mother-hood, she took a fancy for gathering scalps. Want the full list?'

'Please.' There might a new name on it, Georgia thought. So far it wasn't looking good for Tom's innocence.

'That nice US sergeant for one. Harold probably, David for sure, and I've a feeling Sandy got drawn into the honey-trap. She had Micky where she wanted him, though probably without bothering to open her legs for him. He thought Joan the greatest thing since powdered egg.'

'Were both you and David at the Black Lion that night?'

'We were. It was too bad we had to give evidence that Tom wasn't. So did Micky and Sandy. Harold too, but I think he left early. Not nice for any of us, but we couldn't lie. Even if we'd wanted to, we couldn't have risked it with so big a group including us women.'

'Tom couldn't have been in the snug as Cherry claims?'

'No. Cherry was there for a while, but we never saw Tom.'

'Did you stay till closing time?'

'Matter of honour. We'd had a rotten performance that evening, so we stayed on to drown our sorrows. Closing time eleven, plus drinking-up time, and we fell out of the doors about twenty past eleven. David and I went home, and Sandy and his then girlfriend, Jeannie, came with us to drown a few more sorrows. They stayed on until the small hours.'

'So you all four had a complete alibi.'

Mavis chortled. 'Good of you to say so, dear. You can't

think David or Sandy would have killed her? Jeannie and me, now, well, wish we'd thought of it.'

'Just checking possibilities, ma'am,' Georgia said lightly.

'Then we're off the list. Anyway, Sandy's too cunning a bastard for a crime of passion like that. Unless someone did it for him, of course. But he'd have no reason to kill Joan. How could she be a threat to him? Tell Jeannie? No threat at all, and Joan would know that. Jeannie adored Sandy, and she was as tough as he is. Micky? No way. He hadn't the guts to take Joan on in a big way, and little Miss Muriel would know that.'

'Was Muriel there that night?'

Mavis thought for a moment. 'I don't remember, and that's the truth. Probably not, because they'd have had to get a babysitter. Micky was, but I think he left early to get back home to his loving spouse.'

Georgia tried another tack. 'You told me David said there were nasty things going on at that time. What did you mean? Joan's sex life or something else?'

Mavis frowned. 'Did I say that? Must have been drunk. In vino veritas. Mark you, it was a funny time. We'd won the war, but there we were, worse off than ever. Rationing and gloom. It made some folks bitter. Our lot had mostly missed the war, David did a year I think, so did Tom, Sandy and Harold. There were no jobs around afterwards, when David came out, so lucky he had this voice of his. "Tides of Love" – remember that one?' She seized a tissue and mopped her eyes. 'Sorry, dear. It gets to me sometimes.

'Anyway, as I was saying,' she continued briskly, 'they were hard times. Remember the razor gangs of the fifties? The Teddy Boys? The black market? There we all were, kicking up our heels in the chorus line and singing about sunshine and true love, and all the while the crime rate was soaring. Yet it was only a few years later that nice Harold Macmillan declared we'd never had it so good. Maybe he never came down our way.'

With one leg in her car and one leg still to go, Georgia remembered to check her mobile phone before she left to return to Haden Shaw. There were seldom any messages, since she preferred to take calls on the landline, but nevertheless it was a routine she tried to keep to. Just as well. Today there was a message from Peter on voicemail awaiting her. 'Georgia? Damn this thing (a routine opening for Peter). On your way home through Canterbury, call in at the charity shop in Hurst Lane. Ask for Mrs Robin.' End of message. Thanks, Peter, she thought crossly. And just what am I to say to Mrs Robin when I accost her? Ah, well, perhaps Mrs Robin herself would know.

By the time she had successfully fought the battle of Canterbury parking, she was in a thoroughly irritable mood. Ten to one, Mrs Robin was merely keeping something on one side for her father and Georgia had been selected to be the courier. That was fine, but not at rush hour. The shop smelt of boot polish for some reason, but nevertheless there were a lot of people in it, heads bobbing up and down between rails of clothes. Behind the desk she could only see a girl with long black hair who looked too young to be Mrs anything, but it was worth a try.

'She's having a cup of tea,' was the accusing answer, as though Georgia had deliberately chosen this moment in order to annoy her.

'Shall I call back later?'

The girl looked amazed. 'What for? She's in there.' She pointed to a door at the rear of the shop that announced it was 'Private' in such stern letters that Georgia wondered how much of the country's gold reserves was hidden inside.

Very little it seemed. When she knocked and entered, she found a small room holding two chairs, a table with an electric kettle and tea paraphernalia and a pile of boxes. One chair was empty, the other, a wing armchair, had its tall back to her, and presumably Mrs Robin must be within it, hidden from her view.

'Mrs Robin?' she called experimentally.

A tiny face peered round the corner of the chair and beamed. 'Come in, come in. Who are you?'

'Georgia Marsh. My father told me to ask for you.'

Georgia felt as though she were looming over the tiny Mrs Robin, who looked lost in the large armchair.

'Marsh . . . Marsh . . .', she muttered. Then suddenly she smiled. 'You'll have to forgive me,' she said briskly. 'I was dozing off, and my brain comes to slower than my eyes when I wake up.'

Indeed she looked as alert as her namesake now, although her size made her seem as though the next breeze might waft her away.

'I'm not sure what I'm here for,' Georgia warned her.

'There now. If you don't know, how should I?' Another beam.

This was hopeless. Georgia was about to give up, when Mrs Robin chuckled. 'Just my bit of fun. I know why you're here. I talked to your dad earlier on this afternoon.'

Georgia waited expectantly.

'About Tom Watson,' Mrs Robin added uncertainly.

Immediately Georgia's hopes rose. 'Did you know him?'

'Know him? Of course I did. I lived next door.'

The neighbour. This was the *neighbour*. 'Your daughter was babysitting?' Georgia asked in excitement.

'Good gracious me, no. Mum's been dead nearly twenty years. I was the babysitter, Alison Wetherby.'

'Of course.' How stupid. 'I didn't do my sums right.'

'I wish I didn't,' Alison said feelingly. 'I'm Alison Robin now, of course, though Steven's been dead nearly as long as Mum. That's why I came to work here. He died of cancer too, and I wish there'd been all the support around then that there is now. Sit down, Miss – Georgia you said your name was? Pretty name that. "Georgia on my Mind"? Know that song?'

'My husband –' that word still sounded strange to her '– sings it when he wants to annoy me.'

'And when he wants to please you, he sings "Sweet Georgia Brown".'

'Right.' Georgia laughed, feeling at home amid this chaos, especially as her chair brought her knee to knee with Alison. 'What did you tell my father? Was it just that night you were babysitting, or were you the Watsons' regular sitter?'

'Regular. I was seventeen when Joan got herself murdered, but I'd been babysitting for them on and off for three years.'

'You knew them well then. Did you like them?'

'Liked *him*. He was a sweetie. Used to do his clowning act for my young brother. But Mrs Watson was a bit of a madam. Mum said she was no better than she should be – silly phrase, isn't it? How good *should* you be? I was mostly there on my own, but I'd stay on a bit if Tom was there alone. Cheer him up. He was always wondering what was keeping Joan so long. As if I didn't guess. It was more a case of *who* was keeping her, if you ask me. Fancy stockings, cigarettes galore, flashy cigarette case, perfume, clothes. And drink! Couldn't buy all that on a seasonal clown's money plus a chorus girl's, and there's the fact they weren't available except on the black market.'

'Apparently she had several lovers though.'

'Even if they paid her, she still had to get hold of the stuff, and there wasn't much silk in Broadstairs' shops. All black market, Mum said, and who's to say she wasn't right? There was some Yankee soldier used to come visiting her. Mum reckoned he was handing the sweeties to her.'

Buck Dillon, Georgia thought. Mrs Robin had probably confused soldier and airman over the years. 'Do you think Joan was expecting a lover the night she was murdered?'

Alison shook her head. 'Sorry, dear, but no. She came in with one of those looks on her face that the world wasn't giving her what she expected of it. That wasn't her usual expression if there was one of her fancy men expected. They usually came during the day, or if she and Tom were in different shows, because it was safer.'

'How did you know? Did she talk to you?' At least two of her lovers were in the show, which could have been why she was 'dressed up' as Brian James had told them.

A snort from Mrs Robin. 'Her face wasn't looking like no lovers coming. As soon as she got back, she said I could go, so I did. Said she'd come home for an early night.'

'Was there any sign of Tom when you left?'

'Not a whisker. She said he was at the pub.'

'Or of anyone else?'

'No.'

'If she was tired, it was odd she didn't go to bed immediately, and she can't have done, because she was still fully clothed when she was killed.'

'Probably wanted to empty the rubbish – Mum said she saw Tom speaking to her later on at the bottom of the steps.'

'The bottom? What time was that?' That rang an unpleasant bell. Perhaps Tom had returned and met her going out – no, that wouldn't work because of the time element.

'No idea. Mum didn't say. After I was inside, anyhow. Maybe little Pam woke up and stopped her going to bed earlier.'

That was possible, Georgia supposed. 'Do you keep in touch with Pamela?'

'No. Mum did though. Right to the day she died. Pam was a nice little kid.'

'Tom liked her?' Pamela had denied all knowledge of the neighbour, which confirmed her feeling that Pamela had a story to tell.

'He was her dad. Of course he did. It's my way of thinking that's why he came back.'

'Came back from where? The pub?' Georgia was lost.

'No. Years later it was. Mum was still alive, still living at the old place.'

Came back? 'Your mother met Tom years later?' Surely she had misunderstood. 'When?' she demanded.

Alison looked surprised. 'Not sure. Must have been in the nineteen seventies sometime. I know I was living in St Peter's and I didn't move there until seventy-three or four. Mum popped in for a cuppa and told me. He'd been to where the Dickensons were living, but they'd moved away.'

'The who?' Georgia's head was spinning.

'Joan's parents. But it was Pam Tom wanted to see, not them.'

'But what happened after that? Who else saw him?'

'I don't know. Mum never said. She didn't tell me for ages. It had slipped her mind, she said.'

'Have you told Cherry this?'
'Cherry who?'
'Tom's sweetheart, Cherry Harding.'
'Oh, her. No. Least said, soonest mended, Mum said.'

EIGHT

'Excellent. You got my message then?' Peter opened the door as Georgia arrived straight from the Canterbury rush-hour jams. It was Friday afternoon, so she had decided to report back to him immediately, even though it was six thirty. A nice smell was coming from the kitchen, which Georgia assumed meant that the dinner Margaret would have left was well on its way to being ready. She was wrong.

'Hi, Georgia.'

Janie's face was so open and welcoming as she emerged from the kitchen to greet her that Georgia was annoyed to find herself apologizing for intruding. Even more annoying was that she could not find any rational reason for her irritation.

'Like to eat with us?' Janie asked. 'We've plenty for three if Luke's working late. Or four, if he'd like to come over.'

'No, thanks so much, but I've a date with a stove myself.'

Georgia watched as Janie bent solicitously over Peter. Don't do that! she wanted to shout. He hates it. Fortunately Peter was concentrating on her news and didn't notice.

'I deduce that you have something of interest to tell me, Georgia, or we wouldn't be honoured by a visit this evening.'

'I do, and guess what? Your Alison – how did you come across her, by the way?'

'I didn't. Janie did. She discovered the Broadstairs connection. I spoke to Alison Robin on the phone, and hey, presto. So tell us your news, daughter mine.'

'Well done, Janie,' Georgia forced herself to say, hoping this did not sound condescending.

Luckily Janie looked pleased. How far was she part of this establishment? Georgia wondered. Should she go ahead and discuss the case in front of her? As if anticipating this problem, Peter turned back into the living room and Janie disappeared

back into the kitchen. Georgia ran quickly through what
Alison herself had said, and then at last she was able to add
a nonchalant:

'And there was a sighting of Tom in Broadstairs in the
nineteen seventies.'

A long sigh. 'Magnificent, truly magnificent news.
Sighting by whom?'

'Alison's mum again. Mrs Wetherby.'

'Did you speak to her direct? She must be a fair age.'

'No longer alive, but Alison is quite clear about it. It just
slipped out – it wasn't something on her main agenda.'

'The question is: had her mum been quite clear about it
too? She could have been rambling.'

'Possibly, but it sounded too specific for that. Tom had
called on her to ask what had happened to baby Pamela.
So far as Alison knew, the good news hadn't been passed
on to anyone else, including Cherry.'

'Obviously on the grounds that Mum would presume
Tom had obviously already gone to see her.'

'Obviously?' Georgia queried sweetly.

'Objection upheld,' Peter said crossly. 'If he hadn't seen
Cherry for twenty years or more, why bother? There would
be some point to his seeing Pamela.'

'Even if she was David's child, not his?'

'Yes. Starved of affection from the lovely warm-hearted
Joan, he could well have poured all his love on to Pamela.
If you're right and Mrs Wetherby stayed in touch with her
until her death, then she's holding out on us in a big way.
She must have some memories of her at least, and we can
ask her.'

'Sure we can, if the guard dog lets us through.'

'Ah, it seems there might be a chance. Cath rang while
you were out today.'

'News of Buck?'

'No. But she thought we'd like to know that the annual
fête for St Edith's in the Field is being held in the Trents'
garden tomorrow. Apparently it's quite a do. It's a small
church, but the fête has grown in prestige over the years
and has become a money spinner not only for the church

but the local hospices too. It's the thing to do, Cath says. Everyone who is anyone must be there.'

'Do we count as "everyone" in the circumstances?'

'I see no reason why not. It's a big place apparently. The Trents own a couple of meadows behind their garden, and I gather the fête takes place in one of them; the other acts as a car park, and a highly expensive cream tea is usually served in the garden itself.'

'I can't wait. Do I wear my best hat?'

'Of course.' A quick glance at her. 'Janie's coming too. I'll tell her it's best hats to the fore, and I'll don my favourite Panama to live up to you both. And meanwhile, Georgia, why don't you fill in the breathless period of anticipation by checking out our website? We've had some response to the new photos I put up. Most of it is probably rubbish, but there are one or two replies that might be worth following up.'

'What do we say at the fête about Tom's possible return home?'

'Nothing, until we know more.'

'I suppose you're right. If we broadcast the news, it could hurt Cherry if there turns out to be nothing in it.'

'Bear in mind that one swallow doesn't make a summer,' Peter said darkly.

'Meaning?'

'If he came once, *why* only once?'

'Either he didn't find Pamela, or he did and that was sufficient to say what he needed to. Then he returned whither he had come.'

'Accepted. So the next step is . . .?'

'Pamela Trent and,' Georgia added, 'Matthew.' She told Peter about her creepy meeting with Greg Dale. 'He seems very protective of the Trents.'

Peter frowned. 'Because he fancies Gemma perhaps. She's probably grown up in the mystique of the murder being something that mustn't be talked about, let alone investigated. What on earth did he think you would find out all this time? There's precious little in the way of physical evidence likely to turn up.'

'The Trents wouldn't know that if they encouraged him to keep an eye open.'

'True. Did anything Alison say change the way you thought about the night of the murder?'

'Only the reminder that Joan was dressed up to the nines but had no date awaiting her at home, except one with the rubbish bin, where Tom must have met her on his return.' Georgia hesitated. She couldn't mention fingerprints in front of Janie. Instead: 'I suspect she was dressed up because she was hoping to meet her current flame *at* the show but was disappointed. So she came home in a huff by herself. That fits . . .'

Her voice trailed off. Here they went again. Round and round the mulberry bush – and only one ripe fruit falling from it: Tom had probably not committed suicide in 1953.

It felt almost as though this was purely a social occasion, Georgia thought as she and Luke drove to the fête the next day. She felt better about Janie now and had Luke to thank for this. Tired after the Canterbury trip, she had exploded to Luke over supper, and being Luke, he had listened sympathetically but in silence. Then he had put his 'oh so gentle' boot in.

'Why does it worry you that Janie is around so much? Is it professional or personal?'

'Professional,' she had snarled.

'What's she done?'

Georgia had poured out a list of wrongs, culminating in Alison Robin.

'Sounds rather like you and Frost & Co,' he commented. 'You put in the odd comment, in other words – and highly helpfully too. That's all Janie seems to be doing.'

'Nonsense,' Georgia had replied, but then caught his eye. 'Oh hell,' she admitted, 'you're right.'

When they went to bed, he came back to the subject: trust Luke to catch her off guard. 'Okay, so why does it worry you personally? Are you jealous?'

'No . . . yes,' she admitted.

'Why?'

'She's too damned possessive.'

'So why are you jealous? Marsh & Daughter is enough for Peter, is it? You don't want him to have another partner or wife.'

'It's not that,' she had almost shrieked. She had not even got that far, but now the point had been raised, she was forced to consider it. The idea had come completely out of the blue – hadn't it?

'Why then?' Luke persisted. 'Because Peter's in a wheel-chair, and you've looked after him for so long with Margaret's help?'

She could not believe this. And yet was there a kernel of truth in what Luke was saying? Because her father was in a wheelchair, that didn't mean necessarily he was incapable of sex or sexual desire or that he didn't need companionship.

'A daughter can only do so much,' Luke murmured.

She wanted to tell him he was being sanctimonious, that he was wrong, that he did not understand. Instead she found herself weeping. For Peter, for herself – and for Rick. Peter had contacted François Décourt, who was still working with the Brittany police, to ask him to check his records to see which parts of France he had covered in the 1994 search. That had been a week ago, and so far they had heard nothing.

Luke had held her, cradling her in his arms until he'd rocked her to sleep. When she woke in the morning, she saw things clearly for the first time. 'I can,' she announced as she plonked the milk jug on the breakfast table, 'see it all.'

'Good,' Luke remarked. 'What exactly?'

'I *am* a little jealous that Peter's and my relationship might change, but I can conquer that.'

'Good so far.'

'What worries me is that Janie might be substituting Peter for her mother. Without Clemence to care for – although she never really needed care – Janie's turned to Peter to mother him. Peter must hate that. He needs to be loved for himself alone. So it worries me.'

'It worries me too,' Luke admitted, reaching for the cornflakes. 'Don't worry about this afternoon. I'll take her under my manly wing so that you and Peter can get on with the work.'

The sun was tentatively condescending to shine as they reached St Edith's, which was a small village behind Broadstairs, so close it formed a suburb. What it lacked in sea views, however, it made up for in charm. Hidden on a minor road, its red-brick houses and beamed cottages made a pleasant sight. Filberts, where the Trents lived, was set well back from the lane, almost next door to the church. Georgia was looking out for a nameplate, but balloons and placards proclaimed they had arrived, even if the cars parked in a field at the side had not indicated the fact.

Luke whistled. 'You were right. No standard fête this.' There were even disabled parking spaces nearer the impressive early nineteenth-century house, and Georgia could see Peter's car already parked there. Arrows directed them to the scene of action. They reached the garden ready for the teas first, and beyond that she could see the field with the haunted house, the trampoline and doubtless a hundred other attractions awaiting them. When they reached the fête, she could see that no expense had been spared. There was also a magnificent Edwardian carousel with gilt-painted proud horses and a splendid organ, together with plenty of old-fashioned game booths. Impressively, there were no commercial stalls at all, which must have been a policy decision, she thought. An area was roped off for children's races, and programmes of a delicate pink were being handed out. These were sponsored, she noted, by Trent Cars, of course.

Georgia had finally decided against wearing a hat, especially if Janie was going to wear one, but had made some effort towards traditional frilliness in her dress. She was glad of that, as although plenty of casual clothes could be seen, there were also a fair number of people definitely 'dressed up' and not all of them elderly. She could see that Gemma, for instance, was wearing a large pink picture hat. Then she spotted Peter, looking more relaxed than she had feared, and made her way towards him. Janie was at his side – and in a posh hat, though it was a smaller affair than Gemma's.

'I know this is a working day for us,' Peter said, 'but would you mind if I got lost for a while? I rather like throwing coconuts.'

Georgia laughed. 'Win all the cuddly toys you like – you too, Janie, although they'll look a bit odd in the Fernbourne Museum.'

True to his promise, Luke ambled off with them, leaving her to study the programme. It was traditional in approach. 'Conjuring Display with Alexander Smith' caught her eye, and 'Singalong' with Gemma Trent. The fête was to be opened shortly by Matthew, she noted, which was hardly a surprise. She had now done some homework on Mr Trent. Born in Canterbury, brought up in Broadstairs, he had worked in London for some years but had returned to open a car business in Medway in 1972. It was obviously a highly profitable one, judging by this house. There was nothing to suggest he was other than what he seemed, a prosperous businessman and councillor. It was clear from this fête alone that he filled the role of unofficial lord of the manor – not a big parish, but an influential one, Georgia guessed, listening to the smooth charm with which the words fell from his lips as he began his speech. It was hard to believe that this was the same man who had spat venom at her on the telephone so recently.

Pamela was at his side in a silk turquoise two piece, fulfilling her lady-of-the manor role splendidly. Don't stereotype her, Georgia warned herself. At the funeral, after all, she had seen another Pamela Trent, a nervy woman probably dominated by Matthew. Perhaps she had been judging her harshly. The terrible death of her mother, young as Pamela was at the time, must have set her apart from other children when she was old enough to understand. In a town the size of Broadstairs, she might have been marked by a constant reminder that she was the daughter of Joan Watson, and no doubt Pamela's attitude to Tom was similarly coloured. Had Tom tracked her down on his nineteen seventies visit, assuming there had indeed been one? She would have been in her twenties and able to think for herself.

There was no sign of Peter, so Georgia strolled over to watch Sandy's conjuring show, which had drawn a large crowd of both children and adults. There was no Fenella to be seen, although she could see Vic Dale onstage with Sandy. So he was conjurer's assistant as well as chauffeur. Fenella must have caught sight of her in the crowd, because when the show was over, Georgia saw her coming towards her. She immediately felt guilty about comparing her to Janie, because Fenella was a much stronger, even pig-headed, woman than Janie could ever be.

'Are you never tempted to share his limelight?' Georgia asked lightly after she had greeted her.

'Dad prefers to go it alone, with Vic hovering in the background in case. Besides –' she flashed an unexpected smile at Georgia '– I'm hardly a grade-one decorative object at my age. Let the young folks take over, that's my view.'

There was no honest reply to that. 'Sandy's good, isn't he?' Georgia said instead.

'Do you mean for his age – or just good?' Fenella asked with ironic eyebrow.

'Good,' Georgia said firmly and truthfully. 'Does he practise at home?'

'All the time. You were lucky not to be commandeered as audience when you came. Always one for party pieces is Dad. Which reminds me: how is the Tom Watson investigation going?'

Georgia suppressed the reply that her own son should be able to enlighten her. 'Progressing nicely, with new leads,' she rejoined. Two could play at being non-committal. 'You know all about the Watson murder?'

'Of course. Dad rarely talked about it, but Mum rattled on and on.'

'Was she a Joan Watson fan?'

'Hardly. Few women were, as I'm sure you know. She was all right to work with, I gather, but when a man came on the scene, it was a different matter.'

'Was your mother jealous of Sandy working in the same show as Joan?'

Fenella shot a glance at her. 'Let's say wary. But it was a crowded field round Joan. It's my guess that Dad and Joan were amicably disposed to each other, but no bed. She was a bright lady, by all accounts, and Tom, so Dad says, was lacking in the quick wits department.'

'Although he was a clown?' Georgia decided not to enlighten her that her guess was wrong, according to Sandy himself.

'Dad led the trio.' Fenella began to look uneasy. 'Look, if you'll excuse me, I should get back to Dad.'

As she set off, either with duties as carer in mind or to avoid further questions, Georgia took the opportunity to follow her on to the stage. Fêtes and fairs were fascinating events. They often had two layers, the gaudy, noisy message of universal enjoyment that they put out – but also the undercurrent of an unstoppable roller coaster that could so easily obliterate the individual response. What nonsense, she told herself – and yet the idea lingered.

To her left the carousel was in full swing, and the rise and fall of the horses made a colourful sight. It would not seem incongruous if a clown called Tom rode astride one, his private face hidden.

'We enjoyed the show, Dad,' Fenella congratulated him as she and Georgia reached the stage. Vic was busy clearing up props, and Fenella began to help him.

Sandy winked at Georgia. 'What did you think?'

'Terrific.' It was the truth. 'I liked the vanishing parrot.'

'Ah, yes. I was born too late, you know. I should have been one of those great nineteenth-century illusionists, vanishing ladies, magic cabinets – masterpieces, they were, filling the whole theatre with one great illusion. Trouble is, that takes money, too much for today's budgets. I can't even afford to vanish Fenella now, can I?' He grinned at his daughter.

'Good job you don't want to,' she retorted.

'I'd do it in a flash,' Vic joked.

He was eyeing Georgia speculatively, whether sexually or otherwise, she could not tell. Perhaps it was part of his carer's job to study every comer. Perhaps putting his son Greg on her tracks was also part of it, but on second thoughts, Greg's mission was more likely to have stemmed from the Trents, not the Dale household. On the whole, Vic looked a lot jollier than his son, even if she wouldn't want to meet him in an alley on a dark night. He was a big man, well suited for his job – and for Fenella.

'You still on about Tom Watson?' Sandy asked her.

'I'm afraid so.'

'She'd like to know if you slept with Joan,' Fenella put in meanly.

Sandy roared with laughter. 'I told you I did. Straight out, didn't I, love? I was only one of many though. Too many other fingers in her pie.' Another guffaw. 'She was a good sort, was Joan, but as she told me, when you've got one clown round your neck – meaning Tom – you don't need another. Not Micky, not me, not for longer than a quick one. We were more mates, Joan and I. She needed a listening ear. She was cut up over David. Determined to punish him by doing well for herself and making him see it. That sergeant—'

'Buck Dillon ?'

'Yeah. I told you about him. And there was our Harold. Joan had a good eye for men going places. She was serious about him, but he wasn't. He had an equally good eye for avoiding trouble, and Joan had it written all over her. Still, he wasn't above taking what was on offer, and like me he wasn't married then.'

Sandy was taking rather too much pleasure in this banter, Georgia realized. This case, she decided as she left them, was becoming very much like that carousel, with Joan in the centre conducting the music and at least four of her cavaliers circling round and up and down on their colourful prancing horses.

But then the music had stopped.

'At last, Georgia. Cherry was looking for you.' Cath Dillon pushed her way through the crowd to join her. 'She's over there, talking to Harold.'

'Good. I'll go now. Is your grandfather here?'

'No way.' Cath laughed. 'I mentioned it, but when I said that Sandy and the gang would be here, he opted out. He's taken a fancy to you though. He said if you wanted to see him, you knew where to find him.'

'Did that imply he had something to tell me?'

'No idea.' Cath pulled a face. 'He won't talk to me, anyway. How are you doing generally on the case?'

'One lead.' Georgia hesitated. Should she risk this? Peter had said they should keep it under wraps, but Cath was a special case. 'But off the record. Agreed?'

'Yes.' Cath looked surprised. 'Don't look so anxious. I'm used to it. Scouts' honour.'

'It came from Alison Wetherby, who was the babysitter that night. Her mother told her years afterwards that Tom had come back sometime in the 1970s.'

Cath pounced immediately on this new lead. 'You mean Ken and Cherry were right? Was that Ken's scoop? Any proof?'

'Give me a chance. This only happened yesterday.'

'Is that my role then?'

'Not yet,' Georgia said hastily. 'And particularly no word to Cherry.'

'Wot me? Never.' Cath laughed. 'Truly, Georgia, I'm not daft. I see and hear evil, but I'm mighty careful about what I say. Ken wasn't – and look what happened.'

There was no sign of Harold by the time Georgia reached Cherry. She was chatting to a group of women Georgia did not recognize and looked as if she would be installed for a long time. No help for it. She'd have to deflect her.

'Cath said you wanted to see me,' she murmured lightly.

Cherry spun round in pleasure. 'Oh, yes, I did. I wondered how you were getting on. Georgia,' she explained to her companions, 'is investigating where my Tom is now.' The group looked both interested and embarrassed but luckily decided this was a hint for them to leave, especially when Cherry suggested they should have a nice cup of tea so that Georgia could tell her all about it.

Not quite all, Georgia thought as they sat down at one of the white-painted tea tables set out on the lawn. A real tablecloth, she noted. A very special fête, this. 'My treat, Cherry. In return for that lovely walnut cake you baked.'

'I like making cakes,' Cherry said simply. 'It will be a forgotten art soon, the way the world's going. Everyone is so frightened of getting fat, but they forget that cakes are a great comfort, and that's important too.'

'You're not fat and you eat them,' Georgia pointed out.

'Nicely filled out are the words you're looking for.' Cherry giggled. 'You wait, Georgia, it will happen to you too. No gym in the world can compensate for age.'

'You don't look old. Do you feel it?' Georgia carried on the small talk to ease her way in.

'I'm seventy-four,' Cherry announced with pride, 'but I feel just the same as when I was a girl in love with Tom. Time stands still inside you, doesn't it?'

Pamela Trent was helping to serve teas, but Georgia saw a look of anxiety cross her face as she noticed her. The hostess role immediately came into play. 'Now, what can I get you two ladies?' Once it had been established that the two ladies would like a cream tea apiece, she promptly departed. No way was she going to linger there.

'With extra cream for the elderly,' Cherry called after her.

Pamela turned to smile, but the gesture didn't reach her eyes, and it was with some difficulty that Georgia forced her mind back to Cherry. She decided to continue small talk in the hope that when Pamela returned with the tea she would feel more like sitting with them, but once again she whisked off on hostess duties.

'What did you want to see me about, Cherry?'

Cherry looked surprised. 'I wanted to know how your search for Tom was going, of course.'

How could she answer that? Truthfully, but not completely, Georgia decided. 'We've put his photo on our website, but there's been no significant response yet.'

'Oh.' Cherry stared at her teacup, now full of milky tea. 'Harold doesn't think he's alive any more, but he's wrong.'

'You were married to him—'

'Very briefly,' Cherry interrupted, almost indignantly. 'I came back here in 1960, and I married Billy Johnson a year later. He was a dear man. He reminded me of Tom, but Harold never did. Billy died twenty years ago. He was older than me, so I was on my own again. We never had children, you see. I think it was meant, as Tom wouldn't have wanted me to marry anyone else. It seems disrespectful to have done so, when he's been waiting all this time for me.'

A chill ran through Georgia. This was taking it too far, but Cherry seemed quite serious.

'I used to pretend sometimes that Tom and I had a child,' Cherry continued. 'He had lovely fair curls like Tom, and his name was Angel. But I'm afraid –' a nervous look at Georgia '– he grew up. Just like Peter Pan. He didn't want to, but he had to, and so he left me too.'

Georgia made the appropriate noises, but she could see what Harold meant by her living in dreamland.

'Harold wasn't married when you were all in *Waves Ahoy!*,' Georgia began, uncertain what effect this would have.

'No,' Cherry said happily, helping herself to a large dollop of cream on a scone, 'and he was a very naughty flirt, I'm afraid. He flirted with me during the show even though he knew I loved Tom.'

'Perhaps that was just his way,' Georgia said tritely.

She received a slightly frosty look. 'It was a very strange *way* if so. A woman knows, you know. I could tell. I told Tom that Harold was after Joan—'

'You *what*?' Georgia nearly choked on her tea, and Cherry looked startled.

'Why shouldn't I? It was his wife after all, and I loved Tom. We were going to marry as soon as we could.'

'When did you tell Tom about Harold?'

'Well, it's such ages ago, I can't be sure,' Cherry replied, looking perplexed. 'I'm really not. I don't think it was long before she died.'

Georgia waited – and sure enough it came.

'In fact,' Cherry looked close to tears, 'it could have been that night. I really don't remember. But if it was . . .'

'Don't worry,' Georgia forced herself to say quickly. 'It couldn't have made any difference.'

But it might have done. Talk about last straws. That evening Tom might have heard that Pamela was not his child, or perhaps now that Joan might have had yet another lover, or both. What would that have done to him?

It would have to be Matthew Trent she met first, not Pamela. Georgia took the bull by the horns, and in this case a particularly nasty bull. He had been friendly enough at the funeral, but this was his own turf, and she didn't rate her chances highly. 'I thought your speech was excellent – and it's such a good fête. Sandy's show was great fun.' Nothing wrong with gushing every now and then.

'Thank you.' It wasn't exactly gracious, but it was an olive branch, or at least a twig. 'He's a great chap, isn't he?'

'Yes,' she agreed. He hesitated, and she thought he was about to give her another earful. He did not, however, but simply murmured, 'If you'll excuse me . . .'

Time to attack. 'We're progressing on Tom Watson,' she told him, 'but I do want to assure you I wouldn't want to upset your wife.'

Matthew Trent did not look angry as she had expected, but he muttered something in reply and hurried on to the next group. He clearly had something on his mind, and out of curiosity she followed him as he walked towards the tea garden, where he sat at a table with Sandy Smith. Sandy was in his wheelchair, but there was no sign of Fenella or Greg. Vic Dale made a third at the table, however.

Did that mean the Tom Watson case could not have been quite so far from Matthew's mind as he pretended? Georgia decided she was going over the top. Vic worked for Matthew after all. However, it did mean it might be an excellent moment to speak to Pamela. There was no sign of her on the tea lawn, and she tracked her down eventually to the coconut shy, where she was talking to Peter and apparently enjoying having a go at the coconuts herself. Peter was now accompanied by a giant teddy bear, but not by Janie, who must have been with Luke. As Georgia joined them, they seemed to be talking about Charles Dickens, but on her arrival, Peter promptly changed tack. 'Georgia met Alison Wetherby the other day.'

'Who?' Pamela looked blank.

'She used to babysit at the Jameston Avenue flat when Tom and Joan were at the show.'

Pamela stiffened. 'Yes, you mentioned a neighbour. I don't remember her.'

'She remembered you, naturally enough, and so did her mother.' Georgia waited to see if this would bring any results.

Pamela swallowed. 'I don't remember anything about an Alison. I do remember a Beryl Wetherby. That must have been this neighbour. I only remember my grandparents clearly.'

'They must have hated Tom, if they still believed he killed your mother, despite the trial verdict.'

'They did.' There was a silence, which Georgia was determined not to break, and nor did Peter. It worked, for Pamela gave way. 'I suppose I should tell you, but please don't quote me on this, as they say.' She gave a nervous laugh. 'I'd like you to see it from my point of view.'

'No quoting without permission,' Peter said.

Pamela seemed reassured. 'My grandparents never talked to me about the murder. People didn't in those days. All I remember were the heavy silences if my mother was mentioned as I grew up. The general atmosphere of mystery and hatred. They were at such pains to tell me my mother was married twice and Tom was not my father that I knew something was wrong. As I got older, I found out, of course, but not through them. I tackled them about it, and then I did get the story – after a fashion.

'My mother was the most lovable, dutiful, beautiful girl in the world, according to my grandparents,' she continued, 'and Tom a monster who beat her and finally killed her. Of course I believed it, but then I discovered he had been acquitted, which didn't tie up. In my adolescence I began to get more inquisitive. Nothing made sense. I talked to

Micky, Sandy, Harold and even poor Cherry, though at home she had been branded as a scarlet woman who doubtless drove Tom to murder on her behalf. I got an overall picture of my mother being promiscuous, and Tom a henpecked husband who wanted his freedom and probably murdered to get it. But I could see for myself that Cherry was no scarlet woman, just a kid who'd never grown up. What I didn't find out until Ken Winton's funeral was that David Maclyn was my father. I guessed there'd been no first marriage for my mother, but I'd presumed my father must be Tom and therefore that I had either a wimp or a murderer, or both, for a parent. So I put the whole thing behind me.'

'And then we came along.'

Pamela managed a smile. 'Don't blame yourselves. Ken was always buzzing around like a wasp waiting for his big coup.'

'Did you know what it was?'

'No.' She hesitated. 'Well, if he told me, I've no recollection of it.'

'Did your grandparents ever give you reason to think Tom wasn't dead? And did they move home in Broadstairs?' Interesting, Georgia thought. Pamela wasn't in eye contact any more.

'Yes, to the latter,' Pamela replied. 'They moved to Ramsgate to get away from the gossip. That's the home I remember. As to Tom not being dead, he had every reason to kill himself. Cherry never believed it, of course, but when Ken Winton started questioning me about it, I did get upset.'

Pamela stopped speaking, as though she'd gone a step too far, so now was the time. Peter must have realized that too, for he said, 'We have a witness who said that Tom Watson came back in the nineteen seventies, especially to see you. Did Ken know that?'

Pamela tensed up, and for a moment Georgia thought she was going to walk away from them, but she controlled herself. 'This is most definitely off the record,' she said wearily. 'When Ken pestered me – and he did pester – about Tom, I remembered something that had happened ages ago, which I'd successfully buried. He *knew* about it, or at least suspected, or I wouldn't have told him. He said he'd publish the story anyway.'

'Would you tell us?'

She shrugged. 'It almost doesn't matter any more. What harm can it do? I was married by that time and living in St Peter's, at the back of Broadstairs past the railway bridge. I thought the old story was well buried in the past. Well, it was my birthday, the fourteenth of July, and I think it was 1974. Gemma hadn't been born anyway. I was stopped almost at my doorstep by this peculiar-looking man. Not exactly a vagabond but hardly smart, yet it was his look that alerted me to something odd – wild and sort of despairing. Not violent though, so I wasn't frightened in that way. "Are you Pamela?" he asked. "Pamela Watson?" I was very wary, but the name Watson drew me up. "Trent," I said. "I'm married." "Be careful," he replied. He was looking so anxious. "Do be careful." "About what?" I answered. "Everything," he said hopelessly. I thought he was mad, so tried to walk on home, but he stopped me again. "Are you happy?" he asked. I was, so I told him so, and it seemed to cheer him up. "I'm Tom," he said. "I came to wish you a happy birthday, but I won't come again. Don't be upset." He walked away, but I really was worried by that. "Tom who?" I called, but I think I already guessed. "Tom Watson," he replied. I was so stunned, I just let him walk off, and by the time I'd recovered there was no sign of him. I rang Matthew, and when he got home an hour or two later, we discussed what to do – nothing, was our decision. My grandparents would be upset if we told them. Tom was officially dead by this time, and there was no proof it was him anyway. He could have been a madman who happened to find out it was my birthday. We never told anybody, and certainly not Cherry. If she had seen him, it would have been all over Broadstairs, but there was no sign of that.'

'Alison Wetherby knows. He called at her mother's home first.'

'Thankfully she must have kept quiet too.'

'Thankfully?' Peter queried.

Pamela flushed. 'I'm sorry. It seems cruel, but I'm not good at coping. I couldn't cope if he were still alive. It's best to forget it, so I have.'

The Magic Flute – of course. On this afternoon of surprises, Georgia supposed it was inevitable that there would be one last twist. She could never have guessed that 'Singalong' with Gemma Trent would include the duet between Papageno and Papagena, especially with Greg supplying the baritone role, rather than the audience, for this 'singalong'. His voice hardly matched Gemma's, but he held his own, partly because he turned out to be such a good actor. Too good perhaps, because by the end of the duet, they had ceased to be Greg and Gemma in Georgia's mind. All she could see was another young man and a girl with long blonde hair.

'Why did you choose that, Gemma?' she asked her afterwards, rather shakily. Peter seemed to have had a similar reaction, for he left quickly with Janie. Internet hunting was under one's own control to do as and when one pleased, but this unexpected reminder might have pushed him a step too far. Like Janie, Georgia thought ironically. She had seen Janie put her hand on Peter's shoulder at one point in the afternoon – a hand Peter ever so gently removed.

Gemma looked pleased. 'Greg knew the piece as we do it at concerts, so I thought why not? After all, Mozart was the pop star of his day, and he deserved a whirl here too. How's your Tom Watson hunt going?'

So she knew about that. Hardly a surprise, Georgia thought, and Greg must have picked up on the story from the Trents. 'Lots of loose ends,' she replied lightly. 'Not many knots tied yet.'

'That's what the *Flute* is all about, isn't it?' the girl replied. 'A quest with lots of serpents and baddies and trials turning up en route until you reach journey's end. It's a path to the truth.'

'It never seems as clear as that when you're actually on the path,' Georgia joked, trying to keep Rick well distanced. Greg had come to join them, and she was aware he was sizing up the situation, perhaps wondering how to make his mark on it.

'Maybe you're not using your own magic flute. You need a few guiding boys to show you the way, like in the opera,' he said with a straight face.

'Feel like having a go, Greg?' Georgia shot back.

'Sure. Suits me down to the ground. The lads don't do much in the *Flute* anyway, just hang around and watch where the hero's putting his big feet. Best stick to the straight and narrow and keep your feet clean – don't you agree, Georgia?'

NINE

'What about Pamela's story?' Peter asked on Monday morning. 'Do you put it down as at least part fantasy? Long-lost father who pays her one magical visit and then vanishes?'

Georgia had been asking herself this question throughout the remainder of the weekend and was still in two minds. 'Cherry makes no secret of her fantasies, whereas Pamela most certainly guarded this secret. You still think we shouldn't talk to Cherry about Tom's return?'

'No. Firstly, even if we made no mention of Pamela, Cherry would be round to see her like a shot. Secondly, Tom didn't go to see her or, as far as we know, any other old chums in Broadstairs, apart from Mrs Wetherby. The story would have spread if he had. Thirdly, it doesn't affect our core issue of who killed Joan Watson.'

'It does,' Georgia argued. 'What about Ken? It's a living issue, not a dead one, if his murder was connected with Tom's return here.'

'Point to you.' Peter drummed his fingers on the desk. 'What does Luke think about this case? He sounds committed enough, but is he going to give us a contract?'

'There's been talk of it,' Georgia said cautiously. Work overlapping with marriage was a quicksand area in more ways than just talking shop out of hours.

Luke had been so full of a problem over another book – not one of Marsh & Daughter's, luckily – that she hadn't wanted to distract him. She suspected she was taking the wrong approach, however, and perhaps it was one she would not have taken a year ago. Why had marriage made a difference? she wondered. Had it made her feel more emotionally involved in Frost & Co? Logic said no, but it still seemed a possibility.

'Talk to him some more,' Peter said briefly. 'We need publisher backup.'

She was inclined to agree with him. 'So where next? If the old gang did see Tom in the 1970s, they're holding back for their own reasons, and we won't get any further.'

Peter groaned. 'Nothing for it but to tackle it from the other end. One more dive into the website replies.'

She shared his reluctance. There on the desk lay a hard copy of the list, with added notes based on Peter's email follow-ups. These were always of limited help, as a human voice was needed for them to sum up the potential of each one. So far they were only a fraction of the way through. 'Now?' she asked.

'I fear so. Let colour-coding battle commence.'

Each reply, whether hopeful or not, had to be colour coded accordingly with the sighting and witnesses' own locations indicated on maps, not to mention also be fed into the Suspects Anonymous software. Colour-coding was the quickest way to eliminate the hopeful from the irrelevant. Some ruled themselves out immediately (flagged in green), some were definitely hopeful (red), some less so (blue) – and yellow indicated a grey area. Yellows were the hardest to deal with.

As Margaret brought coffee in, Georgia was still hard at it. 'There's a nice bunch together,' Margaret casually commented.

Surprised, Georgia sat back and looked with some surprise to where Margaret's finger was pointing; she had been too close to it to notice how they were accumulating. On the London map there were four reds in the Edgware Road area and three in Soho. 'Thanks,' she said gratefully.

'I know that bit of the world,' Margaret told her. 'Dave had an auntie and uncle up the Edgware Road somewhere. We used to see them once a year or so and do a show in town.'

'When would that have been?'

She pondered. 'Late seventies maybe? We hadn't been married long. They were just beginning to smarten up the area.'

'It's more likely Tom Watson lived there than in Soho then,' Peter said.

'I'd have thought so,' Margaret replied. 'A good place to disappear. Mind you, so was Soho. You could bury yourself for good there and no one would notice.'

'Now that,' Peter commented, 'is what I call a good omen. *Two* good places to disappear, if Tom wanted to be anonymous. Let's try Edgware Road first.'

With coffee and renewed hope, Georgia tackled the job again and prepared to face ordeal by telephone. More decisions to be made. 'We don't know that the red sightings are necessarily correct,' she pointed out. 'Witnesses are going to know where *they* are but could be less sure about where they think they saw Tom.'

'Unwillingly accepted,' Peter groused. 'Those living in, say, the Soho area may have sighted Tom in the Edgware Road area.'

'Sometimes,' Georgia said viciously, 'I wish life would just be straightforward.'

'Nonsense. Think how dull that would be.'

'Think how much easier,' she retaliated, picking up the receiver. One was a mobile number – no reply, no voicemail. One was a landline with no reply, but the third struck gold. A nervous-sounding man by the name of Ron Eastley thought the photo on the website looked rather like his parents' long-term lodger. He couldn't be sure but it did look very like him. And yes, Ron Eastley still lived near the Edgware Road.

The area between Edgware Road and Lisson Grove was a new one to Georgia, although she knew London reasonably well. That was the nice thing about London; you turned a corner and there was a surprise: something new, something old, but seldom anything to make you blue. Massive roads ran overhead, vast new office blocks adorned the road that had once led to Tyburn gallows in one direction and the open countryside in the other. Off the main streets, it was still surprisingly quiet, however. Beech Road, where Ron Eastley lived, had individual houses rather than large blocks of flats. It had clearly come up in the world since Tom Watson's day, so the fact that Ron lived in the family home suggested he might still be a bachelor. Number thirty-six must have been worth a fortune now, but to Georgia it had the forlorn air of being a bastion to the past in the midst of a new generation. It wasn't neglected, but its steps and windows indicated that nothing had much changed for fifty years, whereas neighbouring houses sported porches, bay windows, a little balcony or two and a general air of going places. Nevertheless, number thirty-six looked comfortable in its skin, as the French say, and the kind of house she liked.

The man who opened the door was about sixty, she guessed, a gentle giant in a pullover and casual shirt and with an anxious expression. 'Are you Miss Marsh? Come in.'

He led the way along a hallway to a room at the rear of the house overlooking the small garden – which was perfectly kept. 'You're a gardener, I see,' she said. Always a good opener, for her as much as for the person she was visiting.

Ron looked pleased at this icebreaker. 'It keeps me occupied. I'll be retiring one of these days. Got to have something nice to look at.' He explained that he worked at a local electrical shop.

He went into the kitchen to get the ritual coffee, which tasted amazingly good, together with some apparently home-made biscuits. 'A cook too, I see,' Georgia murmured, although her eye was already on the pile of photograph albums lying on the table.

'Have to keep body and soul together.' He grinned as he saw what she was looking at. 'I've dug these out. There are quite a few that might interest you.'

'Your family took all these, although he was just the lodger?' She purposely kept the 'he' anonymous, waiting for him to take the lead.

'Part of the family,' Ron said promptly. 'Those were different days. I was only a kid when he first came. Coronation year, Mum always remembered it by. I was five then.'

'The man we're looking for is called Tom.'

'No. Bert. He was Bert Holmes.'

Georgia's heart sank. True, Tom could have changed his name – in fact, she cheered up, he probably did. In fact, Holmes – Watson? Coincidence? Maybe not, and she brought out her own photos of Tom in that period. 'Let's lay them side by side,' she suggested.

She spread hers out on the table, and Ron opened the albums in which the photos had been carefully pasted in by loving hands.

'That's Mum there – that's Dad – ' The black and white photo showed two men and a woman with their arms round each other on an open heathland – Hampstead, Georgia wondered, or Regent's Park? The wide skirt and the trilby hats spoke clearly of the fifties. 'And that's Uncle Bert.' Ron pointed to the second man.

'Uncle?'

'That's what we did then,' Ron explained to her relief. 'Couldn't call him Mr Holmes, too formal when you had your breakfast with him every day and he took you to school or to the playground, but then you couldn't call him Bert either. Disrespectful. So it was always Uncle.'

'He really was considered part of the family then.' She studied the photos of Bert side by side with those of Tom, looking at the hands, the eyes, the angle of the head as he faced the camera, the slope of the shoulders if he was in side or back view. They were of the same man. This couldn't only be her eagerness to get a match.

'Oh, yes, he was a proper entertainer, was Uncle Bert. Always doing tricks. I thought he was the cat's whiskers. Few conjuring tricks, lots of jokes. Said he'd been a clown for a short time, like at the circus.'

So that was surely proof. Although – Georgia had a sudden doubt. Could Ron have looked up Tom Watson's career? To her relief, she remembered that Marsh & Daughter hadn't used Tom's name on their website. 'Did he still do stage work professionally?'

'No. Surprising, really, because he was good. He did odd jobs, though Mum told me he settled down to a job as a washer-up at some club in Soho later on. I had my own life when I started working, so I didn't take too much notice.'

Soho? That was the site of the second cluster of reds on the location map. She thanked her lucky stars that she'd brought all the Soho details with her. It was time to plunge in the deep end, she decided. 'Does the name Tom Watson mean anything to you?'

'Don't think so. Should it?'

'He went on trial for the murder of his wife in 1953 but was acquitted.'

'And you think he's my Uncle Bert?' He couldn't be faking that look of astonishment.

'Tom Watson was a clown. He had regular season slots in shows on the south coast.'

'He talked about the war – he'd been in the army, he said, but never on the stage.'

'Your parents never mentioned it?'

'Not that I can remember, but they might have known and never thought to mention it. Mind you, they wouldn't want me going out with a murderer,' he added doubtfully.

'Acquitted,' Georgia said firmly. Amazing how the word 'murderer' was so emotive that it cancelled out all else.

'There weren't so many murders then, and it would have been in the press. They never said anything, and Bert lived a quiet life here.'

'When did he leave?'

'He was here a good long time, a good twenty years.'

'He left in the 1970s?' Was this coincidence? Not too fast, Georgia warned herself. Take it step by step.

He took his time thinking about this as she looked at more of the neatly captioned photographs, mentally thanking Ron's parents. How would researchers in the future fare now that photo albums were so often stored inside computers?

'Yes,' Bert said at last. 'I reckon I was in my mid twenties when he left. I was busy at work and so on, but I still lived here, and Bert and I were sort of mates.'

'Sort of?'

'Well, he was a lot older than me,' Ron said apologetically. 'I thought of him as Mum's and Dad's friend by that time. Mind you, we went to a lot of opera together.'

Georgia must have looked as amazed as she felt, because he took her up on it, grinning. 'We both liked it. It's so expensive today that it's more for the nobs and idle rich, but back in those days the galleries were stuffed full of East Enders and regular folk like me. Bert took me to my first one – must have been in the mid sixties, when London was supposed to be swinging. Didn't swing much round here though; life went on as normal. It was Leoncavallo's *Pagliacci* we saw. That makes sense, now you tell me Bert was a clown himself. I thought opera a bit daft first off; but it began to get hold of me, and we went to quite a few.'

Georgia had to get a grip on herself. *Pagliacci* – the story of a man who comes home and kills his wife because he fears she's unfaithful. '*Vesti la Giubba*' – 'Put on the Costume' – was the famous aria; once the costume was on, no one thought of the man who wore it, that he had emotions and tragedies in his life like anyone else. But why should this suddenly seem so significant to her? Because, she acknowledged, it brought Tom to life for her so vividly, as a man who had lived and worked here, who had interests outside work and a home that he could return to. She almost knew what Ron Eastley was going to say next. And he did.

'But Bert liked Mozart best though. *The Magic Flute* was his favourite.'

Forget Rick, this is Tom, Georgia tried to tell herself, but the two were merging even more strongly into one. Still no word from the French police about Aix-en-Provence.

'He liked operas in English so he could understand,' Ron continued, 'so we went to Sadler's Wells pretty often and then to the Coliseum when the Wells opera moved there. Sometimes we even went to Covent Garden. That was really something. Bert said he liked Papageno best of all.'

Of course, he would, Georgia thought jubilantly. It all fitted. Papageno the mirth maker, the clown. A step forward on Tom seemed to bring hope for the same progress on Rick.

'I used to tease Bert by asking him if he didn't ever want a Papagena for himself.' Ron looked taken aback. 'Pretty tactless of me, if you say he was accused of murdering his wife.'

'You weren't to know.'

'He used to joke I should find one for myself first, and if there were any left over, he might consider it. I never did find one, of course, but we can't have everything. You married?'

'Newly wed,' Georgia told him. 'At Easter.'

'I thought about it. Still do . . . but somehow –' his eye roved round the room '– this place is a bit like marriage. Know what I mean?'

'It's home and memories. And they're part of marriage.'

He looked pleased. 'I've got a lodger up above too. She's company. We go on holiday together sometimes, or I go with my mates, so I've got things sorted.'

She thought he had, and so, perhaps, had Tom, when he lived here. 'Was Bert happy, do you think?'

He considered this. 'You never ask yourself things like that at the time, do you? I never wonder if my up-stairs' lodger's happy. We just potter on. Answering your question, I reckon Bert was. He looked comfortable just pottering on.'

There was a major question still burning in her mind. 'So why do you think Bert left?'

'I never knew. I asked Mum and Dad, and they were mystified too. Bert said he'd just seen an old friend and was going on a short trip; he packed a small bag, and off he went. I've been thinking it through. This would have been about 1974 or 1975.'

'Did he say where he'd been when he returned?'

'He didn't come back – that was the thing. They had a postcard saying he wouldn't be coming back, thank you very much, and someone would be coming for the rest of his things.'

Georgia went very cold. 'And did someone call?'

'Yes, his brother came round to collect his stuff. Not that there was much of it.'

His brother? In all their enquiries, nothing had turned up any information about a brother.

'And the postcard was definitely from Bert? Did your parents hear from him after that?' *Please, please let the answer be yes.*

'I think there was a Christmas card for a year or two, no address. Mum and Dad never said anything about the postcard, so I wouldn't know. They were pretty upset.'

'They didn't think it strange?'

'They assumed he'd gone back to his old life and that was that. Course they had no idea he was a—' He caught her eye. 'About the murder and all that.'

Georgia took herself to lunch at a local fish and chip shop, which seemed fitting. She wondered if it had been open in the nineteen fifties and tried to picture Tom eating here. Perhaps the connection to Broadstairs would have been too much for him. She tried to make sense of her thoughts. She had no doubt that Bert Holmes had been Tom Watson, but where did that leave Marsh & Daughter? It suggested that Pamela's story was true for a start, but where had Tom gone after that? And what about this brother? He must have known where Tom was. One thing was for sure. She felt more confident about asking Luke for a contract.

She decided a phone call to Peter was in order. Would it be worth checking the Soho connection while she was here? One of the three red-flag contacts had claimed she worked with Tom. On the other hand, Georgia had had an uneasy feeling on leaving Ron's house that she was being watched. Was it Ron peering through the window, Greg Dale even more dedicated to her trail than she had feared or was it just a prickling feeling in her spine that there were uncharted waters ahead? She reassured herself that it could be due to the memory of a former case where she had indeed been stalked on a London visit and that today she was merely imagining a silent watcher. It was ghosts from the past who were following her, not flesh and blood from today.

The number rang – but it wasn't Peter who answered it, nor even Margaret. It was Janie, which surprised her, as this was their office number. Then the receiver must have been snatched by Peter, for he took over peremptorily. 'What news?' he snapped.

'Good news. Almost certainly our Tom. It's worth my trying the Soho contact.' Georgia told him briefly about the disappearance in the nineteen seventies, to which he said, 'Hmm,' and other noises to that effect.

The contact turned out not to live in Soho at all. Soho was where she had known Tom, or Bert Holmes, or of course neither if it wasn't the same person, Georgia reasoned. Dorothy Wild now lived in a flat in Finchley, on the ground floor of her daughter's home. That was an easier journey by underground than Soho, although the house was some way to walk once she reached Finchley station.

Dorothy Wild looked as if she were in her eighties or late seventies, which is what Georgia had expected, given the fact she claimed to have worked with the supposed Tom. She was no slight Alison Robin to look at and was far more robust physically, tall and purposeful.

'It's a long time ago,' she said doubtfully. 'You probably think I'm rambling.'

'No,' Georgia replied truthfully. Those alert eyes wouldn't be rambling for a good while yet.

'That chap on your website was Bert Holmes. I check it regularly just for fun – but I never expected to see anyone I knew. And blow me down, up pops Bert.'

'You're an Internet fan?'

'Not much else to do at my age. Get with it or get lost, I say. I like your books, by the way. That's why I click on the website.'

'I'm glad you do,' Georgia said sincerely. 'Have a look at these photos and see if you recognize him in any of them.'

She passed over three or four and studied Mrs Wild as she looked at them. 'Not sure about these. I knew an older man,' Dorothy said, passing the first test. The words 'not sure' meant she could rely on her.

'Try this one.' Georgia gave her an unidentified photo from the white envelope in Ken's box, and this time the answer, to her relief, was:

'That's Bert all right. I worked with him in the late sixties, early seventies. I was a waitress at this club, the Blue Parrot. Bert did the washing up.'

'He was actually a clown by training – did you know that?'

'A clown?' Mrs Wild looked surprised. 'He was a bit of a comedian in his quiet way, but no acrobatics at the kitchen sink. I suppose he wouldn't, would he?'

'Did he talk about his past life?'

'I didn't know him much outside work, only a "how are you?" sort of relationship. He was a nice chap, got a rough deal from the other staff because he wasn't the mixing sort. He was still there when I left in seventy-two though.'

'Do you know what happened to him afterwards?'

Mrs Wild looked suspicious. 'What do you want to know all this for? What's he done?'

'His name was really Tom Watson, and in 1953 he was acquitted of having murdered his wife.'

Dorothy snorted. 'Not surprised he was acquitted. If Bert was this Tom, he couldn't murder a sandwich, let alone a woman.'

'The jury agreed with you.'

'So that's why he came up to the Smoke, to get over it?'

'I imagine that's the reason. Most people in his home-town still thought he was guilty.'

'Poor old bugger. I never realized. Mind you, we never talked much. Except once. That club was a funny place. I reckon Bert was the only one who didn't know it was a meeting place for half the gangs of London. And I don't mean spotty kids. Soho had all the bright lights then. Not that you'd have seen much light in the Blue Parrot. Know anything about those days, do you?'

'The age of the Beatles, Carnaby Street, rise of pop music, women's lib . . .'

'Crime, ducky, crime. The fifties and sixties were the time for the big gangs. Billy Hill and Jack Spot ruled the fifties and the Krays and others in the sixties. One of them was the Silver Gang. Nasty lot, they were, and for a time they were riding high in the crime charts, until they went a step too far with their rivals and had to scatter for their lives. They used to like the Blue Parrot.'

She paused and looked as if she was doubtful whether to continue, but thankfully she did. 'Bert was in the kitchens, of course, but he used to take a peek at the punters every so often. We all did. One day in comes the Silver Gang together with the big chief, Quicksilver, they called him. Well, Bert freaked out.'

'In what way?'

'He got very excited and said he knew a couple of the guys, and went out to talk to them. Then he came back again, looking rather queer. We all reckoned Bert must have done time or got mixed up with a bad crowd at some point.'

'Could this have been about the time he left?' Even as she spoke, she realized her mistake.

'Oh no,' was the inevitable and disappointing answer. 'This would have been in the late sixties.'

'And you didn't see him again?'

'Afraid not.'

So Dorothy Wild could not have been the 'old friend' whom Tom had seen just before he left for Broadstairs. Two steps forward, one back. Nevertheless, Georgia consoled herself that the Blue Parrot information could suggest Tom had been mixed up with a criminal crowd in London.

She needed Peter's input on this, so risking the chance that Janie might still be with Peter at Haden Shaw, she went straight there after picking up her car at Canterbury. When she reached Haden Shaw, there was no sign of Janie, which might have made it difficult to talk freely. Even so, she was annoyed with herself for feeling relieved. Discussions between three, however, were not as focused as discussions between two, and she could hardly have asked Janie to kindly step into another room.

'No Janie?' she asked as casually as she could.

'She's gone,' said Peter. 'Fire away.'

His voice did not encourage further questions, and Georgia had plenty of talking to do, so she postponed them.

'It's quite likely Tom got drawn into crime in London,' Peter agreed after she'd finished. 'If there had been any connection between the couple he saw at the Blue Parrot and Broadstairs, it would have been under the name of Tom Watson, and if he was anxious to preserve his new identity, he would hardly have jeopardized it by rushing out to greet them. Which suggests they knew him as Bert Holmes.'

'Wrong. He might not have known these chums were part of the Silver Gang.'

'True. As Dorothy Wild remembered it for over thirty years, however, it must have imprinted itself strongly.'

'Or grown in her mind,' Georgia said brightly.

Peter ruminated. 'Let's be optimistic and assume we have a clear-headed witness. Sufficiently so to take us a stage further, at any rate. We could check out the gang, see what's known about them?'

'Even though it was years before Tom returned to Broadstairs?'

'Despite that. Remember that we were told about some odd goings-on in Broadstairs in the fifties. Perhaps it's time we talked to Brian James again. Your favourite misogynist.'

Peter didn't seem overeager about this, however. In fact, she realized, although he had looked impressed, he had not been as delighted at her news as she had hoped. Something must be wrong.

'Is it Janie?' she blurted out.

'No.' He didn't even look surprised, and she realized why. It was worse than that.

'Rick?' Of course it was. Realization hit her like a blow to the stomach.

'I'm afraid so. Décourt has done a good job, but it's bad news. The Provençal police were notified at the time along with every other national police force. He's been in touch with them again, but there were no unidentifieds in Aix or the surrounding area that could possibly have been our Rick – then *or* more recently.'

Her favourite misogynist, Brian James, had apparently been delighted to see Peter again. Georgia had refused to go on the grounds that Peter would get far more out of him than her presence would allow. He agreed rather too readily, but

she wasn't sorry. She was still smarting from the setback
over Rick. So great was the disappointment that neither she
nor Peter had had the will to discuss a next step – if any.
Besides, she had plenty to do at Medlars. His appointment
had been for Friday, and it had suited her well to have an
afternoon off. Early July was no time to be on the computer
all day.

'A Kir if you please.' Peter turned up at Medlars early
on the Friday evening, looking, she thought, more cheerful.

'Not unless you're staying the night,' Luke said firmly.
'I pack a powerful punch in my Kirs.'

'A relaxing tomato juice then,' Peter said sulkily. 'I must
say this is a very welcoming room – apart from its drinks
service.'

'Brian James,' Georgia reminded him.

'He was quite forthcoming about the funny goings-on
in Broadstairs,' Peter told her. 'Not much help on the
Tom Watson front though. When I put my point about Tom
possibly being mixed up with London crime, and could it
link with what was happening in Broadstairs, Brian came
back with the fact that on the south coast there had been a
tradition of funny goings-on for centuries. The other word
for it is smuggling, including just after the Second World
War.'

'For the black market?'

'Indeed. Cigarettes, brandy, booze, this, that and the other,
paintings – you name it.'

'Smuggled in by boat?'

'Chiefly. It came into the Gaps, seven coves along the
coast, and was then taken into the town or through tunnels
to inland farms. The particular Gap that Brian says they
had their eye on in the early fifties was the furthest north
towards Cliftonville, appropriately called Botany Bay. It
was pretty deserted out there then, with only the odd
bungalow around and unmade-up paths.'

'Ideal for Joan's lifestyle,' Georgia commented.

'Not just her. It's an interesting line to follow up. I
wonder if anything other than light entertainment was going
on in *Waves Ahoy!* Talking of interesting lines,' Peter added,

'I forgot to tell you that, as we suspected, Tom Watson didn't have a brother.'

'So who was the so-called relative?'

'Could be the Eastleys' memories at fault.'

'It could,' she agreed, but there was surely a question mark over that. 'There's something I forgot to tell you too.'

'Good. We're quits. What?'

'*The Magic Flute* was Tom's favourite opera.'

TEN

So Tom had no brother. Georgia was still grappling with the implications. Did that mean Tom wasn't Bert or something more sinister? What had happened to him after that visit to Broadstairs? The coming of another Monday morning made the answers no easier. Weeks were passing, and every time she and Peter seemed to be in command of the boxing ring, they were thrown back on the ropes. She did not dare raise the subject of Rick. She had forced herself to spend time on the Internet chasing up Mozart performances in other capital cities of Europe, but increasingly it seemed a hopeless task, when they had no firm evidence that Rick had even gone anywhere with Miss Blondie. Tom Watson seemed an easier option – although not by much.

'Is your Mr Eastley a reliable witness?' Peter asked for the umpteenth time. 'It could have been the same "old friend" who called for the luggage, or even Bert himself. And was the "old friend" part of the reason he went to Broadstairs?'

'Who knows?' Georgia fumed. 'Presuming what Ron said was accurate though – where does that take us? Did Tom do another disappearing act after coming back to Broadstairs and, if so, why?'

'The Silver Gang reared its head again when he got back to London? Presumably it liked to keep a low profile and Bert-cum-Tom knew who at least two of them were. Quicksilver wouldn't like that. It's a nickname that suggests he liked keeping himself and his gang out of the limelight.'

'Bert hadn't come to any harm since he'd seen them in the club.'

'Maybe he became part of the gang.'

'He might have run into the gang again.'

'Sheer speculation.' Georgia dismissed this gloomily.

'Even Suspects Anonymous turned up its nose at that when I tried it on them.'

'It was equally dismissive of the rest of the website replies. It spat most of them straight out again and dumped them in its trash can as irrelevant. We've nothing left for either the period leading up to the Broadstairs visit or after it, except for some "maybes".'

The dreaded maybes. It was always a problem deciding whether or not to follow such replies up, save for acknowledgement and thanks. She usually left it to Peter to settle, since it was a job he'd faced so often in his police career.

'If the few maybes on Tom after the mid seventies don't lead anywhere, are we entering murky waters?' She had to voice what Peter must also have been thinking. 'Could Tom have committed suicide after that, or did he disappear so convincingly that he wasn't noticed by anyone?'

'It's a line of investigation,' Peter agreed cautiously. 'After all, if he had plans not to return to London after Broadstairs, why not tell the Eastleys? I'll check the name Bert Holmes to see how many deaths were recorded around that time, but it's going to be hard to work out which was our Bert Holmes, if indeed any of them were.'

'And if it leads nowhere?'

'We look at the possibility that something happened during his visit either to change Tom's mind about returning to London or which caused it to be changed for him.'

Pleasant though it was for her to be sitting in the gardens on Broadstairs' seafront, it was less attractive to think what it might have been like for Tom after over twenty years' absence, Georgia thought. Here he could be passed un-recognized by former friends, colleagues and acquaintances without a second look. What would Tom have been thinking about? What were his plans, his reasons for being here, besides seeing Pamela on her birthday, or was that really his sole purpose? If so, after achieving it he had walked off into a metaphorical sunset, so far as the record was concerned.

Would Tom have tried to see Cherry and failed – perhaps for the mundane reason that she had been out when he called? No, such a meeting would be too painful for both, unless he meant to settle down here for good. Tom seemed to have been the sort of person who might have sacrificed his own happiness in the interests of freeing his former sweetheart from the taint of association with him. That was unlikely to have changed in the years since the murder, and therefore he would be unlikely to seek her out.

It was far more likely, Georgia reasoned, that Tom would try Sandy or Micky, and perhaps even Mavis. Tom's former home would represent unhappiness, so he would not linger there after seeing the neighbour, and he would avoid the pubs. Where in the town might Tom have been happy? One obvious answer was in *Waves Ahoy!* and on the pier where it had taken place. If anywhere, he would go there after seeing Pamela, Georgia decided, especially as he'd come in summer, when there might have been another show on the pier. He was unlikely to have had a car, so probably would have come to Broadstairs by train. After visiting the pier and the site of the former theatre, he would have walked back up the High Street to take the train back to London. No, that was wrong. Tom had taken a bag with him, so perhaps he intended to stay at least one night.

Tom, like Rick, was becoming an increasingly elusive shadow to pin down, but now Luke had agreed to a contract and it had been signed, Marsh & Daughter were committed to push onwards, however foggy the outlook.

Peter had suggested Georgia should make Christine her first port of call today. Apart from being a friendly face, Christine held Micky's diaries from the nineteen seventies, and so far she and Peter had checked only those for the nineteen forties and fifties. The new information meant there was a slim chance of Micky's diaries from the later period indicating something of interest.

To Georgia's relief, Christine looked much better than she had at the funeral. She needed all her energy for the coming baby. 'Only a month or so to go now,' she said happily as she led the way to the garden, where two easy chairs awaited them. 'So far the hospital is pleased with me. No complications, so full-steam ahead for the big one.'

'Not too big, I hope,' Georgia joked.

'How are you getting on with your Brittany quest?' Christine asked diffidently. 'Any luck?'

'We're more or less at a standstill,' Georgia confessed. 'Just as in the Watson case, there are too many ifs and buts to proceed in a straight line. We've got a lead on Tom though. Could I have a look at the diaries from 1973 onwards?' Better to be on the safe side. Both Pamela and Ron had been unclear about the precise year, although 1974 was the most likely.

'Just in time. We were thinking of chucking them all out.'

'Don't do that,' Georgia pleaded.

Christine laughed. 'Chucking them into the garage, at any rate, just in case the British Library wants to make an offer for them. I'd keep them inside, if they really meant anything to the family, but they don't.'

'I'm hoping they'll make more sense to us now that we know a little more.' Georgia realized to her surprise that with them actually in front of her she was eager to get started. A new day, a new lead, she thought hopefully.

'Nineteen seventy-three.' Christine came back with the relevant diary, and Georgia looked quickly through the July entries. There were the familiar jottings of names and the same cryptic comments, but Christine was right. There was little here to aid the entertainment historian of the future, or even the family researcher, and certainly not Marsh & Daughter. She went through the weeks following Pamela's birthday in case Micky had recorded the visit later, but there was nothing that could possibly relate to Tom Watson.

Christine disappeared inside again and came out with the 1974 volume, on which Georgia was pinning her hopes. Again she was disappointed. There was nothing.

With decreasing hope, she opened up 1975 and turned to the fourteenth of July.

'Hey, jackpot time!' She was staring at a familiar name. 'Bert Holmes.' That was all Micky had written, but it was enough. It was a bullseye. 'Thanks, Christine.'

At least she now knew Tom had called on Micky, and possibly Sandy as well, although Sandy had kept quiet about it if so. Another thought: 'Did Ken ever look at these?'

'He had them on his shelves, but he never talked about them.'

Could Ken have just chanced on this entry and seen the Watson connection there? Even if he did, Georgia thought, excitement draining away, it was surely too slender a clue for Ken to build his entire scoop on. And yet it was tempting to believe he could and that he, like Peter and herself, had found Mrs Robin and even persuaded Pamela to talk, even though she had been annoyed at his pestering.

On the off chance, she leafed through the entire diary and at the very end was rewarded. Micky liked being cryptic, and here was plenty of proof of that. Under 'Addresses', he had written with heavy underlining: *Notes on Sherlock's Last Case*, and a series of notes: 'The Adventure at Wisteria Lodge'; 'Talk about the Three Garridebs' – the Three Joeys, she wondered. Irene Adler was another name noted down – Joan Watson? Micky was devoted to her, as Sherlock was to '*the* woman'. 'The Mysterious Lodger' was another, and at the end a query mark with 'The Giant Rat of Sumatra', the famous story that Sherlock had never recorded, if she remembered correctly. So to what was that a reference? And if Tom had told Micky the story, why the need for a question mark?

'Helpful?' Christine asked, obviously curious.

'Oh indeed it is. I think Tom Watson did come to see your grandfather in 1975, but I need a few months to work out Micky's clues. Could I—'

Christine laughed. 'Of course you can take it.' Then her face clouded. 'Do you think my father read this and that he was as excited as you?'

'It's possible,' Georgia said gently.

A pause. 'So Tom didn't commit suicide in 1953. This diary seems to be proof, and it's probably what Dad had discovered too.' Another pause. 'Does Cherry know?'

'No, and I don't think she should. Not yet, at least. It's unlikely that Tom went to see her, because it would be hurtful for her if he then left again.'

Christine accepted this, to Georgia's relief. She tried to put herself in Cherry's position. Suppose she and Peter discovered that Rick had paid a visit to Kent and not bothered to look in to see them?

Port of call Number Two was Cath for lunch, and Georgia arrived at Marchesi's on the seafront buoyed up with the success of the morning. It was a pleasant place for lunch, and so full of atmosphere that it would be easy to think that the famous Signor Marchesi, who had moved here in the nineteenth century, was still busily baking away in the kitchens. Georgia realized she and Cath had been talking for half an hour without a word of work.

At last, Cath leaned back and said, 'OK. That was good. Now tell me what I'm here for.'

'To have dessert.'

'Sounds good. I haven't got much for you yet in the way of information though. Poor return for your cash if lunch is on you.'

'It is, and you should have some soon, I hope. How about smuggling and the black market in the nineteen fifties?'

Cath cocked an interested eye at her. 'Our lads at it, were they? Uncle Tom Watson and all?'

'Not Tom necessarily, but it would explain Joan's lifestyle.'

'So would generosity with sexual favours. Anyway, you need my help?'

'Yes. We need to know if any of the *Waves Ahoy!* company could have been involved.'

'Ships rowed ashore at dead of night? Smugglers' tunnels – that sort of thing?'

'Do you know the Gaps, and in particular Botany Bay?' She outlined what Peter had learned from Brian James.

'I knew there were a lot of tunnels,' Cath said when Georgia had finished, 'but I don't know which if any were in use in Tom Watson's time, or how distribution was done in the fifties. Actually, we may make light of it,' she added, 'but it can't have been a barrel of fun living on rationing. And there must have been a thin line between the butcher

handing you the best joint and paying for foreign goodies
on the black market.'

'The smuggling going on sounds rather more than that.
Anyway, I suppose fun's what you make of a situation.'

'Are you the family's chief moralizer, Georgia?' Cath
pulled a face. 'If so, warn me now.'

Georgia did a double take. 'Are you implying . . .'

'I'm considering my options,' Cath said hastily. 'Could
you stick me around long term?'

'I could try. Can you stick Charlie, warts and all?'

'I guess it's the warts that attract me, so the answer's
yes.'

'They might not attract you so much with a mortgage to
pay and housework to be done.'

Cath grinned. 'Trying to put me off?'

'No way,' Georgia said fervently. 'You're the great white
hope for Charlie, and therefore for Gwen and also for us.
Keep right on.'

'That's nice. Maybe I'll think about it seriously. Charlie
and I might shack up together for a while anyway.'

'Not a bad plan. That's what Luke and I did.' Georgia
decided not to mention all the agony, the heart searchings,
the 'what ifs' that had preceded their marriage. Cath could
reason that out for herself. Georgia realized with some
surprise that she had difficulty remembering them now. One
step, and on to a new plateau, which seemed wonderfully
good so far.

'This smuggling thing,' Cath hesitated. 'Suppose I have
to take this all the way?'

Georgia knew exactly what Cath meant. Her grandfather,
who worked in the US stores. 'Do you want me to tackle
Buck on it?' she asked.

'No. I'll put my mouth where my heart is. Leave him to
me. That's if you trust me.'

Georgia thought about this perhaps rather too long for
Cath raised her eyebrows, even as Georgia replied, 'Yes.
In return,' she added, 'I'll present you with some information. Maybe Buck could help on that. Strictly under wraps
at the moment.'

'I promise. What is it?'

'We've evidence that Tom came back here, at least briefly, in 1975.'

'What?' Cath looked incredulous. 'You really mean the suicide, the presumed death and all that are all so much hot air? Are you sure? Was Ken on to this?'

'I think so. What we don't know is everything that Tom did when he came back that day, and what happened to him after that. It seems fairly sure he came back primarily to see Pamela, who had been a toddler when he left. What we don't know is who else he saw while he was here, apart from Micky Winton.'

Cath's eyes gleamed. 'Ken's scoop? You mean Micky kept mum all that time?'

'He seems to have done, and it's more than possible that that was indeed Ken's last scoop. We need to know who else Tom visited though.'

'Such as Grandpops?' Cath asked sharply. 'Well, OK. I'll tackle him, but he tends to be rather good at parrying tackles. How likely is it Ken was about to launch the news of Tom's return plus a "where are you now?" appeal?'

'It seems a strong probability. It's even possible that one reason for his return was to spill the beans on who did kill Joan.'

'Then why didn't he do just that?'

'That,' Georgia said, 'is open to discussion.'

'He was stopped?'

'Nothing to rule that out yet.' She had been hoping Cath wouldn't make the connection. Some hopes! Cath was right there.

'Then you – we – might be in for a big surprise, like the teddy bears in the old song. You know what I think?'

'Tell me.'

'If Tom copped it in 1975 and Ken this year, so could you, so could Peter and so could I, if we go probing too far. Unless it's general knowledge that Tom returned here. I'd be in favour of telling the whole damn world or, short of that, everyone concerned with Tom Watson.'

Georgia considered the merits of this approach,

remembering all too clearly that creepy sensation of being followed in London, and of Greg Dale's watching eye.

'The teddy bears are meeting at Sandy's home on Saturday,' Cath continued, 'to discuss the reunion concert next month. If we go and play with them, you could throw in your grenade.'

Georgia reached into her bag for her mobile. 'I'll consult the oracle right away.'

The oracle had agreed. On her return to Haden Shaw Georgia found Peter sitting smugly reading the daily newspaper.

'We can,' Peter said blithely. 'In fact, it's all arranged. I phoned Fenella as soon as you rang off. It turns out Fenella knows Janie through the Fernbourne Museum. She did some of the cataloguing for it. Small world, isn't it?'

'A useful one,' Georgia agreed. 'Is Janie coming then?' She hoped to sound casually interested, but as usual it failed.

'I could hardly say no,' he shot back at her accusingly.

Diffuse the situation quickly. 'I'm glad. Your car or mine?'

He considered. 'Yours.'

She thought Peter was about to add something, but if so, he refrained. 'What about our promise to Pamela to say nothing?'

'I rang her too. I deserve a free dinner at the pub for that. I said we had other sources to confirm Tom had been here in July seventy-five, not seventy-four, as she had thought, but she needed coaxing before she agreed she could be brought into it. I got the impression she was—'

'Annoyed?' she asked when he broke off.

'Apprehensive. It's hard to see why unless she's holding something back.'

'Is there a risk in bringing this into the open?' Georgia asked doubtfully.

A pause. 'When did risk ever stop us? We have to do it, Georgia. I'm getting superstitious in my old age. I have the feeling that if we can't find out what happened to Tom Watson, we'll never know the truth about Rick either.'

He looked at her to see how she was taking this, adding,

'I'm still trying to track down possible leads when I have the heart.'

'So am I.'

'I haven't reached Mongolia yet.'

Georgia managed a laugh. 'Then keep right on.'

There was nothing grudging about Fenella's welcome, perhaps because Janie was with them, Georgia thought. Peter had been silent on the way over, leaving Janie to do the talking and Georgia the driving. The set look on his face had deterred her from asking what he was mulling over.

She was glad he had arranged for them to come towards the end of the meeting, with the plan of joining the *Waves Ahoy!* crew for lunch and social chit-chat afterwards. As she drew up, she could see at least a couple of dozen cars outside the house, and from inside came the sounds of laughter, singing and a piano being bashed rather than played.

'Come in,' Fenella greeted them. 'The action is in the kitchen for you at present. Help yourselves to a drink, make your own instant, pour your own wine. Best to go round the back with the wheelchair,' she told Peter. 'There's an entrance straight into the kitchen. If you go now, you'll beat the scrum. Vic's there if you need a hand.'

Peter turned the chair, and Janie followed anxiously as he manoeuvred it and set off for the kitchen. Georgia could see by the tension in his shoulders that something was still displeasing her father – something to do with Janie? Give him space, she wanted to cry after her, but no. Janie was right there, a hand on the wheelchair back, and when they reached the kitchen, she walked straight in to prepare the way. Vic Dale was more tactful. He stood back, waiting to see whether help was needed. He had obviously had plenty of experience with Sandy.

'Glass of white, Peter?' Janie asked, and without waiting for the answer, 'I'll pour one for you.'

'Thanks.'

A brief exchange, but it depressed Georgia. Peter liked

getting his own wine, his own food, and Janie *still* hadn't realized that. Nevertheless, that must surely be a small matter compared with the companionship that Janie offered him. There was no doubt there was a strong rapport between them. The chemistry was there, even to Georgia's observing eye, but the equipment for handling it seemed to be heading for trouble.

Georgia could see through the open doors that the meeting was being held in the large living room, with people spilling out on to the terrace. It looked informal as meetings go, although Harold was very clearly in command. Sandy was standing at his side with a hand on the piano top, so full marks to him for not using a wheelchair today. All eyes seemed to be on Harold, however, although he was talking quietly, both listening and consulting rather than lecturing his audience. Effective, Georgia thought, as she was sure that if he suddenly cried, 'Enough,' there would be an instant hush. He seemed to have a deft way of unifying a group that must have stood him in good stead in his career. She could see Cherry discreetly at the back of the room, clad appropriately in cherry red, eyes fixed on Harold. In repose it was possible to see in her gentle face the seventeen-year-old sweetheart of Tom Watson.

Mavis was sitting in the window seat, a sardonic look on her face, although not a rebellious one. Sandy was definitely Number Two, watching his producer for the next call for the Three Joeys. There were others whom Georgia did not recognize but who seemed to be contemporaries of *Waves Ahoy!* and so could well have been part of other acts. No sign of the Trents, however, except for Gemma.

Georgia wondered what Harold would do about the chorus line. Surely it would be too pitiful to try to recreate anything like it had been in Joan Watson's day. Did Harold fill in with modern acts, as well as the home movies someone had mentioned? That would be one way of organizing the show, which Cath had told her was for charity in aid of the Benevolent Fund.

Watching them, Georgia found it hard to imagine that any secrets could remain amongst this group. It looked as if it were here solely to pay a tribute to the past rather than being bound up in conspiracy to cover up something that bore little resemblance to nostalgic reminiscences. As the meeting finished, the audience sprang instantly to life, silent faces becoming animated again as they made their way to the terrace where the buffet was laid out. Georgia was swept up in the crowd, aware of Janie again leading the way for Peter, but then her attention was diverted.

'Georgia. How nice to see you.' Cherry had sought her out. 'It's good of you to take such an interest in our doings. You will be coming along in August, won't you?'

Georgia felt her face must be flushing with guilt, as Cherry swept on. 'Harold had such a good idea for those of us who were in the chorus line. Such fun.' The guilt grew. Cherry's fun would not last. Half of her wanted to run like hell, to limit the damage Peter's announcement would cause before it was too late. But it wasn't possible. She was committed.

'We're going to use the old songs,' Cherry chattered on, 'but instead of kicking our legs up, we'll be in a line with our arms round one another's waists, just moving to the music like *waves*. Do you see? And all dressed in the same colour, blue probably, which suits us all.'

Georgia did see, and it could indeed be very effective.

'We'll have to rehearse, of course,' Cherry said. 'Harold wants split-second timing.'

She spoke of him almost objectively, despite the fact she had once been married to him. Such a long time ago, Georgia supposed, and Cherry had been married again since then, as had Harold presumably. But then Georgia's own first marriage to Zac now seemed to involve a different person and era. Zac was in her objective category, as Harold was to Cherry. Whereas Luke . . . Never. Luke was present and Luke was her future.

'Cherry!' Harold came up to them at that moment and deposited a kiss on her cheek. 'Think you can manage the rehearsals?'

'Of course, Harold. Plenty of life left in me yet.'

'Good. I should get some of that salmon mousse, if I

were you. Running out fast. Darling, I need a word with
Georgia here.' A quick kiss, and he turned away from his
former wife.

Cherry looked rebuffed for a brief instant and then trotted
off obediently to collect some food.

'It must have been fun being in one of your plays, Harold,'
Georgia observed.

'Not always,' he joked.

'The quiet voice can be deadlier than the roar?'

For a moment he looked taken aback, then, 'Both work
on occasion, I find. Or rather, *found.*'

'It must be hard adapting from the West End to a retirement community, but I suppose you've directed all these
folk before, and people don't change in personality, despite
the years.'

'No.' He eyed her thoughtfully. 'That's what worries me,
and I have a feeling that Marsh & Daughter isn't going to
give up easily.'

'Give up what?' she stalled.

'The Tom Watson story.'

'Any reason we should – apart from our not wanting to
hurt Cherry?'

He looked at her earnestly. 'I don't think you realize what
you might be getting into.'

'You're wrong. I think we do. That's why, as Peter must
have warned you, we decided to talk to you all together.'

'Sleeping dogs are much happier.'

'Peter and I can't judge that.'

'Look what happened to Ken. Doesn't that worry you?'

He was beginning to rile her. 'Are you saying he was
killed by a sleeping dog? If so, that would seem to belie
your statement that they are happier. Far from it, I'd say.'

He shrugged. 'Perhaps you're right. Guilt can do damage.
Look at the four knights who murdered Thomas Becket.
But to do nothing – isn't that worse?' He glanced at her as
if he'd thought better of what he was going to say next and
muttered, 'I suppose I should have another word with your
father.'

Janie's arrival gave him an excuse to leave, and Georgia's

heart sank. She was not feeling up to coping with Janie and hoped she was going to talk only about Tom Watson. She was wrong.

'I wanted to ask you,' Janie said hesitantly, 'how you were getting on with the search for your brother.'

Georgia gritted her teeth, forcing herself to reply reasonably instead of shouting out that this was her business and Peter's – and perhaps Luke's. 'It's not leading anywhere *yet.*'

'Peter said the police search took place all over France, not just Brittany.'

Every word brought the agony back more clearly. 'Yes.'

'But nowhere else?'

How long was this inquisition going on? 'I don't know. Anyway, Rick wasn't in the habit of just wandering off without letting us know roughly where he was.'

'But he did,' Janie persisted.

Damn her. 'That last time, yes. Where does one start looking though? Beijing? Sydney? New York?'

Janie wasn't going to give up. 'Did Rick leave belongings behind him at the farm where he stayed in Brittany?'

To Georgia's horror, her mind went blank and her defences were gone. 'I don't know. I don't know if I ever knew. And yet I must have done.' Only fourteen years ago, and she *couldn't remember*. She had thought every detail was indelibly stamped on to her memory. She forced herself to think back to the weeks she and Peter spent in Brittany hunting for him.

'I don't think so, but I can't be sure.'

She remembered going to the farm; Peter was then on two active legs and ran up the stairs with her behind him to look at the room where Rick had slept. But then came a blank. 'No. I don't think so,' Georgia managed to continue. 'He was hitch-hiking so he wouldn't have had much.'

Not much. Just one rucksack to carry belongings while he followed his dream. Images flashed through her mind: the Pied Piper, rats, the Giant Rat of Sumatra, Miss Blondie, Mozart. A magic flute. Rick had gone with Miss Blondie into the Pied Piper's mountain and taken the magic flute

with him. Tom Watson and Papageno. Georgia began to
feel giddy and then sick, just as she had at Ken's funeral.
Rick and Tom were intertwining themselves in her mind.
She felt herself swaying, and then Janie was grasping her
arm, talking urgently to her.

'Come away from the crowd for a few minutes.' Janie
led her quickly from the terrace and down into the garden,
where Georgia took several deep breaths and gradually
began to recover.

'I'm sorry,' she said, aware her voice was trembling.
'Sometimes it gets too much. I can handle it normally, but
now – knowing we have a lead but being constantly frustrated is terrible.'

'It's bad. You must be thankful you have Luke and Peter
to share it with. I could never share anything with my
mother,' Janie said matter-of-factly. 'I had to pour it all into
my novels.'

'Are you writing again?' Thank heavens, normality
restored, as perhaps Janie had intended.

'Oh, yes. It's the only way. Keep going, keep going. It's
where to is the problem.' Janie looked sad, but when she
noticed Georgia's attention on her, she flushed. 'Maybe
that's what Tom Watson felt,' she added.

As Janie left her to rejoin Peter, Georgia wondered what
had made her raise the subject in the first place. Kindness?
Fellow sympathy? Janie had both. If only she would use
them at the right times.

As the party began to thin out, Georgia started to feel more
and more on edge. Peter must have been leaving his 'grenade'
until only the hard core, those who had known Tom or had
been involved in his life story, remained on the lawn. Among
them were Matthew and Pamela Trent, who must just have
arrived. The die was about to be cast, she thought, if only
because she could see Janie leaving Peter to join Fenella –
at his request, she suspected. She was right, as Harold called
the group to attention, and she listened to what followed
almost as though it were a play in itself.

'*Waves Ahoy!*' Peter began without preamble. 'That's

where this story began for Tom and Joan Watson. But it didn't finish there.'

'Of course not,' Cherry cried out brightly. 'I know—' She was hushed by Harold.

'Tom is thought to have committed suicide,' Peter continued, 'but we know that didn't happen. Not in 1953, anyway.'

'That's right.' Cherry's voice was shrill with excitement. 'Have you found him?'

'No,' Peter answered so that all could hear. 'I'm afraid I think he is no longer alive, but I could be wrong. The truth is that to save you hurt, Cherry, Tom made another life for himself under another name in London.'

Everyone looked very still, which made this seem even more like a play, Georgia thought. But this was real, and it was worse than she had feared.

'Tom did come back to Broadstairs for a day at least in 1975.'

Georgia heard the general intake of breath but her eyes were on Cherry who was very white. 'He obviously did not want to hurt you, Cherry,' Peter repeated, 'and that's why he made no attempt to see you. After all, you were married, and he might have thought you still were.'

Harold looked totally detached, Georgia noticed. He wasn't looking at Cherry, far from it, although there still seemed to be feeling between them. What had attracted Harold to marry Cherry? She supposed she might have had a helplessness that would have appealed to a young man eager for power, and on Cherry's side protection and a chance of leaving Broadstairs might have been irresistible.

'But where is he now? Tom must be alive,' Cherry cried out. 'You *know*, don't you? You have his address.'

'Nothing has been heard of him since that visit,' Peter explained. 'It's possible he died very soon after it.'

'Nonsense. Of course he's still alive,' Cherry shouted indignantly. 'I'll advertise in *The Times*. Tom will want to come to the reunion to see me dance. He may not know we have one every year.'

'The first question is,' Peter continued gently, ignoring this outburst, 'whom did Tom see when he came here? We know he met an old friend in London, which might have been connected with the visit. We know he saw Mrs Trent.' He nodded at her, but she did not respond. 'And we know he met Micky Winton again. Ken may have discovered this, but it seems that Micky did not tell his son himself. Why not, I wonder? Did he come to see you, Sandy?'

Sandy shook his head. 'I'd like to have seen the old blighter, but I haven't set eyes on him since he vanished in October 1953. I moved away, so I reckon Tom didn't know I was back in Broadstairs – otherwise he would have dropped in.'

'I was living in London,' Harold said. 'So rule me out.'

'Mavis?'

Georgia saw Pamela flinch, and no wonder. She must still be coping with the blow of finding out who her real father was.

'No. Why should he, dear?' Mavis replied.

'Are you sure Tom came back?' Cherry asked doubtfully.

'It looks almost certain that he did.'

'And he thought I was still married?'

'Very probably.'

'But I'm not. So I could advertise now. Yes.' Cherry nodded vigorously. 'That's what I'll do. Advertise. He's out there somewhere.'

ELEVEN

'What on earth did you say to him on Saturday, Luke?' Georgia asked. Something must have sparked Harold Staines off to send what amounted to a threatening letter to Luke of all people. Why send it to Frost & Co and not the offending Marsh & Daughter? It was not only puzzling but somewhat sinister.

'Nothing.' Luke looked as much at sea as she was. 'We passed a few idle words about the Frost list. How much he enjoyed our books and so on. There was nothing that could possibly have provoked this reaction.' He passed the letter back to Georgia, who rapidly scanned it again.

'I enjoyed our pleasant chat on Saturday. However, I understood that it is still your intention to publish in due course Marsh & Daughter's book about *Waves Ahoy!* and the murder of Joan Watson. As the show's producer, I am naturally concerned that such a publication might rake over old embers but would fail to reach any provable conclusion; this would cause great harm to those of us who still remember those days. The authors seem to be entering the world of speculation rather than re-examining the established facts, and although I applaud a positive approach in general, I fear that in this case they may be using a hammer to squash a nut and in the process injure some very frail shells. I do plead with you to discuss this matter very fully with the authors, both for their sakes and yours.'

Georgia frowned. 'What does he expect you to do?'

'No idea.'

'Did you discuss the Watson project with him?' It was the last straw to return to this shock after yet another frustrating day scrabbling to join up loose threads that seemed to have no intention of being tied down.

'Of course not. I'd have been way out of order.'

'So Peter's announcement sparked this off. Are you going to reply?'

'Of course. It's what I'm going to say that's the problem.'

'You won't be put off by this veiled threat?' She was getting into deep waters here, prejudiced by her own position as author.

'Doesn't that rather depend on what it's based on? He's right in one respect, Georgia. What you've told me about the case provides very little new evidence about *Joan's* death, even though it gives much scope for speculation. Tom still seems the only person likely to have murdered his wife.'

'Put like that,' Georgia said sadly, 'no case in the world could progress.' There was a wall between them now, which chilled her. She had often imagined such a clash between author and publisher and how it might differ or affect the clash of husband and wife, but now the reality had come, she felt unable to cope with it. She could see no way through.

'Maybe that's just as well.'

This was even worse. Could it be Luke saying this? She had always believed that she would be able to divide the personal from the professional in such a conflict, but now she feared she could not. 'Is this the publisher talking or you?' she asked.

'I hope,' Luke replied evenly, 'that it's the former.'

'So do I.' But the wall was still there.

'Shall we leave this until tomorrow to talk over with Peter?'

Even as she answered him, she knew it would be a risky move, but it was done. 'Let's get it over with. Let's go now.'

It was still light as they drove in silence through the lanes to Haden Shaw. Luke doesn't believe in us, Georgia was mentally saying over and over again in shock. She could not rid herself of a sense of personal betrayal, even though she knew this was unfair. It was only the publisher in him speaking. She told herself that he had always been doubtful about this case – and now he was seizing on this letter to justify it. True, Marsh & Daughter had a contract for the book they were intending to write, but the contract contained the usual libel clause. In any case neither she nor Peter was ever stupid enough to publish without firm evidence, whether the people concerned were alive or dead. Nevertheless, it was hard to tell whether it was her mind or her stomach churning so hard as Luke drew up outside Haden Shaw's one and only pub.

'I'll prop the bar up here,' Luke said, 'while you talk it over with Peter. Then you can give me a ring to summon me over.'

Always practical, always so *right*, damn you, Georgia thought. If Peter exploded in fury, as was highly likely – as Luke well knew – it was better that Luke should not be present. After he'd done with explosions, Peter would present his case for Marsh & Daughter in a more reasoned way than she could. Another failing of hers, she supposed. There might be an overdose of emotion in any case she presented, and that would be a big mistake. Nevertheless, as she walked down Haden Shaw's main street towards Peter's home she fervently wished she too were tucked up cosily in the pub.

She gave her special evening ring at the door of three short buzzes, and then went straight in, as she often did on an evening call. Only this time it was not a normal call. She had been concentrating so hard on the Harold Staines letter that she forgot Janie might be visiting Peter. And tonight she was – this was all too clear as Georgia entered.

She stopped abruptly as she heard a first class row in progress, appalled to hear Janie sobbing and Peter's irate shout: 'For heaven's sake, leave me alone, woman. Stop fussing.'

Should she retreat? Georgia wondered. They clearly hadn't heard the doorbell. Too late, as Janie came rushing out of the living room, and beyond her Georgia could see Peter fuming and red-faced.

Janie didn't even look surprised to see her. She just cried, 'Whatever I do, I annoy him. I try and try, but he doesn't want to see me.'

'Let him calm down.' Georgia put her arm round her. Ineffectual probably, but she could try. 'He often gets like this. It's only the frustration.'

'No, he doesn't.' Janie detached herself and opened the front door. 'No, no, *no*. And anyway, I can't take it any more. I really can't.'

What would Luke do or say? Georgia tried frantically to think. He was usually good at calming situations down. Or was he? Today, he might run like hell from another confrontation.

Peter was wheeling himself furiously towards them. 'What the blazes do you want, Georgia?'

Janie first, Georgia thought, taking her arm and leading her out to the car. If she could find the right words . . . 'What do you want, Janie?' she asked her gently. 'Do you know? If you want someone just to look after, you're right that Peter's not for you. If you love Peter, then give him what he needs, not what you need. Is that possible?'

At least she succeeded in stopping Janie in her tracks, and the sobs stopped too. Janie pulled herself up with obvious effort. 'Of course you're right. But you've had years to adapt to Peter's situation. Didn't you struggle at first? I've had less than a year. It's not so long.'

Was she talking about Peter? Georgia wondered. Or the death of her mother? She watched Janie get into her car, her mind full of mixed emotions. Who could blame Janie if she needed someone to take her mother's place? Georgia forced herself to think back to how she had felt when Peter was first confined to a wheelchair. Her mother, Elena, couldn't cope. First Rick's disappearance and then Peter's accident. Georgia was now able to concede that Elena had tried, but she had failed. She had given up after six months of Peter's unrelenting tantrums interspersed with silent spells of depression. Then Elena had left and Georgia had taken over – hardly the best of carers, considering that her own marriage had broken down. She and Peter had coped together – somehow. He had dealt with her problem by ignoring the subject of Zac. His view was that her marriage had happened and it was over.

And she supposed she must have treated his accident in the same way. Had she mothered him? No. She thought she could truthfully claim that she had treated him as she always had. She could take no credit for that, however. She had needed him because Zac was in prison and her divorce was going through. It had been a mutual acknowledgement of a status quo with no requirement on either side for pampering. It looked as if this balance was way out of kilter where Janie and Peter were concerned, however. Janie did all the pampering, but Peter was ignoring her needs.

Watching her drive off, Georgia wished she could do the same, but she couldn't. There was Peter to face, and Luke, and Harold Staines's letter. First, an angry and no doubt guilt-filled father awaited her inside.

At least the guilt was uppermost when she reached him. 'Sorry,' he muttered, 'but I had to do it sometime.'

'You hardly chose the kindest way,' Georgia said, trying not to sound tart.

'Perhaps it was the only way. It wouldn't have worked. You know that.'

'I don't know that,' she said crossly. 'Stop trying to put it on to me. It's your future at stake. You and Janie get along fine. It was only—'

'I love that word *only*. If one thing drives you crazy, there's no *only* about it.'

'Yes, there is. You're forgetting she needs fussing over too.' Georgia ground to a halt. 'Sorry, Dad. I'm not in good shape myself this evening.'

'Luke been beating you?' he joked.

'Not physically. Have a look at this.'

He snatched the Staines letter so quickly that Georgia realized she might by chance have hit a nerve over Janie. Peter never liked to feel himself at fault and was hoping that by switching to Marsh & Daughter business he might be able to avoid examining his attitude to Janie more closely. He was wrong, of course, but at the moment it suited Georgia. She wasn't up to long talks about Janie tonight. She needed more preparation. Work was therefore a relief to her too, and Peter must have agreed, because signs of emotional turmoil subsided as he finished reading the letter.

'What did Luke make of this?'

'He's very disturbed. He won't say anything until we've had a chance to discuss it though. He's waiting in the pub for me to summon him when we're ready.'

Peter's eyes gleamed. 'Make it waiting for *us*. It's Margaret's day for vegetarian only, and I need to get out of this hellhole. Luke can take us to dinner.'

'*Luke* will. I'm not sure whether Luke the publisher would though.'

'As bad as that?'

'Yes.'

'So we've got to sing for our supper?'

'If you feel up to it.'

Peter muttered something she could not hear properly, but which might have been 'blasted women'. What he allowed her to hear was: 'Of course I do. What's behind this letter?'

That was what was so good about working with Peter. He cut straight through to the chase. 'Something to hide?' she suggested.

'Possible. Such as?'

'Harold knows what happened to Tom both in 1953 and 1975.'

'Possible. Protecting his own involvement?'

'Or someone else's.'

'Does he feel so close to his old chums that he would turn a blind eye to murder?'

Georgia blinked. '*Murder* in 1975?'

Peter looked startled. 'I meant Joan Watson. But we can't rule out Tom being murdered later, even though it's a leap into the dark with the facts we have so far. It would certainly account for no one seeing him after that. It's bothered me as to why he should cut himself off from the family where he'd been so happy in London.'

'What about suicide?'

Peter gave some thought to this. 'Unlikely,' he said at

last. 'His seeing Pamela was a positive action. He wouldn't have bothered if he was depressed to the point of suicide. And by all accounts he wasn't. But if suicide or murder, why no body?'

'Because the name Bert Holmes was attached to it when found?'

Peter sighed. 'Here we go again. I fear Luke would be fully justified in pointing out that this is speculation in a big way. Not what the publisher ordered. We have to admit to ourselves that we're still floating along on this case, just as we are on Rick.'

'Luke won't accept any more floating.' Ignore the subject of Rick. She just could not bear it. She was forcing herself to keep the Internet search for Mozart venues going, but each click of the mouse became more painful as the constant foreboding that it would lead nowhere grew stronger.

Peter looked glum. 'That's all we can offer him, if we have to make a declaration right now. We could tell him to wait until we deliver the script – we've a contract, so we would be within our rights. He can then have a free choice as to whether to publish or not.'

'Is that fair? He has advance schedules, jacket-design costs and budgets to fix.'

Peter considered. 'The other option is to tell Luke he can cancel the contract, and we'll present a script as and when.'

'Which course do you prefer?' She knew which she did, but then she was biased.

'Cancel the contract.'

Relief. 'That's my choice too. You never know, it might bring good luck, and evidence will come flooding in.' This solution would cut the Gordian knot nicely. There would be no more clashes with Luke the publisher.

'Agreed,' Peter grunted. 'Right now I'd like a dose of good luck. But this evening a dinner at the White Lion would do me. And a stiff drink.'

The White Lion served good food, and one of its many advantages was that Peter could get there easily by himself in the wheelchair. Luke was sitting on a bench inside with a half of bitter before him, looking up apprehensively as they arrived.

'Is this joint deputation ominous?' he asked.

'Only if you don't buy us a drink,' Peter assured him. 'On second thoughts, buy me dinner and you're off the hook completely.'

'Dinner, yes, but what particular hook might this be?' Luke asked him cautiously.

'The Watson case. Georgia and I have decided to give you your money back—'

'So far so good,' Luke quipped.

'And cancel the contract. If we finish the Watson book, we give you first option of publishing it on the same terms.'

'Ah. I'll have to think about that,' Luke said, then went over to buy their drinks.

Peter looked taken aback. 'I thought he'd jump at it.'

'So did I.' Georgia watched Luke returning with the two glasses. Peter had elected to have a whisky – always a sign that he was in turmoil, since he never usually drank spirits.

'First,' Luke said, plonking glasses in front of them, 'I don't like threats like this letter from Staines. Second, why the hell should I cancel a contract when I don't yet know and can't guess whether the text is defamatory or not? I haven't seen it, and you haven't even written it. Third,' he added, as Georgia began to laugh, 'I *really* don't like threats. So fourth, things stay as they are for the moment.'

Thank heavens for Luke, she thought. Another cutter of Gordian knots. And glory be, publisher and authors were on the same side again.

'I tell you what,' she said to Luke amiably, 'Marsh & Daughter will buy *you* dinner.'

'Done,' Luke said promptly. 'Is Janie—' He broke off as Georgia's foot landed firmly on his. He looked at her in bewilderment. 'What did I say?'

'I imagine,' Peter said gently, 'that Georgia wished you to know that Janie left me rather abruptly this evening.'

'Ah.' Luke glanced from one to the other. 'Was she pushed or did she run?'

That stopped Peter in his tracks. 'Pushed,' Georgia

answered crossly. Torn as she was over Janie, Peter had acted far too impulsively – at least to the observer's eye, she conceded.

'Pity,' was Luke's comment.

Peter glared. 'I do not need sympathy – *or* a nurse. Is that clear?'

Perhaps the good luck had been kick-started by the reconciliation with Luke, for when Georgia arrived the next morning, Peter was beaming. Had Janie returned? Apparently not from his opening greeting.

'There's a message on your phone, Georgia. Hope you won't mind, but I listened to it. We might be on our way to that hard evidence our publisher will require.'

'Good. Who? What?'

'Or even why. Cath rang. She'd lost your mobile number, which is why it was on the office phone. Ex-Sergeant Buck Dillon wants to talk to us. *Us,* kindly note, not just you. He was prepared to come over here – no doubt,' Peter added sarcastically, 'in view of the fact I'm wheelchair bound. I explained that no special treatment is required. The chair merely represents my legs, not my brain.'

'Was he happy about that?'

'He was. He even laughed. I like the sound of Buck Dillon. I've arranged for us to go on Monday.'

'Any idea what he wants to talk about?'

'He doesn't sound as if he's about to confess to anything, let alone murder.'

'How about smuggling? Just a guess, but you did ask Cath to follow up that line.'

Georgia noticed Peter's sardonic eye on Cath, who kept protectively near her grandfather. Obviously protective ladies were still in Peter's mind, although the name *Janie* had not passed his lips since Wednesday evening. Georgia was sorry for Cath, who must feel rather as she did with Luke, torn between her job and her family loyalties. She only hoped that whatever Buck had to tell them wasn't going to destroy Cath's faith in him.

Fortunately Buck and Peter seemed to hit it off immediately. 'My wife's out today, and that's good,' he told them.
'She doesn't know too much about my misspent youth. I'd
have preferred this young woman here –' Buck glanced
affectionately at Cath – 'didn't either, but there you go.
She's got a job to do, she says.'

'Whatever you tell me,' Cath retorted, 'I won't believe
you're a monster.'

'See what I mean, Georgia?' Buck replied. 'She tells me
she might be joining your family, so I wanted you to see
the kind of thing you'll have to put up with.'

'Charlie's a lucky fellow,' Peter said.

'Not yet he's not,' Cath shot back. 'I'm still thinking it
over.'

'Don't think too long,' Buck suggested, 'or the fat lady
will start singing.' Then he turned to Georgia. 'You'll have
noticed that I keep my distance from the old crowd nowadays. No reunions for me.'

'Because of Joan's death?'

'Maybe. I guess you still have me in the frame for that.'

'You, Tom Watson and the whole wide world at present,'
Peter answered frankly. 'But I'm afraid that Tom is still
way out in front. Motive, means and opportunity. He didn't
even have a credible alibi except for Cherry's evidence,
and that's hardly reliable.'

'She's out in cloud cuckoo land, that one,' Buck observed.

'Did you know her then?'

'Depends on what you mean by know. I remember young
Cherry being around, making eyes at Tom, and I guess he
liked that. It was a change from the way Joan treated him.
I should tell you that I was a lot further in with that gang
than I let you think, Georgia. And I had to cut myself off
sharpish. The US Air Force wasn't too keen on its men
being murder suspects or even giving evidence. We were
supposed to be the good guys.'

'*Were* you a suspect?' she asked.

'I was interviewed by the police, but that was all, thanks
to good old Uncle Sam. I was in camp that evening. No
pass. That's a good enough alibi, I reckon.'

'Could be,' Peter said politely.

Buck laughed aloud. 'Sure, I could be lying through my teeth, but I'm not. I brought you folks here to confess, but not to murder.'

Georgia diagnosed the look on Cath's face as resignation rather than opposition.

'My turn to speak,' Cath said firmly. 'You asked me to look into post-war smuggling, Georgia. The trail led me straight to Grandpops, as you feared.'

Georgia had indeed, but nevertheless it was a shock to hear Buck himself confirm it.

'It was just fun at the time,' he said. 'Beating the system. It was a gloomy time all round in England. The USAF was sharing Manston with the Brits, as I told you, but we had our own supplies and did a heck of a lot better than they did. The war was only just over for us both, but you were still suffering more of the consequences. But it was tough for us Yanks too, dumped into a strange depressing place like this. We had to brighten it up. The war in Korea was still on, and so entertainment off duty was high priority. I met Joan, as I told you, and used to pinch a few cigarettes for her or the odd can of food. I'm not proud of it, but I was thousands of miles from home and it didn't seem like thieving. She began to ask for more and more, and she was drinking and smoking stuff I hadn't gotten for her, so I began asking questions like the dumb fool I was. Darn it if she didn't try to blackmail me. Turned out there was an organization running smuggled stuff in by boat from the continent. Don't know how much you know about the Kent coast, but way back smuggling was big business, with stuff landed at coves – the Gaps they're called at Broadstairs, aren't they? – and then run through tunnels to safe houses. In 1952 it wasn't so widespread, and this organization centred on Botany Bay out towards Cliftonville, which was nicely deserted back then.

'Joan insisted I get drawn in on the distribution,' he continued. 'As a US sergeant I'd be less likely to be caught, and the damn woman said she'd go straight to my CO if I didn't cooperate. So I decided to stay right on the sidelines, plead camp rotas in order to do as little as possible and keep my ears and eyes closed. I knew some of the *Waves Ahoy!* folk were mixed up with it because I'd overheard conversations at the pub. I kept out of them. It wasn't long after I joined that Joan was killed, and I was out of that circle like a shot, putting it round that I was being transferred. By the grace of God, I was, so I heard no more about it. So that's why I keep my distance now. I never thought I'd be back in this neck of the woods. But what happens? I meet Mary over in the States and find out she lived here. When my air-force time expired, I came back to find her, and here we are. I heard no more about the smuggling ring, but now you two come along,' he added without rancour.

'Was Joan the ring's organizer?' Peter asked.

'Good grief, no. Joan was a good-time girl. Rotten to the core, but then she was young, in her late twenties, I reckon. Maybe she was just weak. I was even younger, twenty-two. She was proud of her looks, and no wonder. She was useful to the ring, she knew so many folk and could distribute stuff without eyebrows being raised.'

'Who was the organizer then?' Peter asked.

Buck chuckled. 'That's where I bow out, Peter. I settled here because it's far enough from Broadstairs not to cause any problems. I sure as hell didn't want my new life mixed up with my old.'

'You must have had contact with some of them over the years,' Georgia said, despite Cath's frown, which was saying, 'Don't push it.'

'I stumble across them from time to time, but we're all older now, so we don't talk of the past. It's history now – even to journalists,' Buck added, grinning at Cath. 'Never wake up a sleeping dog.'

'Ken Winton did,' Peter said evenly. 'And he died. Any connection?'

Georgia could see Cath looking uneasy as Buck replied, 'I don't know, and that's the truth. Knowing I was around at the time, Cath mentioned Ken's theories over Tom so often over the years that I knew them inside out. I didn't take them seriously – and nor did I you, Georgia. Guess I was wrong there. Cath told me you'd found out that Tom came back to Broadstairs in 1975. That was news to me, and mighty hard to believe.'

'We've good evidence for it. Could he have been mixed up with the ring?' Peter asked.

'No way. Joan made it clear that he wasn't involved. Are you thinking her death might be mixed up with it?' Buck frowned.

'It's on the cards.'

'It's possible, I reckon. Joan was a greedy lady. Maybe she got too greedy and threatened the organizer, as she did me. So, Peter, here's my stake. You bring me proof that that's why she was murdered, and I'll come clean. Otherwise no way. It might be history, but I take no chances. I aim to stay alive to see Cath and Charlie's kids.'

'Grandpops,' Cath complained instantly, 'you make it sound as though there's one on the way. And for the record, folks, there isn't. Yet. Happy everyone?'

'For you, yes.' Buck grinned. 'Charlie's a good bloke and he'd be even better if he ever stops in one place long enough to think what's good for him, which is Cath. He'll settle down.'

'Not likely,' Cath declared. 'I'll be travelling with him.'

Georgia was watching Peter, who was clearly awaiting his moment to pounce. Then it came: 'You implied the organizer is still alive, Buck.'

For the first time Buck looked thrown. 'As I said,' he answered shortly, 'bring me proof that's why Joan was murdered, and I'll sing like a nightingale.'

'Would proof that he or she killed Tom in 1975 do?'

Trust Peter to float an idea as though it was a near certainty, Georgia thought. Nevertheless, it was a good ploy, on a par with beating woods to see which birds fly out. It was working in this case.

Buck looked very shaken. 'You reckon old Tom was *murdered*?'

'We've found no one who has seen him since then,' Peter replied. 'Of course that's no proof at all, but he didn't return to his previous life in London after his visit. Even so, it's hard to see to whom Tom could have been a threat by that time. If he knew who killed Joan, he would have told the police at the time, and though the smuggling ring opens up another possibility, it seems a weak motive after all those years.'

'Who knew about his return in the seventies?' Buck asked abruptly.

'So far as we know, only his former neighbour, Micky Winton and Pamela Trent.'

'And Pamela told her husband,' Georgia added. 'None of them seems likely to have killed Joan though. Pamela and Matthew are ruled out through age, and neither the neighbour nor Micky seems to have had any motive.'

'Whatever that was,' Buck commented.

'The Giant Rat of Sumatra,' murmured Peter. 'That's a cryptic clue Micky wrote in his diary for 1975. A story for which the world is not yet ready, according to Conan Doyle. That could have been the smuggling ring.'

'Or the Giant Rat. That you, Grandpops?'

Cath was joking, but there was no answering grin from Buck this time.

TWELVE

Awarm beach. Luke at her side, the sun beating down – Georgia stirred uneasily. Or was it fireworks? The sky seemed to be lit up to celebrate – celebrate what? With a start, she was fully awake, aware of the patterns dancing on the curtains and the crackle – of what? Immediately she was out of bed and rushing to the window.

'Luke! Fire!'

Flames were leaping and flickering from the oast house. Even as she dashed for the phone, she heard a grunt and the sound of his moving as rapidly as she was. Why, oh why had she left her mobile downstairs? No, it was here, thank heavens. As she punched in 999, Luke rushed past her down the stairs in a towelling robe; by the time she joined him he had already seized the small fire extinguisher from the wall. Grabbing a coat, Georgia hurried after him, desperately trying to think as she did so: water, blankets, buckets, water—

'Luke, *don't* go in!' she shouted. Too late.

It looked as if the fire had reached only the storage end of the oast house and not yet the office itself. How long before the fire engines would be here? As she reached the door to the oast house, the heat was already intense, with small flames greedily licking their way towards her. Seeing her there, Luke passed his computer to her, but then to her horror he went back in. Long seconds ticked on by.

'Come on, come out, Luke,' she pleaded, and at last, at blessed last, he did, clutching another computer.

'I could get another one—' He was gasping already.

'No!'

He glanced at her and thankfully saw sense.

Time ticked by agonizingly slowly as she watched it burn. They were helpless to achieve anything more than the fire extinguishers had already accomplished, but at last she could hear the wonderful sound of a fire engine siren. That must mean it was still on the Canterbury Road, she thought; another few minutes before it would arrive here; she blinked tears of frustration from her eyes. Luke was the calm one now.

'Think of the bright side. Only unsold backlist gone. The new ones aren't in yet.'

It gave her no comfort at all. What did was the arrival of not one but two fire engines.

The rest of the night was punctuated only by cups of coffee and tea as the firemen's assessment officers went about their work. At least the fire hadn't been at Medlars itself, she tried to comfort herself, but with the smell of the aftermath of fire in her nostrils it was hard. Offices could be replaced, she told herself, even oasts – and looking at it now that the flames were mostly out, the oast itself looked as if it might survive, even if the attached storeroom had not.

As dawn came, the smell and desolation seemed to get worse. There seemed an endless procession of firemen, police and insurance and assessment officers, while she and Luke remained mere onlookers. At last Luke went out with the police, but came back with a grim face.

'The good news is that my office and the staff office in the oast are mostly OK. It's chiefly confined to the back room, with minor singeing to the oast. We were lucky the clapboards didn't catch.'

'And the bad news?'

'They're pretty sure it was started deliberately. It seems to have begun at the rear access door.'

'A random arsonist?' She couldn't believe that and was not surprised when Luke replied, 'Perhaps. But a co-incidence we should have a threatening letter one day and only a week later a fire. The PC thought I was barking to consider that letter a threat, but I'm afraid we might think otherwise.'

'It doesn't fit with Harold Staines, Luke,' she said wearily. 'He's well over eighty. He wouldn't be prancing around with accelerants in the middle of the night.'

'No,' Luke agreed, 'he'd send his lawyer.'

A feeble joke, but Georgia managed to laugh.

Sleep, when it came at last for a brief hour or two, provided nightmares of flames and heat, but at least when she awoke at ten o'clock she felt marginally rested.

I'll be late for the office, was her first thought. This suddenly seemed inordinately funny as the full horror of the night came back to her. Then, realizing that Peter would be worried by her no-show, she dragged herself downstairs to telephone him. The smell of the fire was so strong, even in the house, that she wondered if any of the sparks could have reached as far as Medlars' ancient wooden beams, but she decided to put the thought aside. She couldn't cope with everything at once. Medlars seemed its usual comforting, solid self, however. Getting breakfast on the table provided reassurance today, rather than routine. Luke had already come down, she realized, and must already be outside. Should she join him? No, a quick bite and drink first after ringing Peter. She needed sustenance to face what lay outside.

Peter snatched up the phone so quickly that Georgia felt guilty, knowing he must already have been worrying. She told him what had happened, and he just said, 'I'll be over.' The receiver was replaced.

At that moment Luke returned to announce, 'Frost & Co will survive to publish a few more books. The flames had reached further than the structural damage they had caused. Quite a bit of stock has gone, but the metal shelving must have helped slow the flames a little.'

'Can you still work in the office?'

'Not yet. I've sent Cheryl and Dinah home today. Will's out there helping clear up.'

'And it still looks as if it was deliberately started?'

'Let's say there's no sign of accident yet. Over to the insurance folk now. Then Frost & Co can get back to its autumn programme.'

It sounded comforting, but they were only brave words, and both she and Luke knew it.

Peter was longer than Georgia had expected, and when

she heard his car draw up, she realized why. He was not alone. Detective Superintendent Mike Gilroy was now inspecting the damage. As she and Luke went out to join him, he grimaced. 'Not as bad as it could be, but nasty,' he commiserated with them.

Peter joined them, explaining, 'Mike told me some nonsense about a police luncheon he had to go to, but he saw my point that he was needed here.'

Georgia caught his eye and controlled an insane desire to laugh. His next words stopped that. 'Think it will happen again?' Mike asked.

Luke looked aghast at the very idea, and it was Peter who answered gravely, 'It could do.'

'Thanks,' Luke said gloomily.

'Unless,' Peter added meaningfully, 'we get a move on with police help and get this business sorted.'

'By which you mean my business or yours?' Luke asked wearily.

'Both. I know you think I'm barmy, Mike,' Peter said mildly, 'but we're all involved. Luke because he's an easy target with the office here, with the result that a threat can be made to him without physical danger to him or Georgia, and Georgia and myself because if that does not deter our determination to continue this case, we could be the next target.'

'It's our fault, Luke,' Georgia acknowledged. 'You're the victim because we chose this case.'

'If I remember correctly,' Luke said, 'I accepted the risk.'

'You'd better tell me all, I suppose,' Mike said in resignation. 'Can we go inside?'

Once back in Medlars, the situation assumed slightly more normality. 'This Broadstairs case of yours isn't in my patch,' Mike pointed out, 'but this one is.'

'Good,' Luke said.

'I'm not sure I agree with that, but I can't change the situation, so shoot, please. And before you ask, Peter, I had a word with DI Jenkins at Thanet HQ about the Winton murder. It's still ongoing. They've got their eye on some connection with a shooting in south London last year.'

That was a point in favour of Ken's death being uncon-
nected with the Tom Watson case, Georgia thought, although
she still could not believe it was. 'Any link between the
victims?' she asked.

'None found yet. But,' Mike added sourly, 'if Ken
Winton's death was linked to the death of that fifties case
you were talking about *and* this fire, a whole different picture
might emerge. So spit it out, Peter.'

He listened patiently as Peter duly spat out the Tom
Watson story, including his return visit in 1975, but then
Mike picked on the obvious objection. 'So you don't know
where Tom Watson went after then. Tried advertising for
connections?'

'Of course. He's on our website now under both Bert
Holmes and Tom Watson. Nothing after seventy-five.'

'Your website isn't viewed by the entire population.'

'That is true,' Peter admitted, 'but it did bring forth two
fruitful lines of enquiry for the period *before* seventy-five. So
if Tom Watson *was* killed on that visit to Broadstairs—'

Mike knew Peter's thinking of old. 'You'd like us to
check all the unidentified bodies between Broadstairs and
John O'Groats for the last quarter of a century. Certainly.
Easy as anything.'

'More locally would be acceptable,' Peter said hastily.
'And perhaps up to 1980 would be reasonable.'

'Easier,' Mike grudgingly agreed. 'Any DNA to help?'

'No chance. His only relative, his daughter, turns out not
to be his.'

'Naturally,' Mike remarked. 'It's one of your cases.
Nothing ever is simple.'

Luke was fully occupied with his own problems and had
made it clear to Georgia that her help was not wanted.
'What you can do to help is get on and solve the Watson
case,' he told her in a rare fit of irritability.

This, she acknowledged, was a reasonable request. The
problem was how to translate it into action the following
day when she was trying to grapple with an elusive Tom
in the Haden Shaw office.

'Let's assume that Tom Watson did disappear in July 1975,' she said at last. 'To recap, there's no known reason for any of the four people who knew about his visit to want to get rid of him.'

'There may have been others,' Peter pointed out. 'Micky or Matthew could have casually mentioned it to anyone. Acquaintances could have seen him in the street – Tom made no secret of his visit.'

He was right, of course. 'So where does that leave us?' she asked.

'I was struck by a word Mike used: connections. Remember that story of the Silver Gang?'

'Yes, but I also remember that was years before Tom came back here.'

'Agreed, but nevertheless there are interesting possibilities. I've been looking into it. Firstly, let's assume John Silver, the leader, was nicknamed Quicksilver for his powers of vanishing off the scene whenever he chose. The gang disappeared abruptly as a unit about 1969.'

'And the point for us?' she asked patiently.

'It's believed that each member disappeared into a different hole, but there would still be a price on their heads, whether offered by the police, or by those with old scores to settle, or by those ensuring they never challenged the new kids on the block.'

'If you're suggesting they wiped Tom Watson out for that reason, then why wait for years to do so?'

'I don't *know*. Maybe Tom hadn't been a threat when he met him in the restaurant, but he was by 1975.'

'But that was in London, not Broadstairs.'

'He could have been living there.' Peter stared at her as the idea took hold. '*Yes*. It has to be that, surely. Oh *yes*. Not the smuggling ring, the Quicksilver gang.'

Georgia tried to think logically. It was her job to question, and question she must. 'What threat could Tom have posed?'

'Plenty, if on his trip to see Pamela he recognized someone who was trying to live down a past as a member of the Silver Gang.'

'He met Mrs Wetherby, Micky and Pamela herself. No scope there.'

Peter looked smug. 'Matthew. Pamela rang *Matthew*.'

Caution needed. 'He fits the profile a lot better than Micky,' she agreed. 'He's a respected man now, but he's had a long time to polish his image. In the late sixties he would have been a young man in his twenties. Oh.'

Peter groaned. 'A hitch?'

'Matthew *didn't* meet Tom in 1975. Pamela told him by phone. Even if Tom had seen him in the Blue Parrot, he would hardly have recognized him from Broadstairs days, as he would have been only about ten or so when Tom left Broadstairs in 1953.'

Peter glared at her. 'Any more bricks you'd like to throw?'

'Yes. If Tom came back because he knew his wife's real killer, then again Matthew Trent is ruled out on age.'

Peter was about to retort when the phone rang. His expression changed as he listened for a moment or two. His voice was definitely cool as he said, 'Thank you. I'll pass on your condolences to my daughter, although of course it was her husband's office that was set on fire. Deliberately.'

'Who was that?' she asked curiously as he put down the phone.

'Our friend Harold Staines. So sorry to hear the news on the radio. At least, he *says* it was on the radio.'

'We shouldn't jump to conclusions that he was responsible. The fire could have been coincidence. He wouldn't have done it himself or even arranged it, surely.' Even as she spoke, the thought of Greg Dale came into her mind. Greg – *and the Trents*.

'Wouldn't he?' Peter shot back at her. 'Harold's last words were: "It seems my letter wasn't quite forceful enough. I do beg you all to take care."'

Cleaning up after the fire was a dreary process, despite Georgia's best efforts at keeping positive. Luke had relented and enlisted her help – not altogether to her pleasure. Sorting out damaged stock from mint, not to mention the files that were singed or burnt, was depressing. So was the sight of

the charred beams and blackened bricks; they had been
made safe but awaited restoration work. She and Luke were
here alone, as it was Saturday morning, and somehow that
made the problem all the starker.

'And we've got the Christmas list coming in soon,' Luke
said. 'I'll have to make other arrangements. Should I build
temporary storage or hire other premises?'

She and Luke were still in the midst of this discussion
when, of all people, Janie appeared. Georgia saw her through
the window as her car drew up and groaned. What now?
Janie looked nervous, glancing cautiously up at the window
before she knocked on the door, as if she expected an iron
portcullis to descend on her head.

'I heard about the fire,' she said awkwardly when Georgia
opened the door. 'It's my day off, so I thought I might be
able to help.'

And you might be able to drop in on Peter too, Georgia
thought meanly. A natural enough hope on Janie's part, but
today? Then, feeling ashamed, she put herself in Janie's
shoes: wouldn't she be tempted to do just as Janie had done?
Probably. She resigned herself to her fate, especially when
she saw Luke retiring to the far office. The hint was taken.

'You can come over to Medlars and help me have a cup
of coffee. The rest of the gang have got iron rations here,
but I could do with a break.'

'I know I shouldn't have come,' Janie said, following
her into the house, 'as Peter and I have split up.'

'On the contrary,' Georgia said as cheerily as she could.
'It's kind of you. And I was very sorry about the split.' It
was true enough. Peter had been distinctly grumpier since
it had happened.

'Don't be. It was my own fault, wanting too much too
quickly. I was thinking of myself, not Peter, I suppose.
Actually I came about something else, in addition to a
genuine offer of help. I didn't feel I could go to Peter with
it, so I thought I'd come to you.'

'About Tom Watson?' Georgia asked guardedly, remembering their last chat.

'No. About Rick.'

Her worst fears. How could she cope with this *now*? But she had to try. 'We've still got no further. It's all been negative information so far.' Then seeing Janie's look of sympathy, Georgia tried to explain. 'I feel as if I'm walking through cobwebs. Each time I make it through one, there's another to battle through. None of them goes anywhere.'

'I felt like that after my mother's death. It was the shock, but in your case it must be different. The experience of now he's there, now he's not, but where is he?'

'You're right.' Georgia looked at her in some astonishment. She'd never seen this side of Janie before.

'About Rick,' Janie continued diffidently, 'do you think you could be working the wrong way round? You're taking the story as told by Christine and trying to narrow down where they went and who this blonde lady could possibly be. I wondered if you should try it the other way up.'

Georgia was totally confused. This was getting more Kafka-ish every minute. 'I don't understand.'

Janie tried again. 'Think of the best Mozart performances —'

'Which is what we've been doing.' Not again. They'd been through all this.

'Yes. But you've been looking at Miss Blondie as she was when he vanished. Remember Rick's view of her – a *real* singer. Suppose she was the best – an exceptional person and singer. That means she would be going somewhere in her career. Of course a thousand things could have stopped her doing so, but suppose nothing did? Suppose she's right at the top of her profession now. She'd be in her mid thirties like Christine. Suppose she's another Janet Charing or Josephine Mantreau?'

Georgia sought to make sense of this. 'But what then?'

'Take the ball and run with it.'

'You mean look at early photos of them and see if they have long blonde hair?' She seemed to be making heavy weather of this.

'Why not?' Janie said. She flushed, as she must have sensed Georgia's disbelief. 'Don't give up, that's all.'

'Nor you,' Georgia found herself replying, and was rewarded by a smile.

'Physician heal thyself?' Janie asked.

'Why not? It's happened before.' Georgia had meant just to be polite but was surprisingly heartened.

'Matthew Trent,' Peter was muttering as Georgia reached the office on Monday morning. Nearly the end of July and still no sign of any answers. Her father was hunched over Suspects Anonymous. 'Why should he want to murder Tom Watson? Revenge? Highly unlikely. He's a man motivated by money, not emotions.'

'I thought we had dismissed him as a suspect.'

'Car business established 1972. I still think he's involved.'

'With less foundation than the Loch Ness monster.'

'You're very frivolous today. Perhaps this might appeal to you if you need evidence. Mike emailed a list of unidentified bodies that might fit our guidelines. This one caught my eye.' He pointed to his printout. 'Barn fire with male body, near Margate, July 1975. Badly burnt. Never identified, presumed to be a vagrant. Farmer's employees all accounted for. No one missing locally. Fire due to arson. Culprit never found.'

Arson? That had an unpleasant ring of familiarity. 'Any indications of suspicious death?' she asked. It did indeed sound on target. 'Presumed overcome by fumes. And there, for my money,' Peter added soberly, 'lies poor Bert Holmes.'

THIRTEEN

'DNA. That's what you're going to ask me, isn't it?' Peter asked soberly. He seemed as shaken as Georgia was at this possible, even probable, link between their missing clown and a burnt unidentified corpse.

'Actually—' What she had been going to ask was whether the police had had any leads at all in identifying the body.

'Checking DNA is a chicken and egg situation,' he interrupted. 'Mike says if we get a definite link with its being Tom Watson, Thanet Area will put its hand deep in its pocket to go for exhumation and DNA check. But how do we get further if we can't start on the sure footing that it was Tom's body?'

'We—'

'Harold Staines is mixed up with this. That's for sure. The boss—'

'Come off it.' It was her turn to interrupt. 'I agree he's obviously involved, otherwise why the threats to us. But the boss? Quicksilver? He couldn't have been king of the London underworld *and* an up-and-coming West End producer.'

Peter looked injured. 'I meant boss of *Waves Ahoy!* But now you come to mention it, why not of the Silver Gang too? You need money for West End productions, and Harold didn't hit the big time until well into the seventies.'

'Problem,' Georgia retorted smartly. 'He could hardly vanish as king of the underworld and pop up immediately as king of the theatre. Don't you think someone might have noticed?'

'That,' Peter snarled, 'is true. So we're back with Buck Dillon. He might be more inclined to talk to us now that we have this tentative link to Tom Watson's fate.'

'Unless Buck himself was the Giant Rat organizer,' Georgia felt obliged to say.

Peter took his revenge. 'Locally perhaps, in the nineteen fifties, but he couldn't have commuted to London as king of the underworld. Buck was living here all the time.'

'That rules out Sandy Smith too for big boss. We're left with Harold very tentatively, and perhaps Matthew.'

'You're wrong,' Peter instantly shot back. 'Sandy was no longer in Broadstairs in the late fifties and sixties. He said he was travelling the country with seasonal shows, but we've no proof that he wasn't based in London – just as we've no proof of whether Matthew was. I *still* think he's involved.'

She sighed. 'We've been over this ground before. Assuming he was sitting at that table in the Blue Parrot, when Pamela rang to tell Matthew about Tom's visit in 1975, he would just have lain low to avoid being recognized.'

Silence. Then: 'Let's go back to Tom,' Peter said. 'He returns to Broadstairs for his daughter's birthday on a mere whim.'

'It happens.'

'Feeble, but agreed.'

'He also wants to tell her he really was innocent of Joan's murder, and even who he thinks the guilty party was.'

'Pamela didn't mention that to us.'

'Perhaps for good reason.'

'Accepted.'

'His mission also involved a visit to Micky. Why?'

'To get Pamela's address?'

'Wrong. Alison Robin's mum had kept in touch with Pamela. She would have told Tom her whereabouts and married name. And there could be another reason . . .' He looked at her speculatively, and Georgia guessed where this was going.

'I can't believe it,' she said firmly. 'Micky was a family man—'

'Who adored Joan. He wrote in his diary for sixteenth August "The day it happened". Sparse words, but they surely indicate involvement to some degree – even as a murder suspect. Mavis didn't give Micky an alibi. He could have killed Joan through jealousy at finding his adored goddess had clay feet.'

Georgia shook her head. 'I can't go with that theory. Ken would have winkled that out and his scoops would have stopped abruptly.'

'The last one did. But,' Peter added, 'I suppose I agree with you. But where do we stand on Sandy?'

'He's a strong alibi for the time of Joan's death. And do you see Sandy tottering into town late at night to commit murder?'

'No, but I could see that son-in-law of his doing it.'

'Agreed, but why should he? Protecting his father-in-law? Weak.'

A pause. 'Isn't there any way round that alibi? Why don't you tackle Mavis again? And make sure you ask about Micky.'

'Do you want to come?'

'No, I'll take Buck Dillon out to lunch if he's free. Let him know about the Margate vagrant. You know, Georgia, I can't help feeling we're missing something – the link that binds all this together. It's like that fox finial on your oast: we need a strong wind behind us to swing us round in the right direction.'

Georgia tracked Mavis down via her mobile to a local charity shop, where she said she was a volunteer. She found her on her own surrounded by black bags stuffed full of people's unwanted offerings. Unwanted on both sides, by the look of some of Mavis's piles.

'I have to get this done, dearie,' Mavis informed her. 'The van's coming for the stuff in an hour. Don't mind, do you?'

'I could help,' Georgia suggested.

'Offer accepted,' Mavis said promptly. 'I'll be kind to you. You can sort the books. They need to be separated into rubbish, sellable rubbish and those worth a bob or two. We keep the sellable rubbish here and get shot of the other two piles.'

'As good as done,' Georgia said promptly. She certainly had the easier option, looking at the vast array of offerings lying around. Nevertheless, it was hard to concentrate on the grey areas of whether a tatty paperback was really tatty

and out of date, making it unsaleable, whilst trying not to lose sight of Tom Watson. In this cramped shop, surrounded by clothes, china and every manner of ornament, old records and videos, she found it hard to think of Mavis as a chorus-line dancer of yesteryear. She looked as if she had always been roly-poly and beaming. Fortunately there was no sign of a bottle today, so presumably that was only a leisure-time indulgence.

'Now what can I do for you today?' Mavis asked at last.

'Guess what.'

'That's a no-brainer,' Mavis observed. 'What's up this time?'

'We think Tom might have been killed when he returned in the seventies.'

'Sounds nasty. Pushed off a cliff, or did he jump?' Mavis was busily sorting her piles of clothes, but Georgia sensed she was more shaken than she appeared. 'Poor old sod, Tom didn't deserve that, even if he did kill his wife. Who do you think killed him?'

It was a natural enough question, but it seemed to Georgia not to be as casual as it sounded.

'Whoever killed Joan Watson would be the obvious answer.'

'But you don't know who that was, do you? Not still thinking it could have been my David, are you? Anyway, he didn't get rid of Tom. He'd been dead three years by 1975. Killed by Elvis Presley and Bill Haley. Funny, if he'd hung on, I reckon he'd have had a comeback. You should have heard him—' There was a catch in Mavis's voice, and Georgia hastened to say:

'No, not David, but the answer might lie in *Waves Ahoy!* So I wanted to double-check that Sandy was with you *all* the evening, first at the pub and then at your home, which would have taken the time past the point when the murder was reported and the police arrived.'

'That's right,' Mavis agreed. 'I can't help you, much as I'd like to. I know it was over fifty years ago, but when you have an evening like that, it tends to stick in your memory. Whatever else fades, it's glued on. So that – and

the evening when my David died – won't go away. David gave the police the same evidence as me.'

'And –' Georgia wondered how to put this – 'you didn't forget something then. Perhaps, for example, Micky was more in the picture than he seems, and because—'

'If you're asking,' Mavis cut in, 'whether David and I glossed over something because we were all one big happy family at the show, forget it.'

'They were your friends though.'

'Micky yes, Sandy no, Harold was so-so. David and I both loathed Sandy Smith. Couldn't understand how Tom, Micky and Harold could work with him. David hated being in the same show as him, let alone having the amount of contact that poor old Tom did. He was a creep of the first order, David said. Shagging Joan, roping her into his nasty little smuggling ring.' She ignored Georgia's immediate reaction and swept on. 'David said all the trouble in the show was down to him. He might look a jolly old gent now, but leopards and clowns never change their spots.'

Georgia could wait no longer. 'So Sandy was the ringleader of the Botany Bay smuggling ring?'

'You know about that, do you?' Mavis looked impressed. 'Not sure he was Number One, that might have been Harold, but he was in it all right.'

'Was David involved?'

'No, he was not,' Mavis said firmly. 'He was straight, and so was Tom. As for me, I'd have liked to snaffle a bit of the fancy stuff – they were grim days – but I knew David would go spare if he found out, so I kept well away. David said he was going to make his money through his voice and his career. He liked Harold but didn't like the way he was dabbling in the black market. Wouldn't think it, would you, to see him so high and mighty now? No, dearie, my David died of drink, but at least he died straight.'

'And Tom? Did David think Tom died a murderer?'

Mavis grimaced. 'We differed there. I thought Tom was a weakling who killed Joan in a fit of rage, poor devil. David thought he'd been set up, but he couldn't see how.

David wouldn't lie though, and he knew Sandy and Jeannie had been with us all the time. Believe me, do you?'

'Yes.' She wished she didn't, but there was no doubting Mavis's account.

'We walked back from the Black Lion together, and Sandy and Jeannie were locked together in front of David and me,' Mavis said. 'I reckon Sandy would have fallen down otherwise. He'd had a skinful. Once back at the house he collapsed on the sofa, had another drink and proceeded to become life and soul of the party again, with Jeannie hanging on his every word.'

'Why, if you and David didn't like him, did you invite them back?' A chink of light here? Georgia wondered. If so, it was quickly extinguished.

'Jeannie and me were good mates, so we put up with his lordship for her sake. She thought he was as magnificent as he did himself. So, sorry, love, but no vanishing for Sandy that night. You and your dad coming to the reunion, are you? Only two weeks to go now.'

'We are.'

'Good,' Mavis said. 'Funny thing, us old codgers getting together every year for so long. And what for? To remember an old show that's brought about two murders. Maybe three. Some show, eh?'

'You've done better than I have,' Peter conceded gloomily. 'Buck still wouldn't budge. He was shaken but not stirred by the news of the body.'

'Despite the fact that it could have been linked to the Silver Gang? After all, suppose that had links to the local post-war smuggling ring Buck was involved with?'

'Despite all that. Anyway, it's not smuggling we're interested in. We began with Joan Watson's murder. Fingerprints, remember them?'

'I do. At the bottom of those steps though, not in the room where the murder took place. I still think that's odd,' Georgia said.

'Probably where Tom first encountered Joan that evening. She might have been going out – and he tackled her as to where she was going and whether the child had been left alone. Going back to more solid ground, with Sandy out of the picture, we're left with Harold and Micky who left the pub early, and Buck with a question mark. He too has a strong alibi—'

'Probably uncheckable,' Georgia felt obliged to point out.

'Accepted. For Tom's murder we also have Matthew hovering in the frame – especially if Tom had killed Joan. Revenge, although highly unlikely.'

'Cath won't like the question mark over Buck.'

'Nor do I,' Peter agreed, 'but I've been playing with Suspects Anonymous—'

Georgia groaned. 'It can't do more than we can at this stage.'

'You're wrong. It is of the opinion that Matthew Trent is more prominent in this affair than we are giving him credit for. Several question marks appeared. So I went on the Web to do a bit of investigation about his company. There was nothing immediately obvious, but with the help of a few suggestions from Luke I winkled out some information. Nothing in the list of directors was particularly interesting, but one of our *Waves Ahoy!* chums has a forty-five per cent interest in the company.'

'Harold?'

'No, Sandy Smith.'

Georgia blinked, thinking back to that meeting at Sandy's house. Nothing had seemed to indicate close contact between Matthew and Sandy, but then why should it? she reasoned. And was it even material to the Tom Watson case?

'It could be just that Sandy helped Matthew get started for Pamela's sake,' she suggested. 'It would be quite natural if he could afford it. The business began in 1972. If Sandy was back from his travels by then, he could have looked up Pamela for old times' sake, seen a good business opportunity and bingo.'

'I don't know how much it would cost to set up a car dealership, but is it likely that a jobbing clown would have that kind of cash available?'

'It's possible. Maybe Sandy's dad was a millionaire and Sandy a dropout who later inherited.'

'Kindly depart from fantasy land, Georgia.'

'Very well. There's the arson attack. That followed quickly on from Harold's letter.'

'But was that a threat or a warning? And if a threat, Harold was unlikely to have committed arson in person.'

'More likely Greg Dale. And he,' Georgia was forced to point out, 'is Matthew Trent's stooge. Remember his stalking me on that visit to the Watson flat?'

'Back to Matthew,' Peter said in triumph. 'I told you so. Daughter, the reunion is in two weeks' time. Wouldn't you agree this case has to be settled by then?'

She did. At some point Marsh & Daughter had to come to a decision as to whether they should continue this case or not. So far they had never had to back out of a commitment at such a late stage as this. 'We'll have to force some kind of resolution.'

'Big words,' he answered her. 'How? Just stroll up to Matthew or Harold and suggest they confess?'

She thought for a moment. 'Words, Peter, stray words.'

'Carry on,' Peter said ironically. 'You're gripping me with excitement.'

'That word "connection" again. And something Janie said: now you see him, now you don't.' Mistake. She sensed an instant loss of rapport.

'And when did Janie let this little gem drop?'

Georgia tried to redeem the situation. 'That doesn't matter. The case does.'

'Janie is nothing to do with this case. *Or* with me.'

'She is. You're making a big mistake—'

'Did I presume ever to say that about Zac?'

'Yes.'

A pause. 'Nevertheless, I don't need your views on Janie. Or her daft statements.'

'I think perhaps we both do. Now, listen. Now you see him, now you don't. What do those words mean?'

'Magic,' was Peter's dour answer. 'And thus Sandy Smith.'

'And what did you tell me about the Silver Gang and Quicksilver himself?'

'He vanished with a price on his head, and so did the gang.'

'He *vanished*. Let's assume Sandy is Quicksilver himself. He became an anonymous clown again hiding behind his job. Suppose Tom went to see him in Broadstairs. He went to see Micky, so surely he would see Sandy too for old times' sake? Yet Tom might be the only man who could link Sandy Smith with the Silver Gang, and this is a man with a price on his head who has successfully hidden from his enemies for about five years.'

Peter looked at her pityingly. 'Anything strike you as wrong with that thesis, Miss Marple?'

What had she missed? Then she realized. 'Oh, damn. Tom would not have been stupid enough to seek Sandy out if he knew he was the leader or part of the Silver Gang. And someone at the Blue Parrot would have been sure to have enlightened him, even if the two men Tom recognized there wouldn't go out of their way to mention it.'

'Two people?' Peter picked up.

She realized what she'd said. 'Harold?' She was beginning to see the pattern now, and surely, surely it was right.

'Could be. Hold the horses, Georgia. Let's think about Sandy Smith being Quicksilver. Apart from the police with a few murders still unpaid for, there are going to be people with a grudge against him. The underworld has a long memory. No wonder he hides away in a house with "magician" displayed all over it.'

'With a handy henchman as a son-in-law,' Georgia added.

'Dale – yes. He's old enough to have been in that gang when he met Fenella. Micky Winton's Giant Rat?'

'No, that must be Sandy.'

'Agreed. If Tom told Micky about Smith's London life, Micky would be very wary, as Sandy was living in the town, hence the cryptic clues. But, dammit, there's Joan's murder,' Peter said crossly. 'I take it Mavis isn't lying about Sandy being with her that night? He had motive enough if Joan was threatening to expose his moonlighting activities.'

'Unfortunately I don't think she is.'

'Hell,' Peter muttered. 'We'll sleep on it.'

'It's only ten o'clock in the morning.'

'Metaphorically. Anyway, what's Janie doing poking her nose in? Have you two been chatting about me behind my back?'

'No,' Georgia said crossly. 'She came about Rick.'

'What about him?' Peter asked wearily.

Georgia had not wanted to tell him, but now she was forced to. As she explained, Janie's suggestion sounded weak, and Peter clearly thought so too.

'Whom did she suggest you ring up? Dame Nellie Melba?' he asked.

'No, Janet Charing, Josephine Mantreau . . .'

Peter began to groan but stopped, his interest caught. 'There was a Josephine in Mozart's life too, wasn't there? Josephine Dušek? She and her husband lived in Prague and had a country villa where Mozart used to stay. Isn't she supposed to have locked him in his room until he'd finished writing some piece for her – some say she was locked in with him?'

'It rings a bell,' Georgia said doubtfully. 'But that's just a coincidence. Miss Blondie called herself Pamina, not Josephine.' On second thoughts? 'And yet . . .'

'It just might fit.' Peter whirled round in excitement and clicked on to the Web. 'Damn these safety passwords – they take forever. Hurry up, damn you . . . What a wonderful thing the Internet is!' A whoop of joy. 'Look at this – Bertramka, that was the Dušeks' villa. It was in the countryside in Mozart's time, now on the outskirts of Prague. Glory be, there's a website . . . in English too.'

'Peter—' Georgia tried to calm him down, but it was impossible. Even her own pulse was racing.

'And they run Mozart concerts in the summer, sometimes in the gardens.'

'Let me look.' She looked over his shoulder, ordering herself to be logical. 'Coincidence, just a common forename, that's all. Even if a famous soprano happens to be called Josephine, that doesn't mean there's any connection with Josephine Dušek.'

'But there might be. Suppose Miss Blondie had a special interest in the Dušeks because of it? Mrs D was a singer, after all. Did you check out Bertramka?'

'No. Did you?'

'No. But I'm going to. Right now.'

Peter was right. Computers could never go fast enough sometimes. Come on, come on, she willed it as Peter first searched for the website, then clicked. She almost turned away as the prospect of this thin chance proving positive became too much, especially as Peter's voice dropped. 'Hardly surprising, I suppose. There don't seem to be details of past concerts.'

Plenty else though. One look at the website showing the elegant white-painted low building, and the green, green gardens stretching away behind it made it seem just the sort of place Rick would have loved.

She was the one to be excited now. 'They were giving concerts in 1994 though. Look. Bertramka's been a museum since 1956. Concerts in the garden in July and August.'

'No mention of opera.'

'Perhaps we were wrong about that. But just look at this site. Mozart stayed there, composed there, was inspired there. What more special place for a concert?'

'We could telephone them.' Peter began to rally.

'Before we do that, shouldn't we do as Janie suggested: see if Josephine Mantreau is the right age and blonde? I know it's illogical, but . . .'

'But what?'

'I feel there's something magic about this lead,' Georgia said diffidently. 'And this isn't a case like Tom Watson's; it's about us, so magic is permitted.'

A glance at her, and Peter fed Josephine Mantreau into the search engine. 'A million entries,' he cursed.

'Pick her own site,' Georgia urged. She knew he was as eager as she was, but equally fearful of taking this last step when the potential for disappointment was greater.

She could not bear the waiting, and she leaned over his shoulder so far that she was almost breathing down his neck – a thing he usually objected to. Not today.

'She's thirty-six,' he said as the website came up. 'Look, that's blondish hair, surely. Graduated in 1994.'

She couldn't speak and nor for a moment could he. Then he said nonchalantly, 'Her agent's address is here. It might be worth risking the cost of a first class stamp.' And then a casual: 'I should ring Janie to thank her.'

FOURTEEN

'Did you send that letter?' Over a week had gone by, and Georgia had not dared to ask in case Peter had changed his mind. She could not bear the thought of exposing this fragile hope to scrutiny all over again, and yet now the time had come when she must know.

'Yes.'

Relief, but she wanted to be prepared for the worst. 'We won't hear anything of course.'

'No.'

She caught his eye. 'We might. We just might.'

'It's a one in a million chance. Even the Tom Watson case has better odds than that. In fact, I woke up this morning feeling quite optimistic about him – I suppose it's the music.'

'What music?' she asked blankly.

Peter looked embarrassed and then to her amazement began to sing. Peter's fine voice had entranced her as a child, but after Elena had left he had exercised it less and less. She'd suggested he joined the local choir, but the idea had been scorned. He was too busy for that sort of thing, he had stated. Now, however, he was letting rip with:

'I have a song to sing, O!
Sing me your song, O! . . .
It's the song of a merryman, moping mum . . .'

'That's from Gilbert and Sullivan.' She identified it after a moment as he ended up with a baritone roar of 'for the love of a ladye'. '*The Yeomen of the Guard*,' she added. Janie? she wondered. Had there been a reconciliation and this was the result?

Peter looked even more embarrassed. 'Yes. Jack Point's song. Strolling jester. Reminded me of Tom Watson, clown.'

No Janie then. 'But is Tom's lady Joan or Cherry?'

'That's what I keep coming back to. If Tom killed Joan after a row, was that about her lovers or his sweetheart? It was one of the first questions we asked ourselves on this case, and still we don't know the answer.'

'What if he didn't kill her?'

'Then surely he must have worked out who did – although if so, why not speak out at the time?'

'He worked it out later.' Round that damned mulberry bush again, Georgia thought despairingly.

'Then what brought him back? Nothing connects.'

That idea again: connection, links – and a sudden thought. 'Suppose it *doesn't* connect? Suppose Joan Watson's murder was entirely separate from Tom's return visit, which stemmed only from a longing to see Pamela again? Assuming Tom was murdered because he could identify Quicksilver and/or his accomplice, Sandy is squarely in the frame.'

Peter brightened. 'I like that. But if we also assume Tom wasn't daft enough to call on him, how did Sandy know Tom was in Broadstairs?'

'Either Micky or Matthew rang through to tell him.'

'Not Micky. *Matthew*,' Peter agreed. 'He heard of his return from Pamela, but why should either he or Sandy advertise their presence by seeking him out?'

Georgia saw the answer. 'For all they knew, Tom might be planning to move back permanently. And neither of them would have needed to present themselves in person to Tom. They could have sent in the heavy mob.'

'Vic Dale?'

'Why not? He could even have been in the Blue Parrot that night. Think about it. Vic marries the boss's daughter and returns with her and Sandy to this area. Which—'

'Means he could have continued his role of heavy hit man.'

'Killing Ken when he got too near the truth?'

'Yes.'

'It fits,' Georgia agreed.

'Except,' Peter said sweetly, 'that Vic can't be sixty yet. Which means that he would have been in his teens at the

Blue Parrot, if he'd been present that evening, a young bridegroom indeed. Possible but unlikely.'

'This,' she replied savagely, 'is turning into a caucus-race.'

'No, it isn't. It *was* Matthew whom Tom saw at the club with Sandy. *Matthew* who came back to Broadstairs and opened a respectable business in 1972 with Sandy's help. *Matthew* who has a position to lose, *Matthew* who rang Sandy in a panic to say that Tom was back. And—'

'Matthew who killed Tom?'

'No, my money's on Sandy, who saw the risk and decided to eliminate it. He took action right away, either alone or with Vic's help.'

'That figures. And Ken?'

'Ken got too near the truth. Action was needed before Ken filled in the gaps. Sandy is too old to traipse around late at night so it would have been down to Vic or Greg, and my money's on Vic.'

Georgia drew a deep breath. 'No more questions.' At last they had reached a stage that satisfied them both. One jigsaw at least was complete.

Proving it unfortunately was often a different matter – and it was in this case. 'Where next?' she asked. 'Mike? DI Jenkins?'

'Obviously both. It's out of our hands then, and in the meantime—'

'The reunion show.'

'On Saturday, sixteenth August, tomorrow week, which—'

'Is the anniversary of Joan Watson's death.'

'A murder,' he pointed out, 'that still remains unsolved.'

Only four days to the reunion now. She and Peter had been preoccupied with the police over Tom's murder and the supposed vagrant. Perhaps it was the coincidence of the date that made Georgia so convinced that there would be some resolution of the case today. There was no logical reason there should be, but Peter too was pinning his hopes on it.

'Something,' he declared grandly, 'is going to happen,'

and increasingly Georgia began to share his conviction but with mixed feelings. With all the *Waves Ahoy!* cast together, emotions could run high.

'We need to speak to Harold before the show,' Peter decided. 'If there's any snag to our conclusions over Sandy, he'll know what it is.'

'If he was involved, he's hardly likely to be helpful,' Georgia objected. 'Remember our fire?'

'I do. If you agree, however, Harold wants us to meet at Medlars. He'd hardly do that if he'd just burnt your oast down.'

She stared at him, trying to take this in. 'You think it was Greg after all? But his letter—'

'I still think that was a warning, not a threat.'

She was by no means convinced but reluctantly agreed to the Medlars' meeting, provided that Luke did too. He elected to be out, hardly surprisingly. The idea of the letter and fire being a warning hadn't gone down well with him, and she was decidedly edgy as the time for Harold's arrival came. She watched him get out of his car, walk over to the oast and gaze at the ruins of the storeroom. Rustling up all the control she could muster, she walked over to him.

'Would I be right in thinking that Armageddon is getting nearer, Georgia?' he asked. 'Perhaps even expected at the reunion on Saturday?'

'Yes. At least as far as Tom's visit in the seventies is concerned,' Georgia answered him as she led him through to Medlars' living room, where Peter was waiting, and established him in a comfortable chair.

'Ah. So Joan's death still remains a mystery,' he continued after he had greeted Peter. The armchair she had picked was a low one, in the hope that it might diminish his control of the situation. It didn't seem to work.

'I'd be annoyed,' he continued, 'if my reunion were hijacked, even though I do agree this investigation can't go on. Ken's death alone proved that. I came here to confess to you both that I've not been entirely frank.' A disarming smile. 'And before you ask me why, let me tell you it was for old times' sake. If the story about my involvement in petty smuggling in the fifties comes out, it would only be a few days' wonder, so I can live with that, and I've no doubt you have worked out who organized that little deal. Not me, I hasten to add.'

'Sandy Smith,' Peter said matter-of-factly.

'Correct. However, there's another matter,' Harold continued. 'It came as no surprise to me that Tom visited Pamela in the seventies. I had met him not long before in London.'

'By chance?' Georgia asked. So he must have been the old friend whom Tom had mentioned to the Eastleys. At least that was established.

'No. He asked to see me at the theatre one day. He gave his real name, which meant nothing to my staff, but of course it did to me. I had believed him dead long since, so it was a shock.'

'Did he tell you why he had cut off ties with his earlier life?'

'No. He just said the only person he really regretted leaving behind was Pamela. He didn't want her to think that he'd abandoned her. He adored her, for all she was David Maclyn's child, not his. Funny that, you'd think there'd be bad blood between David and Tom, but there didn't seem to be. Pamela was officially Tom's child, although quite a few of us suspected she wasn't.

'What Tom really wanted to know that day,' he continued, 'was if I knew what had happened to Sandy. Well, I didn't, except that he was back in Broadstairs still doing the odd show. Tom asked me if I knew Sandy had been living in London, and I told him no. Tom had always refused to join Sandy's smuggling ring in Broadstairs, and Sandy was suspicious of him because of that. Sandy liked the excitement and the big lights, and there was no way I could see him eking out a living for the rest of his life as a kids' conjurer. After I'd got over the surprise when Tom visited me in the seventies, I decided I didn't want to poke my nose in too far. I had a career of my own to think of, and it wasn't going to include crime, especially major crime. Tom told me he thought Sandy had been mixed up with one of those

big London gangs but had given it up. He was thinking of
going down to Broadstairs on Pamela's birthday, and he
seemed worried about running into Sandy. It would be only
a brief visit.'

'It was,' Peter said baldly. 'We think Sandy murdered
him.'

Georgia's was one of the first cars to arrive at the Broadstairs
hotel on the Saturday, as she and Peter had decided to lunch
in the bar before the show began. Perhaps they were relying
too much on this reunion. Its importance seemed to have
grown in their minds, and even Mike had declared his intention of being present if Sandy Smith was to perform and
Vic Dale to be present. What's more, DI Jenkins would be
with him. Dale was apparently the suspect for the shooting
in south London last year, and therefore possibly in the
frame for Ken's murder too. A full investigation was under
way, Mike had told them. Perhaps, Georgia thought, Sandy
Smith had still not fully retired from crime, if Vic was in
full operation.

She was glad to arrive, despite the tension building up
inside her. Peter's humming and singing in the car had
grown worse. 'All for the love of a lady . . .' He had blushed
as she asked him to lower the volume. 'Sorry. Janie's
persuaded me to join the Fernbourne Choir. She's a rattling
good alto.'

The odd thing about working closely with other people,
Georgia thought, was that the closer one grew, the more
one's thoughts drew closer together. Ever since Peter had
begun to sing Jack Point's song, it had stayed in her mind,
and one day she had caught Luke humming it too. The song
seemed to be haunting all of them, bringing not only Rick's
disappearance but also Tom Watson constantly into her
mind. Romantic fancy? Perhaps, but every time Peter
hummed the tune, both Tom and Rick swirled round and
round in her imagination. It could indicate a path forward
at last, she thought hopefully.

It was sorely needed. Luke had postponed publication
plans for the Watson book – or lack of it. After all, he had

pointed out to her, you don't know the ending yet. Galling but true. This afternoon might change that.

Making Waves, as the reunion show was called, was to be held in the same room as Ken's funeral. Perhaps lunching in the bar had been a mistake, for it simply increased her edginess, which Peter was sharing. Did he have a plan? She had no idea, and she knew that if she asked him at this stage, he wouldn't tell her anyway. Since Harold had told them about Tom's visit to him in London, she had begun to form her own ideas of how Joan Watson had died and longed to know if Peter was working in the same direction. The sooner the afternoon began, the better, so far as she was concerned.

'Now?' Peter said at last as they finished lunch.

'Yes. Let's go.'

They had to reach the hall through the hotel corridors, as the doors to the terrace were closed, presumably for noise reasons. The one door open led to what must be in use as the changing room for the cast, a tiny room squeezed on the end of the building. This had an entrance both to the outside and to the wings of the small stage. All very efficiently planned, although on a rather smaller scale, Georgia imagined, than Harold was used to in the West End.

As they took their places, she could see the room was well filled, although there were another fifteen minutes to wait before the show began. Automatically she began picking out familiar faces: the Trents, Fenella, Greg . . . No Christine, but then Georgia had not expected her to be there. She couldn't see Cath either. From behind the red stage curtains there came the sounds of furniture and scenery being dragged into position and a buzz of conversation. To her, the closed doors now seemed symbolic; there was no turning back now. And yet never had she wanted fresh air so much.

'No Mike yet,' Peter observed. 'What's keeping him?'

'I'll try and track him down.'

It was just an excuse, and Peter probably realized it. Four walls could get claustrophobic when one was waiting on tenterhooks – especially when she had no idea exactly what they were waiting for.

She hurried along the terrace and down the steps to the gardens, intending to skirt the hotel buildings to get through to the car park. As she approached the corner, however, something made her glance over to the edge of the far flower borders.

Dear God, it's a *clown*, was her first reaction, her heart leaping into sudden fright. *It was Tom Watson*. The ghost was here.

No, it couldn't be. She felt herself swaying with shock and had to force herself to be calm. Then she looked again. The clown was still there, sitting motionless on a bench. It was no ghost. It was a real clown, asleep, his head drooping. Not Tom Watson's ghost, thank heavens, but someone from the show. It must be Sandy. A flood of relief. How stupid of her—

But he was *very* still. Perhaps it was a dummy, an inflatable clown – could it really be Sandy beneath that hat and that paint, lolling with the white costume billowing around him, the red—

Red what?

She realized she was running towards him – it – whatever it was, ghost, man or corpse. Even as she ran, she took in the full horror. It could only be Sandy Smith, and he was dead or near to it. She could see a knife sticking out of his chest. Red was for blood, the red spatters that stood out on the white of his clown's costume. Better that than to look at that ghastly red paint of the clown's face, which still grinned on, although Sandy would never smile again.

She tried to scream, but she couldn't; the sound seemed frozen in her throat, and she heard nothing, lost in her own terror. But it must have made some noise after all, for people were running towards her now, and one of them, thank heavens, was Mike.

'How are you feeling now, Georgia?' Mike came to sit by her on the far side of the gardens. It seemed only a few minutes, and yet white tape denoted a crime scene and the whole garden was now swarming with police and white-coated Scene of Crime Officers. Even Mike was in white. They looked almost like clowns themselves, she thought crazily.

'Better, thanks, Mike,' she said truthfully. Cups of tea weren't the be all and end all to recovery from shock, but they most certainly set you on the right path. She had some way to go though; her mind felt completely clogged up. She remembered talking to Mike earlier and to DI Jenkins; and to everyone else, including Peter. He had seemed to be doing most of the talking, but she had tried. Luke had arrived too, summoned by Peter, she gathered. But they seemed to have vanished temporarily, leaving her stuck here on a bench with a couple of legs that didn't seem as though they wanted to take her anywhere.

'You'd be better inside now, Georgia,' Mike said. 'If you can take it, Peter's sitting with a group of those most involved, waiting for Jenkins to get round to them.'

'Involved in Sandy's death?' Surely Jenkins wouldn't permit that.

'No. Jenkins has those tucked away. Peter's with the Tom Watson group. It's Jenkins's call, but I persuaded him to agree, provided Peter sticks to Watson and not the Winton and Smith murders. I'm still not sure it's wise, but you know what Peter's like.'

That raised a faint smile on her lips. She did. Peter wanted to end the story of Tom Watson and its terrible consequences here and now. Was this always his plan, or had the events of the afternoon precipitated it?

'Pamela Trent is in the group,' Mike added, 'but not Matthew Trent, councillor.'

'I take it you don't like him.'

'Smarmy git.'

Unusual language for Mike, Georgia thought, and she could understand why.

'Jenkins is pretending to observe the niceties,' Mike continued, 'but he's of the same opinion. He'll give him a hard time.'

'Do you think he did it?' Georgia asked fatuously. Of course Mike couldn't answer.

Mike duly gave her what she would call an old-fashioned look. 'Did what? Anyway, I think you'll find Peter will have something to say on that. Shall I give you a hand? You look a bit rocky.'

With Mike's hovering support at her side, she returned to the hotel. He led her to a small private room, where she found Peter and Luke superintending tea and cakes for Mavis, Harold, Pamela, Cherry – and Cath. It all looked very homely, but her heart sank. With Peter raring to go, it wouldn't stay that way long. She thought Mike would disappear, but instead he sat back from the main group in a window seat. In plain clothes, he didn't stand out as a police presence – except to her. Was he keeping an eye on Peter? No, that wasn't Mike's style, so he must have had some other reason.

Cath leapt up to find her a chair – and another cup of tea. Well, why not, Georgia thought. Tea and cakes pinned you to the real world, unlike murdered clowns sitting on hotel benches. 'Christine had her baby today,' Cath told her.

That too was good. Something positive amid the wreckage of today.

'It's a boy. They're naming him Kenneth.'

'Ken would have liked that.' Georgia felt her voice wobbling even more. Something even more positive to hang on to.

'Very nice,' Mavis observed, 'but why are we all sitting here like dummies, Peter? Waiting for Tom Watson, are we?'

'Can't we just forget Tom?' Pamela pleaded. 'If stirring up the old story has led to today's atrocity, surely you should stop meddling in it?'

'Unfortunately, no,' Peter replied soberly. 'There's Ken Winton's murder to take into account. If that was brought about by Ken's enquiries, don't you think Christine deserves to know how it came about? And Tom Watson is the key to that,' he added to Georgia's relief, in view of Jenkins's guidelines. 'But I appreciate your coming here, Mrs Trent. I take it that you do want to know who killed your mother?'

A silence, then a whispered, 'Yes, but that's nothing to do with today's murder.'

'Oh, but it is,' Peter said. 'It's all the same sad story, and it's time it was told. You agree, Harold?'

For a moment Georgia thought he would leave, because his face darkened, but if so, he decided against it.

'Go on,' he said.

A story of lost love, Georgia thought dully. Tom Watson's, Rick's and Jack Point's. No. *Don't* try to fit them together, she told herself. Try to think logically, because in a way these murders had been logical, even Sandy's.

Peter wasted no time. 'Don't think of what you've heard and read or what you remember about Tom Watson. Think of it as a story about someone you've never heard of before. Tom was just an ordinary sort of fellow, except when he was onstage and had an identity. He was a clown, but underneath the paint he had an emotional life that no one knew about. At first he poured his love out at the feet of his wife, but then he found out she was disloyal and unfaithful. Then he met a girl who adored him and thought he was the best thing since ice cream.'

Georgia, sitting next to Cherry, heard her quiet moan, and Harold, on her far side, put his arm round her.

'Being an ordinary fellow,' Peter continued, 'Tom fell in love and wanted to marry her, although he was a lot older than her. Divorce was more difficult in the 1950s: his wife could not divorce him because she had no evidence; he did not want his sweetheart's name to be used in court, nor would he fake evidence of another woman in his life. Nor did he really want to divorce his wife, because once he had loved her. Moreover he adored his daughter Pamela.'

Georgia could see Pamela's eyes fixed on Peter, her expression unreadable, whereas Cherry was whispering, 'No, no . . . he did . . .'

'Then on the sixteenth of August one year matters came to a head,' Peter continued. 'I believe *his* story is this: Tom told his wife that her affairs must stop or he would divorce her. She laughed at him. So he poured his woes out to his sweetheart and they arranged to meet at a pub, knowing his wife had gone straight home. This wasn't the Black Lion, because they wanted to talk the situation over quietly.

'But something went wrong, and his sweetheart did go
to the Black Lion. Not knowing that, he sat there waiting
for her in the hope she would arrive. When Tom at last
reached his home, he found his wife dead. He was distraught.
He called the police, but he did not confess to killing Joan.
He allowed them to think that he had, and he allowed them
to go on thinking that all through the trial and afterwards.
He let it be thought that he must have committed suicide,
but instead he created a new life for himself in London. It
was his bad luck that during that new life which brought
him comfort of a sort, Tom ran into one or two of his former
associates and recognized them.'

Peter must be holding back because of Sandy's death,
Georgia thought, or was he for once taking heed of police
instructions?

'Years later,' Peter continued, 'when Tom decided to give
his daughter a birthday present by reappearing briefly in
her life, he was attacked and killed. His body was driven
some distance away and put in a barn that was then set on
fire. Without identification, our Tom had disappeared for
good, or so it was thought. But now it's possible for Tom
to have justice and a burial at last. His DNA can establish
whether that burnt body was Tom's or not, because, although
he has no living relatives that we know of, his sweetheart
kept a lock of his hair.'

What was Cherry making of all this? Georgia wondered
uneasily. She was showing no reaction.

Peter had not quite finished. 'This is only Tom's story,
of course. His sweetheart, however, has a quite different
one, a story that has finished today with Sandy's murder.
Hasn't it, Cherry?'

Cherry threw off Harold's arm and stood up, smiling at
them vacantly. 'I had to do it, you see,' she explained
earnestly. 'Once I realized that Sandy had killed my Tom,
I had to do it for Tom's sake. Just like the first time.'

It was a much smaller group now. Mike had stepped forward
to escort Cherry as she left the room, with Harold anxiously
following them. Of course, Georgia realized, Mike must

have known all the time that it wasn't Matthew who had killed Sandy; it had been Cherry.

She still had to battle to believe it, even though the process had begun when Harold had told them about Tom's visit to him. There had been no mention of Cherry, and surely Tom would have asked after her, whether or not he knew of her short marriage to Harold. But Harold had not mentioned her, because he was protecting her. No longer. Unlike the night when she murdered Joan, there was no one to deal with fingerprints today, no one to save her, and that was as well, for she was surely certifiable. Georgia had wondered whether Harold would go with her to the police station, but he did not. Looking his full age, he had come back into the room again.

'I'm sorry,' he said to Peter in particular. 'After you had told us all about Tom's return visit, she became convinced she was going to meet Tom again at today's reunion. She came to me to ask – I'm afraid – what I thought she should wear. I decided enough was enough and told her what I had always thought had happened to him. That he'd met a sticky end after his Broadstairs visit.'

'Including Sandy's name?' Peter asked.

'I'm not that stupid, but then neither is she. She's highly intelligent in some ways, and I now realize that from what I did tell her she could guess who I thought was responsible for Tom's death. I'm not proud of myself.'

'It could have happened anyway,' Peter replied. 'At least this way she'll be in safe custody. There'll be plenty of evidence that she killed Sandy, whereas there would be difficulty in proving she killed Joan Watson.'

'I tried to warn you.' Harold looked helplessly at Georgia.

'It was her who set fire to the barn?' she exclaimed in horror. 'I thought it was Sandy who organized it.'

'No. I suspect she got the idea into her head and told herself she was doing it for Tom.'

Georgia shuddered. 'I suppose we were lucky it wasn't Medlars.'

'It might have been next time.'

Pamela had been very quiet. 'How did she kill my mother?' she asked Peter. 'I need to know. I *liked* Cherry.'

Peter looked as if he had no taste for this, but it had to be done. 'She probably thought Tom would be pleased at what she had done. From her viewpoint she had solved their problem so that Tom and she could get married. She might not even have realized that Tom would be blamed. She was entirely focused on her own desire to be with Tom. Joan probably made fun of Cherry as she did her husband, and even if Cherry had gone with the purpose of pleading with Joan, that could have been the last straw. She seized the knife and poured out all her hate on the unsuspecting Joan, who had no doubt dismissed her as a nonentity.'

'Mistake,' muttered Harold.

'My theory is that she had deliberately sent Tom to another pub so that he would wait for her there. If they'd gone to the Black Lion and she had then made an excuse to leave early, then Tom would have gone home straight away. Instead, she put in a brief appearance at the Black Lion, then made an excuse and left. When Tom came home, he found her waiting at the foot of the steps to tell him all about it. He rushed up to the flat with her following him and found Joan's body. She told him that she had done it for him, so he believed that he was to blame. How could he give her away to the police? Cherry was probably still looking at him with those trusting, hopeful eyes, even though she had committed terrible murder – for him. Tom felt he had to go into action on her behalf, however repelled he was by what she done. He probably gave her one of Joan's coats to hide any blood spatters on her that her parents might spot and bundled her down the steps to the yard. That's when his neighbour spotted Joan, as she thought. Then he called the police. He'd done what he could. He took the knife out of the wound so that his prints would be on it. The blood might have begun to coagulate by then, but even if not, it wouldn't matter if the blood spattered him. He realized he had no alibi, because if he asked the people at the pub he'd been in to confirm his presence there, it would be clear that Cherry had not turned up, which would automatically put her under suspicion. So he said he had been in the Black Lion and awaited the inevitable – which he might have thought was only right, as he had been the cause of her actions. Tom was acquitted but then realized that his love for Cherry had completely vanished because of her actions. He had no wish to marry her. He decided instead to find a new life and returned only once on Pamela's birthday. Meanwhile, Cherry waited on in vain.' Peter paused. 'Is that right, Harold?'

'Nearly,' Harold replied, stony faced.

'And the rest?'

He sighed. 'I've told you most of it. What I didn't include was that Tom came to me in London not only to ask about Sandy but about Cherry's whereabouts. He'd found out that she'd married me but that we were divorced. He seemed worried when I said she had returned to Broadstairs. He didn't want to run into her by chance. After we were married, I began to suspect she might have killed Joan, and once that idea was in my head, it killed the marriage. I couldn't stand her, but I still felt an obligation towards her. I still did – up until today, and perhaps even now. I wanted to warn you off with my letter to you, Luke, because I knew she wasn't functioning on all cylinders. When Ken died, I was terrified she'd been responsible, but that isn't the case, is it?'

'No, Sandy organized that because he was getting too near the truth of Tom's return and murder, and once she had guessed that Sandy had killed Tom, there's no doubt in my mind at least that she murdered him in revenge.'

'You didn't have it right, Peter. Nor you, Georgia,' Harold continued. 'Cherry's not a soft little thing with a blind spot: she's dangerously amoral. You two were safe until it looked as if you might get too inquisitive. Then I think the idea of burning down your barn, Luke, seemed a great idea to her.' A pause. 'I blame myself. I couldn't have stopped the death of your mother, Pamela, but once I realized, perhaps then I should have spoken. Salvaged Tom's name if not his life.'

'It's not your fault, Harold,' Pamela said.

He looked at her sadly. 'It's Nobody's Fault. Isn't that what Dickens was originally going to call *Little Dorrit*? When does nobody become somebody?'

'Come to Medlars for dinner, Peter,' Georgia urged on the way home. Luke had gone back in his own car, but now that she felt up to driving, she could take Peter back. 'Stay overnight if you prefer.'

'You know, I think I will,' Peter said. 'I'm exhausted.' He looked very drawn. 'But you look all in too, Georgia. Finding Sandy's body like that was a shock that takes time to get over. You and Luke would be better on your own.'

'No. We don't have to talk it about this evening, but we should all be together. Luke agrees with me.'

Peter quickly gave in, so thankfully it was clear where his preferences lay. 'Let me pick up a bag then, if you don't mind the detour to Haden Shaw.'

She drove along through the village and parked outside his house. All seemed dark and quiet, and she longed to be safely at Medlars. She watched as Peter swung himself out of the car and into his wheelchair. He was beginning to move towards the door when she saw a figure crossing the road.

'Someone seems to want you,' she called to her father as the smartly dressed woman hurried towards them.

'Mr Marsh? I've been waiting for you in the pub, hoping you'd come back. My name is Josephine Mantreau.'

EPILOGUE

A summer's evening, a garden in Prague and Mozart's music. Not 1994, but today, although Georgia found it hard to remember that. In this glorious setting with Josephine, Peter, Luke and Janie around her, it was easy to believe that it was 1994 and that Rick was but a puff of wind away. Mozart had composed and played his music here in the gardens of Bertramka; he had played skittles on the grass with his friends the Dušeks, relaxing in this tranquil green place, where sloping lawns and shading trees formed almost a theatre in themselves.

'If we could meet in Bertramka,' Josephine had said to them on that evening at Medlars two weeks earlier, 'I would hope to know the ending of the story. Rick and I spent our last evening together there. We made arrangements to meet again, but he did not come. Your letter to me told me why at last. I still do not know the whole truth, but I shall shortly. Please, please come to Bertramka. It would give me great happiness and I hope spare you a little of your sadness.'

And now they were here.

'Come,' Josephine said as the last notes of the orchestra died away in the Bertramka gardens. 'The audience is leaving and I think it is time.'

'Do you know the end of the story now?' Georgia asked.

'I believe so.' She led them through the house to the Sala Terrena, which overlooked the terrace and gardens. 'It's warmer inside and I have arranged for us to sit there for a while.'

Of course. Josephine Mantreau was one of the most famous sopranos in the world now, but looking at her delicate features and sensitive face, Georgia saw only the young French girl on the brink of her career whom Rick had known.

'I always think of Rick as Tam.' Josephine flushed. 'Jokes are always so silly when you look back at them later. I was

Pamina, he was Tamino – Pam and Tam. I knew his name was Rick, but not his surname or exactly where he lived. That seems strange, I know, but we had little time together and spoke only of the future. He was not a trained musician, but Tam had such love for music. He understood it, and he understood what it meant to me. Our time together was very short. We had perhaps four days together in Brittany and fell in love. Do you believe that?'

Oh yes, Georgia did, now that she had met Josephine.

'I had a singing engagement in Prague,' Josephine explained. 'I wanted Tam to see Bertramka, for it is still possible to believe that Mozart was here, although two hundred years have passed.'

Georgia could see she was speaking with an effort, but when she made a sympathetic move towards her, Josephine shook her head. 'Do not think of me. It is I who should think of you now. I had many appointments in Prague, but Rick wanted to see more of Carnac, so we agreed to meet in a week's time in Prague.'

'And he came?'

'Of course. We were in love,' Josephine said simply. 'I'm married now, as you perhaps know, but then I was twenty-two and single. You love differently at that age. Intensely and forever, or so you believe, and perhaps it is true. Tam and I had three days, three nights together, the most magical of my life.'

Georgia was remembering her brother. Rick of the bespectacled and gentle face, and a smile she would never forget.

'And then?' Peter asked, his voice choked.

'It was all so foolish,' Josephine continued. 'I had to fly to Venice for the next stage of my training. Rick said he needed to return to England to look for a job and also –' Josephine put her hand out to Georgia – 'because it was his sister's birthday and he had promised to be there. He felt guilty because he had not telephoned as he usually did. Everything else went from his mind, he said. It was the music – and, I think and hope, me.'

Georgia was appalled. She'd forgotten that. How could she have done so? She had been expecting Rick to be present at her birthday. Her surprise, her shock, when he had not come back, the first suspicions that something was wrong. The intervening years had wiped out that memory, but now the misery flooded back in full force, even though it brought a sharp happiness that he had been thinking of his family.

'So we parted. Where shall we next meet? I asked him,' Josephine continued. 'But this is the worst part, although then it was fun. We were Pam and Tam. Let's do this properly, he said. Let's really be kitsch. Let's meet at the top of the Empire State Building, like the Ingrid Bergman film *An Affair to Remember*. America was far too expensive to fly to, I objected. Then where? he asked. Together we thought of all the silly places we could imagine and decided that nothing would be more kitsch than meeting at the top of the Eiffel Tower in Paris.'

Just like Rick, Georgia thought. Oh, just like him. He thought the Eiffel Tower a monstrosity, a blot on a lovely city.

'So we fixed a day in September,' Josephine continued.

'But Rick wasn't there,' Georgia filled in for her.

'No.' Josephine looked at them helplessly. 'I cannot tell you how dreadful that was. First disbelief, then the thought that there had been a mistake in the day and then the awful truth. He wasn't coming because he did not really love me; it had been a holiday romance. He had not been serious, and that is why *An Affair to Remember* had been in his mind, because one of the lovers did not arrive. Rick was letting me down lightly. I was furious, you see. So unhappy.'

'In the Bergman film there was good reason for her not to arrive,' Luke pointed out.

'Yes, but I did not think of it that way. All I thought was that Tam did not love me. I was so unhappy. I went back to Venice, but he did not contact me there.'

'You didn't try to trace his address in England?' Georgia could not help asking.

'I was too proud. I was miserable and angry and *hurt*. I vowed that never would anyone betray me like that again. I closed my mind to Tam and concentrated only on my singing, and then I met Henri, who became my husband.

When you are young and in love, you think only of yourself and your love. You do not think of the other person's
view. That comes only with time and confidence; it is love
on a different level.'

'So you never knew . . .' Peter looked unable to take all
this in.

'Not until your letter came. Then I realized at last that
something had happened to Rick. He *did* love me. So these
past two weeks I have been very busy. I have looked up
all the air accidents and road accidents that he might have
been involved in, even though they would surely have led
to his identification. I had to help you find out what
happened – I owed that to you, and to myself. But then I
came across the sinking of a boat on the Danube. Many
lives were lost, and some bodies not found or identified.
Then, only then, I remembered Rick saying idly that he had
never been to Salzburg, and I thought that instead of flying
home immediately he might have hitch-hiked down to
Austria across the Danube at Linz and taken a boat trip
while he was there.'

'Have you followed it up?' Georgia's voice didn't seem
to be her own; she was somewhere else, with Rick. A boat
trip sounded so like him.

'Not yet.' Josephine spread her hands out towards them
as if she could embrace them all. 'You might have been
my family had Rick lived. So I dared to hope we might
take that last journey together, just as we have here tonight.
I would like that. *He* would like that.'